## PRAISE FOR *THE MIGRATION*

"Intelligent, dark, wildly inventive, *The Migration* does more than put a new twist on the apocalyptic outbreak novel. It dares to be full of heart and full of difficult, defiant hope."

PAUL TREMBLAY, AUTHOR OF *THE CABIN AT THE END OF THE WORLD*

"This beautifully written fictional blend of biology, history, and the human heart is a clear-eyed, clean-limbed parable of change – a blazing emblem of the transcendent power of hope."

NICOLA GRIFFITH, AUTHOR OF THE LIGHT OF THE WORLD TRILOGY

"A dark fable that somehow feels both timeless and urgently topical."

M.R. CAREY, AUTHOR OF *THE GIRL WITH ALL THE GIFTS*

## PRAISE FOR *GIFTS FOR THE ONE WHO COMES AFTER*

"Helen Marshall is one of my favorite living writers. Her elegant, grotesque stories are best encountered like this, gathered together in a book and in conversation with each other; only then can you appreciate the staggering variety of her imagination. This is life, in all its beauty and sorrow."

NATHAN BALLINGRUD, AUTHOR OF *NORTH AMERICAN LAKE MONSTERS*

"In turns chilling, heart-wren~~~~ Marshall has a way with wo~~~~ seem possible."

KAARON WARRE~~~~ H SPLINTERED WALLS

"Sometimes a bo~~~~omes along that is so original, so vibrantly alive, so beautifully imagined and so much a law unto itself that the only comment or advice a reviewer can offer is to say: go read it."

NINA ALLAN, AUTHOR OF *THE DOLLMAKER*

"Stories subtle and unsettling: Helen Marshall clothes the uncanny in new flesh and then makes it bleed."

KELLY LINK, AUTHOR OF *PRETTY MONSTERS* AND *STRANGER THINGS HAPPEN*

The Migration
Print edition ISBN: 9781789091342
E-book edition ISBN: 9781789091359

Published by Titan Books
A division of Titan Publishing Group Ltd
144 Southwark Street, London SE1 0UP
www.titanbooks.com

First Titan edition: March 2019
10 9 8 7 6 5 4 3 2 1

This is a work of fiction. Names, characters, places, and incidents either are the product of the author's imagination or are used fictitiously, and any resemblance to actual persons, living or dead, business establishments, events, or locales is entirely coincidental. The publisher does not have any control over and does not assume any responsibility for author or third-party websites or their content.

Copyright © 2019 Helen Marshall. All rights reserved.

No part of this publication may be reproduced, stored in a retrieval system, or transmitted, in any form or by any means without the prior written permission of the publisher, nor be otherwise circulated in any form of binding or cover other than that in which it is published and without a similar condition being imposed on the subsequent purchaser.

Printed and bound by CPI Group (UK) Ltd, Croydon CR0 4YY.

# THE MIGRATION

## HELEN MARSHALL

TITAN BOOKS

*For Laura.*

For a while now, Duck had had a feeling.
"Who are you? What are you up to, creeping along behind me?"
"Good," said Death, "you finally noticed me."

Wolf Erlbruch, *Duck, Death and the Tulip*

# BEFORE

When I was younger, I used to play dead.

That was back before I knew what dead meant—what it *really* meant. But when you're a kid you play at things you don't understand. You play doctor. You play house. At ten I didn't know a thing about death. I thought it meant stillness, a body gone limp. A marionette with its strings cut. Death was like a long vacation—a going away.

Mom was pregnant with Kira when my golden retriever, Knick-Knack, got hit by a Buick speeding down Dupont Street. I was six years old, in first grade, still getting used to whole days away from home. Afterward Mom said it was lucky it happened on a school day, lucky I wasn't around.

Lucky, she said, but it wasn't. Knick-Knack was *my* responsibility. There had been long talks before we got him, Dad on his knees, eye-level, saying: "I know you want him, Feef, but he's a living thing. You're going to have to take care of him." And so for two months I had walked Knick-Knack around the block, Mom holding my hand, me holding the leash. I brushed his coat, wiped thick black gunk from his eyes, and slid my hand into the silky white curls that covered his belly. I let him slink onto my bed, his head low, when the crash of thunder left him shaking.

But even when Mom sat me down at the kitchen table with a glass of water to tell me what had happened, her round belly pressing against her cotton dress and me in my navy Hudson College jacket and tie, knee-high socks rolled down to my ankles because it was a warm September and my legs got so itchy in the heat, I still didn't really understand. What it *meant* for something to die. Dad never cried much, and the day Knick-Knack died, he was true to form, no waterworks. He's a tough guy, Dad is, poker-faced. But he kept rubbing his sleeve against his chin. His gaze wandered toward the half-empty dog bowl, the leash hanging from a hook next to the door. I don't know if he hugged me—maybe he did.

By the time I was older, I understood more of the way the world worked, but it still wasn't *real* dead I was playing at. It was something else. Something mysterious and deliciously terrifying. Like kissing a boy for the first time.

This is what I remember about the last time I played: late summer, the morning thick with humidity. A storm was coming and the air had that eerie electrical charge that made the hairs on the back of your arm stand up. Murky blue light streamed through the filter of my curtain.

The house on Dupont was old but gorgeous, a beautiful,

nineteenth-century bay-and-gable with two-and-a-half stories of red brick. A bedroom each for Kira and me, mine in the attic where the steep roof came to a point above me. Skeleton beams all musty and sweet-smelling.

I pulled up the covers snugly around my neck, halfway in and out of sleep. The grandfather clock chimed from downstairs. *Bong, bong, bong*. Back then the chiming was a part of what it meant to be *home*. I loved listening to it in the morning. Counting out the hours until everyone else came awake, thumbing through the books Aunt Irene had sent me from England where she lived now. *The Ladybird Book of British History*, all those complicated family squabbles spilling into death, the rise and fall of the nation. A complete set of Susan Cooper's The Dark Is Rising series, which must have come from a used bookstore because some other girl had scrawled her name on the inside covers. I loved those stories for their strangeness. They offered a vision of *somewhere else*, the past opening up like a fairy tale, filled with wondrous happenings, signs and portents.

But that morning I wasn't reading. My eyes were shut, my breath shallow. "I'm dead," I whispered to myself. Outside the window grackles and robins and chickadees hummed above the traffic sounds of the Annex waking up. They felt so close, like they were nesting in the attic with me. The air was full of light, movement, the anticipation of things to come.

And then I heard Kira, three years old, toddling on her pudgy legs. She opened my bedroom door a crack. "Sleeping, Soff?" she asked. I didn't answer, not right away. I listened to her feet padding across the carpet, waited to feel her finger hovering right above my forehead. And then, like a butterfly landing, the nail scraping gently between my eyebrows.

"No, Kiki, I'm playing dead."

Kira was seven years younger than me, Mom and Dad's darling—their stopgap measure against a divorce that loomed on the horizon even back then. Kira didn't fix things but she bought us all time together. Time for me to grow up. It wasn't Kira's fault that she couldn't build a bridge between my parents. She was beloved regardless.

I felt the bedsprings give way as she climbed up and slid her feet beneath the covers. She curled into me and whispered into my ear so that the little hairs moved: "I gonna play dead too, Soff."

I couldn't help smiling, my lips twitching though they weren't supposed to. Kira's hair was a cloud of velvety down against my cheek. She smelled of milk and soap. She snuggled up, warm like a hot water bottle, and placed her ear against my ribcage. I tried to slow my breathing but I knew my heart was still beating a loud *thumpa-thumpa-thumpa*.

"Soff, am I dead?"

"No, Kiki-bird, the dead don't talk."

"Why?"

"Because they can't breathe anymore. You need air to talk."

"Oh." She thought. "Like fish?"

"Not like fish."

"Last night, Soff, um, I was an octopus. We were underwater and everything was blue. You were a fish, and Daddy was a fish, but I didn't eat any of you." She brought her palms up to her face to hide her giggles.

"I'm glad you didn't eat us."

"I wouldn't eat you!"

Her knees tucked into my side. Her toenails touching my thigh through the thin fabric of the pyjamas. "What's being dead like?" she asked me.

"I don't really know, Kiki."

"I play too," she whispered.

And we lay together, side by side. My breath went in and her head rose gently. It was the first time I let Kira play dead with me, and somehow it made things different. I'd been imagining a kind of passage, crawling through darkness into a very bright light where everything was new and beautiful. But with Kira beside me all I could think of was Knick-Knack's empty bowl, the hole in our lives he had left behind.

I remember how Kira looked that morning. Her long eyelashes and her clear blue eyes hovering on the edge of grey. A smattering of freckles around her nose. Her face so like my own, but smaller, rounded in baby fat. I didn't want her to play dead with me.

"Everything born will pass away," Mom had told me when Knick-Knack died. "Sometimes it's sad, and sometimes it's scary but that's just the way the world works." It frightened me to think that everything I knew would one day be gone. I didn't want to see Kira as still as that so I ran my fingers over the ticklish bit of her tummy until she squirmed. "Read me a story, Soff," she begged when I finally let her go.

I miss the house in Toronto. I miss how my life was before everything changed.

Last August—just before the start of my senior year—Kira caught the chickenpox. Half her friends had it but she was the only one left dizzy. The light from the window bothered her. Her hands shook when she tried to turn the page of her book. A week later she collapsed.

The doctor at the intensive care unit said she'd had an episode—that was what he called it. He was handsome in a craggy-faced way, the hair at his temples threaded with grey. In a calm voice he told us her immune system had gone into overdrive and was attacking her brain. Kira stayed in the hospital for weeks. After they released her she was prone to bursts of temper, violent fits. She would start to cry for no reason.

There were more tests. Protein electrophoresis.

Something to do with her cerebrospinal fluid. They didn't know what the results meant. Then two of her friends developed the same symptoms. The school year resumed with a strange air of dread and quiet, everyone glassy-eyed, some wearing face masks, others wiping their hands again and again with antimicrobial gels. But Kira never went back.

Mrs. Burnett told me in one of the counselling sessions Mom recommended that sometimes a stressful event can bring a family together. The shock jolts you out of bad patterns. But it hasn't been like that for us. When Mom said we were going to live with Aunt Irene, a professor in the Faculty of History, for a while in Oxford where there were better doctors, I knew Dad wouldn't be coming. They both said it was temporary but I guessed that was only for Kira's sake. Mom had always been there for us while Dad was away at the office. He had been more of a spectator to our lives. He'd make special appearances on the weekends, serve us breakfast, take us to the zoo once in a while. I'm not surprised he couldn't take it.

Lately I've been telling myself stories about our life in Toronto, trying to fix my memories in place. It's not easy though. Memory is a tricky thing. It isn't a ruler, a hard, straight line for measuring the past, the passage of days, months, years. Memory doesn't work the way my old grade school history books do. It isn't neat and tidy. It's more like murmurs, voices whispering in the darkness. Aunt Irene told me that was how the monks used to remember things. They would whisper the words to themselves over and over again, fixing images, sentences, whole histories in their minds so they wouldn't be forgotten. *Memor. Murmure.* The meanings of the words are intertwined.

A long time ago I used to play dead. Back then I wanted to keep death near me, to imagine what it might be like. Not Death with the robes black as midnight carrying a mirror-bright scythe. Not the death in monster stories, a hand that grabs you in the night. But the feeling of rest after a long journey.

But ever since Kira got sick I've been thinking about things differently. Death is a doorway and I don't want to know what's on the other side.

# ONE

The powers of creation come into violent collision; the sultry dryness of the atmosphere; the subterraneous thunders; the mist of overflowing waters, are the harbingers of destruction. Nature is not satisfied with the ordinary alterations of life and death, and the destroying angel waves over man and beast his flaming sword.

Justus Friedrich Carl Hecker, "General Observations,"
*The Black Death in the Fourteenth Century*

# 1

The episodes always begin the same way, with a strange look in Kira's eyes and that twist of her mouth. Everyone says they're a symptom of her condition, an intermittent twinge of paralysis. "Watch for changes," Mom said, "but don't be afraid. Just write it down, record everything."

It's early January now, a month since we arrived in England. Christmas was a blur of torn paper and scraps of twirled ribbon. Gifts grabbed last-minute from Oxfam to replace things we left behind.

And now this. Aunt Irene has driven us out to Bunkers Hill, a little nothing stretch of road twenty minutes north of where we live. Kira's wearing oversized rubber boots, the thinness of her body hidden by a waterproof jacket, her small hands in ratty purple mittens. She trudges gracelessly ahead of us on the opposite side of the road. It's just the three of us today, Mom absent again because of another meeting with the specialists at the Centre where she's been taking Kira for treatment. When she left this morning I could tell she wasn't expecting good news.

So we're still doing our best at make-believe. Aunt Irene suggested a trip to the countryside, and here we are—just outside Oxford, a place I'd only heard about in stories. I'm surrounded by a tangle of green, gappy hedgerows of hawthorn and blackberry scrub. My aunt has been pointing out features of the new landscape to us: early blooming irises, nettle husks that still sting if you brush them with bare hands, jack snipes, chaffinches, all the other birds I don't recognize yet. The air is milder than it would be back in Toronto this time of year, the wind more like breath. Flowers in January.

On the right is a row of terrace houses, most of them showing signs of abandonment. In front of me an inflatable snowman lists to the side, sagging and dingy. A walnut tree has dropped a branch as thick as my wrist into a tangle of clothes line. Just before Christmas the River Cherwell broke its banks and flooded this area, prompting a temporary evacuation. The water has drained into ditches and culverts but most of the families still haven't come back. Maybe they never will.

Storms have been worsening everywhere. In the airport before we left Mom couldn't tear her eyes away from the monitors, watching the presenters go on and on about the devastation. All over England, rivers have been breaking their banks, or trying to, only held in check by levees and diversion canals. Whole villages in the south have vanished and in Wales the flooding has stripped away the peat, leaving behind ancient animal bones—bears, red deer and aurochs, things that have been extinct for hundreds of years.

"Do you really think it'll be better for us in England?" I'd wanted to know.

"It's for your sister, Feef," she'd said tiredly. "Your aunt said they'll be able to help her. And it's only for a little while."

Kira coughs hoarsely into her fist, another sign of trouble, and her medical ID bracelet jingles. She showed it off like it was a charm bracelet when her clinician first gave it to her, twisting it this way and that in the light. Now she usually keeps it hidden. KIRA PERELLA – JUVENILE IDIOPATHIC IMMUNODEFICIENCY SYNDROME.

"Should we go back?" Aunt Irene asks. There's a muscle over her left eye that starts to jump when she's worried. Mom has the same twitch.

I shake my head, watching Kira. "Let's wait."

Kira plods along the road, stiff-kneed, ignoring us. She sets one foot in front of the other, walking an imaginary tightrope, toe pointed. Then she points to her right, squinting into the distance. "What's that?"

Through the tangle of hedges and brown brambles I see what caught Kira's attention. The silhouette of a tower, at least a hundred feet tall, jutting into the sky. "Well spotted," Aunt Irene says, smiling. "That's the old Cherwell cement works. It's been empty for a good while now. That was the chimney, I think? There used to be all sorts of other machinery around it, and flues for separating the hot gases from the kilns. You can just see the quarry lake from here. I imagine it's drenched down there right now. I used to..." She shades her eyes with her hands. "There was a man I knew who worked at that site, a quarry engineer who sometimes did freelance work assessing dig sites for the School of Archaeology. We went for walks around here."

A trace of emotion crosses her face but I don't say anything. I always used to ask Mom about her life before I was born, old boyfriends, how things were when she was my age. Not so much now.

Before Kira got sick all I could talk about was university. I spent late nights at Jaina Heymann's place, she and I flipping through course catalogues together, looking at media studies or English, maybe journalism. It all seemed within easy reach. Now there's a painful squeeze in my chest when I think about how my future was supposed to be. Mom's trawling for a sixth form college here that will take me at short notice. A whole new system with A-level exams in the late spring I'll need to pass.

I take a breath and let it out slowly but the ache is still there.

"I thought it was, you know, like a castle. Mom said there would be castles around here." Kira stares at the tower, tugging off her mittens.

"Not *here*, Kiki," I tell her. "She just meant in England."

Her grey eyes narrow. "She said *here*."

"I'll show you a castle," Aunt Irene says. "In the summer we can all go to Warwickshire. There's a proper castle near where your cousins live, much older. The cement works was built in the twenties." She grins at me conspiratorially. I like her like this.

If Mom's around Aunt Irene is different, more careful—with Kira especially. I don't think she's used to kids anymore. Before Kira was born, she took a sabbatical year in Toronto and she visited us all the time. I still remember her distracted kindness, the beat-up guitar she gave me when she thought I might be musical, her encouragement even when the lessons didn't take. She was always reading, and she infected me with her love of stories. If she was sitting at the breakfast table she'd read the ingredients on the Rice Krispies box aloud. It used to drive Dad crazy.

I keep quiet. I love the smell of damp stones and moss, the minty musk of nettles. Ivy crawls over every surface, trees and fences and brickwork. All these houses will disappear eventually and no one will miss them. For some reason it feels good to me, being in a place so close to being forgotten.

"Promise?"

A horn from a distant riverboat sounds and all at once the sky is filled with birds.

"Starlings," Aunt Irene cries out. "Look!"

They take to the air making a fantastic noise. Where did they come from? I hadn't seen them on the trees, or I hadn't understood what they were. Just leaves, dead things.

Kira fumbles for my hand. There are moments like this when everything feels the way it used to. I glance at her and she smiles, a brief resurgence of her old self. The strange look in her eyes is gone and I wonder if maybe I imagined it. Still, she's pale and a blue vein glows at her temple.

"Hey now, kiddo." I give her hand a squeeze. "How're you holding up?"

Her eyes are still fixed on the birds, watching the flock twist itself into complicated patterns and ghostly shapes, almost recognizable.

"Maybe it's time to go home," she says.

Home. I wish it were as easy as that.

# 2

It's just past five when Aunt Irene pulls her Renault into the driveway. Her house—*our* house—stands at the eastern edge of Osney, a wedge of barely-island just outside Oxford town, circled by the Thames and its offshoot tributaries. The river footpath runs along the side of the house to the southeast, criss-crossing the waterways down to Christ Church Meadow, a popular gathering place for the students from the Colleges.

Kira's nodded off in the back seat. She only stirs a little when Aunt Irene opens the door and unbuckles her.

"Want me to carry you upstairs?" She's too big but I ask anyway, backsliding into how it was between us when she was younger. All the medical tests and treatments have made her wary of being touched.

"I can walk," she yawns.

Where the Thames flows past the house, thickset men in fluorescent vests are laying sandbags down in case of another storm. "Hullo, my duck!" one of them says to Kira, his vowels slippery and rolling. She smiles shyly and offers a little wave.

"Will we sound like that one day, Soff?" she murmurs to me as Aunt Irene fiddles with the keys on the step. Kira tries on their accent: "*Hulloo, me durrck!*"

"Maybe. Would you want that?" Mom's already got a lilt in her voice I don't recognize. She's starting to sound more and more like Aunt Irene, which I guess is how she used to sound before she moved to Toronto before I was born.

"Nuh-uh. No way."

Inside we all struggle to find somewhere to dump our things. There are coats and backpacks hung on the knob of the banister or piled with the muddy boots next to the front door. Aunt Irene wasn't used to having company much before us. So many things are broken in the house: the kitchen clock, half the electrical sockets. The lower right-hand corner of my bedroom window has a thick crack running through it that lets in the cold. "That's just how it is here," Mom says if I complain. In Toronto Dad wanted our home to be immaculate. But I like how this place seems to say, "There are more important things to be worrying about."

Mom appears in the doorway to the kitchen. "How was it?" She looks worn down, but weirdly it makes her seem more glamorous. She has the striking features you see in certain old paintings, cheekbones made for candlelight, her hair a shade darker than mine, chocolate with hints of copper. She's beautiful in a way that makes it difficult for people to like her, the wrong combination of fragility and hardness. But where Mom is lithe and elegant I take after Aunt Irene: square, compact shoulders and narrow hips.

"Okay," I tell her, "but there was—"

"Nothing *happened*." Kira's glaring at me. I decide to hold off until she's out of earshot.

"How was the Centre? Any news, Char?" Aunt Irene asks as she steps out of her mud-splattered boots.

Kira rolls her eyes. She hates people talking about her. "Going upstairs," she announces and clumps her way up to our bedroom. We share a big room upstairs, a barely insulated extension over the garage that Aunt Irene was using as an office before we arrived. My bed is mounted on an interior balcony I have to climb a ladder to reach while Kira's is tucked underneath, an old wire-framed twin that looks like it came from a charity shop.

Mom shrugs and makes a sign for us both to come into the kitchen where Kira won't hear. "Nothing definitive. Not yet anyway. But Dr. Varghese wants to meet with Sophie after we visit Cherwell College tomorrow." She glances over at me. "Would you mind terribly, Feef? She says it might help for the two of you to get to know each other."

"Whatever's best." I hate visiting hospitals but I know it'll be easier on Mom if I suck it up.

"Good girl." Mom kisses the top of my head.

• • •

Aunt Irene offers to work from home the next day so she can watch Kira while Mom drives me around.

"Most of the students in Cherwell College will be ahead of you," explains one of the teachers, Mr. Coomes, for the umpteenth time in my interview. "You'll have to work hard if you want to catch up." He has sharply parted hair, glossy black streaked with white like a badger's. He reminds me of the men from Dad's office: that clipped way of speaking, the musky smell of cologne.

I grit my teeth and smile for him. "I know. But I don't mind the challenge."

Mom's quick to say how smart I am, how she doesn't think I'll have any difficulty with the reading load. He quirks an eyebrow at me and all I can do is nod while he shows us around. We brush past a group of uniformed girls my age who glance at me without interest. They look identical: red lipstick and too-heavy mascara. Like old-fashioned pin-up models.

Pod people, Jaina used to call kids like that.

When the tour is over Mr. Coomes hesitates before taking my outstretched hand.

"I do hope your sister feels better. Our Centre, I hear, is very good for people with her condition." Our situation was explained before we arrived, offered as a kind of apology. I'm getting used to it. Before I can respond Mom's taking the registration forms from him and hurrying me out into the parking lot.

"God, what an ass. I forgot how condescending people can be over here," she says when we're back in the car.

"He was all right." It's the fourth place we've been to but the only one willing to take me at short notice. If I don't start now I won't be able to take the exams in the spring and that could mean putting off university for a whole year.

"You could imagine going there?"

"The other students seemed nice," I lie.

"There are other schools in some of the nearby towns that might have spaces open…"

"We can register tomorrow," I tell her.

We head west along the high street, passing Brasenose College and the heavy iron gates of the exam schools. As I watch a gaggle of the older students heading toward the Bodleian Library, I feel a twinge of envy. I want that to be me next year.


Perched at the top of Headington Hill sits the John Radcliffe Hospital, a massive complex of grey brick and glass.

"Last stop, I promise," says Mom as she leads me toward one of the side entrances. "We won't be long." From the parking lot I have a stellar view of Oxford. I can make out the spires of the Colleges in the distance to the southwest. To the north is a load of prefab pop-up wards, and beyond that, the countryside, rolling hills sketched out in yellowy green and brown.

This is the part of the day I've been dreading. Mom and Kira have been here once a week since we moved back in December but it's my first visit. I wouldn't have come if I had a choice.

The hospital has chipped blue-green walls that make you feel like you're underwater, slightly rubberized flooring that turns your footsteps noiseless. The same depressing aura as hospitals we'd been to in Toronto. The JI2 Centre's new wing is an annexation of the old blood donor ward. They haven't taken down the old signs. There's something desperate about the whole operation. All the on-duty nurses have the same burnt-out look, as if they've been running triple shifts. There are loads of volunteers in dark blue smocks and posters asking for more to help out at all hours.

"Something wrong?" Mom asks me.

"I guess I thought it'd be shiny and new. Space-aged." I try not to let me disappointment show.

"They're really good with Kira, you'll see—and they've just opened a new set of wards."

Knowing they're expanding doesn't calm the swimmy feeling in my stomach. It just means they haven't found a solution yet and more kids are getting sick.

"Come on you, Dr. Varghese is waiting."

We check in at reception and find the office we're looking for, and a slight, dark-haired woman answers Mom's knock. Back home I got used to meeting different kinds of doctors: the chummy ones who pretended I was their best friend, the sympathetic ones, and the ones so focused on Kira they barely saw me. I try to size up Dr. Varghese but she doesn't match any of these. For one, she's a good six inches shorter than I am and maybe ten years older. So, young for a doctor, and pretty too. She looks me in the eye when she introduces herself. "You must be Sophie. You know you have your mother's eyes, you and Kira both. But then you must be used to hearing that!"

She offers us seats in her office. The room is spare except for a couple of framed photographs.

"Your mother and I thought it would be a good idea for us to meet properly. I'm your sister's clinician—her primary carer here at the Centre. I know this must be stressful for you."

"She's been managing it really well, haven't you, Feef?" Mom chimes in.

Dr. Varghese smiles. "Let's start with what you know about your sister's condition."

I rap my fingers against my knee. "I know something's wrong with her immune system. That she gets sleepy more easily and restless sometimes. That if she gets sick then JI2 can make it much worse."

"That's the gist of it. It took us a while to identify Juvenile Idiopathic Immunodeficiency Syndrome as a single condition because the first cases presented in different ways, as clusters of seemingly unconnected symptoms.

'Immunodeficiency' means the body doesn't fight diseases and infections the way it's supposed to, so sometimes blood doesn't clot properly or the immune system can attack healthy cells. Health problems—even common ones—can be much more dangerous."

"I still don't understand what's causing it."

"That's what 'idiopathic' means. It doesn't seem to be a virus or a bacterium."

"I've heard it's spreading though."

Dr. Varghese sucks in a breath. "Yes, well, that's true. Over thirty thousand cases have been documented in Britain alone." Mom's eyes widen. It's more than either of us had heard.

"What are the recovery rates?" I'm testing her. No one's given me a straight answer so far.

"It's too early to tell."

I grimace.

"Patients with the condition have a statistically higher rate of mortality within the first four months of diagnosis but—listen, Sophie, the numbers never tell the whole story. They aren't a prediction. And we've made some major breakthroughs in the last few weeks."

"Like what?" I've read dozens of online summaries that all say the same thing: we don't know what it is. But Dr. Varghese surprises me again. While Mom listens, nodding from time to time, she explains to me that they've identified a special hormone in the bloodstream of patients like Kira. "It seems to be manufactured by the thyroid, we think, in addition to thyroxin, which plays an important role in all sorts of body functions, like digestion and brain development and bone growth. The hormone interferes in some of those processes. It can disrupt body temperature, blood pressure and clotting, which is one of the reasons your sister's immune system is compromised." When she sees the look on my face she changes tack. "We call it a 'juvenile' syndrome because it only seems to affect young people. We suspect it has something to do with the changes the body goes through in puberty."

"I've heard of kids older than me getting it."

"Most of the changes in your body are over by the time you're seventeen or eighteen but some go on after that. The prefrontal cortex, which handles all sorts of complex processes like reasoning and memory, continues to develop into your early twenties."

"So Kira may grow out of it?" I ask hopefully.

Mom squeezes my hand again but Dr. Varghese's smile is restrained. "We *think* so. But with your mother's help—and yours as well—her condition should be manageable."

She stands and walks toward a large cabinet and she comes back with a small plastic device that looks like a tuning fork with a screen on it. "This is a HemaPen. It's based on insulin monitors so it's non-invasive. We'll use it to track Kira's hormone levels."

She hands it to me. It looks jury-rigged, as if it was pounded out in shop class yesterday. Heavier than I expected. She takes it back and turns it over, lightly flicking a sensor on its base. Then she slides its two prongs around either side of her index finger. "Like this. It should only take a second." The machine makes a crackling sound and flashes green. "It'll automatically send the results to us. I want you to keep an eye on your sister and let me know if you spot anything out of the ordinary—even if you don't think it's important. You may see something I can't."

"Sophie's amazing with her," Mom pipes up, nudging me with her elbow. "The best."

When we get home Aunt Irene is in the kitchen starting on dinner. She doesn't cook much and with all the flooding it's been difficult to get fresh ingredients. All signs point to another night of pasta and red sauce.

"Go check on Kira, will you?" Mom hands me the box with the HemaPen inside. "God knows I'm not her favourite person right now."

"I can try."

I find her asleep in the loft. She's an inert comma beneath the sheets, head turned away from me.

"Kira?"

She twists around, giving me the hairy eyeball when

she catches sight of what I've got. "Will it hurt?" Not *what is it*. She knows what it is, or close enough. It bothers me how used to the idea of being tested she's become.

"Just slide it between your fingers."

She presents her palm to me so I can help her, then yanks it away when I press the button. "Ouch!"

"Are you sure it wasn't just cold?"

"It *hurt*."

She buries her head in the pillow. A minute later the HemaPen begins to crackle softly. "Anything else I should record?" I ask. There's a logbook on her bedside table to track her symptoms.

A mumbled "nuh-uh."

"Please? I'll take you to the pub for pudding."

She pulls the pillow away. "Say 'dessert,' Soff."

"I like saying 'pudding.'" I nudge her foot. "Now you, enough stalling, pudding or no pudding?"

"Fiiine." She tugs at a lock of long white-blond hair. The strands look frayed at their ends. "Out of breath, um, weakness in the right leg. Tiredness…"

"Scale of one to ten?"

She tucks the hair between her teeth and slicks it to a point. "Eight."

"Pain?"

"Hmm." She's fading. I write down what she's said and put the logbook back next to the HemaPen.

The faint sound of snores. Her face has gone smooth, slack, vulnerable.

I let out a breath, suddenly unsettled by the distance I've travelled from Toronto to here. My eyes slide over Aunt Irene's old shelves, still crammed so tightly with her books they creak whenever I try to prise one out. Reference tomes on the Middle Ages alongside old science fiction paperbacks like *The Chrysalids* by John Wyndham, which I remember reading in the ninth grade. It's something at least. I had to leave most of my books at home.

She must have been in here during the afternoon. One book sticks out crookedly and I pull it free, glancing at the title. *A Little Book for the Pestilence.* It's old and sweet-smelling like musty vanilla. The glue has weakened and a frail sheet flutters to the ground, the heading inked in a heavy, monastic-looking copperplate. *In like wise, as Avicenna says in his fourth book, by the air above the bodies beneath may be infected.*

The cryptic words remind me of an old copy of the I Ching that belonged to Jaina's hippy-dippy mother. She loved crystals, burning sage and incense, ley lines and ouija boards. "Every part of the world touches every other part," she used to tell us, clad in a long, loose-fitting skirt redolent of sandalwood. When Jaina and I were alone we'd laugh about it but we let her read our fortunes. "The gentle wind roams the earth. The superior person expands her sphere of influence as she expands her awareness," she would intone.

I turn the page over but behind me Kira stirs on the bed, her voice guttural and indistinct, coming from somewhere deep in her chest. As I slide the page back into the book, the HemaPen stops its processes with a low blip. Numbers in a neutral dark grey scroll across its display panel but I have no idea what they might mean.

After spending most of the day in bed Kira gets up for dinner and won't settle until I take her along the canal to see the houseboats. They're as exotic as gypsy caravans, lacquered in deep purple, oxblood, navy, russet, pink and gold. Kira loves the potted plants and lawn chairs laid out on the roofs.

"One day," she tells me, "I'm gonna live in a boat just like that. What's the ocean between here and home again?"

"The Atlantic."

Dreamily: "Yeah. I'm going to sail across the Atlantic. You can come too, I guess."

"You think we'd both fit?"

"I'd fit but you might have a problem, porky."

It's not until well past ten that she finally nods off. I decide to get a start on the syllabus Mr. Coomes gave me. Aunt Irene has piled some of the books from the list on the corner of my bed. I curl up under the covers and begin working my way through *The Yellow Wallpaper* by Charlotte Perkins Gilman. It's a strange partial autobiography of a distraught woman locked in a sick room:

> *For outside you have to creep on the ground, and everything is green instead of yellow. But here I can creep smoothly on the floor, and my shoulder just fits in that long smooch around the wall, so I cannot lose my way.*

There's a narcotic flow to the words as the narrator's world contracts down to a tiny room she can't escape. I lose myself in the story until the buzz of my tablet interrupts me with a message from Jaina.

Jayhey04: u there soff? got sumthing to show u. u'll wanna see it. Promise.

There's a hot itch of worry in my palms, the back of my knees. I dog-ear my page and set the book down.

We used to message daily, but I haven't been in touch for a while now. The signal's been on and off since the substation blew during the last storm. There are rolling brownouts to reduce the load until things are repaired. Resources are stretched thin everywhere.

**FeeFeesFeed:** Im here.

**Jayhey04:** u seen it yet? Pls tell me u saw it!

A link hovers at the bottom of the message, but I don't click on it, not immediately. There are a load of forums devoted to JI2. Some tracking news reports, others spinning off into conjecture and conspiracy theory. Jaina's been a regular on most of them, ever since Kira got sick. The first time she invited me to one, I lurked for a couple of days, tracking threads about the infection rates in India and China. I finally figured out the users were mostly rubberneckers, chasing disaster. I didn't much like the idea that Jaina was one of them.

I toy with the idea of putting the tablet away, going back to my homework. I want to see how it ends, what the woman will discover in the strange sickly wallpaper of her room. But I know Jaina will badger me with messages until I give in.

**FeeFeesFeed:** hold on

When I click on the link, the page opens to a news video. A shaky mobile camera with a smooth voice-over talking about a kid named Liam Barrett. I can make out a small crowd of people and, beyond them, the expanse of the ocean, grey the colour of wet ash, its surface frothed with whiteheads. Clouds scud the horizon.

*Liam Barrett was on a ferry off the coast of Vancouver when tragedy struck...*

The footage must be from one of the other passengers because at first it focuses on a twenty-something girl waving to the camera. Behind her is a freckly kid a year or two older than Kira with a mop of blond curls peeking out from under a fur-lined trapper hat, leaning against the railing of the boat next to his dad. He's pointing at something in the distance—a pod of dolphins? The camera zooms past him to try to focus on the sleek shapes, diving in and out of the water. Then the angle shifts and a woman is shouting, incoherent. The kid is on the railing, both arms lifted. The shot jerks and blurs, snatches a slice of clouded sky as the boat crashes into a wave and whoever is holding it loses control for a moment. When it refocuses, he's gone.

FeeFeesFeed: i dont get it. Wht happened?

Jayhey04: did u watch it all?

A hard cut to the newsroom. The host and her partner have adopted chatty tones, like this is breakfast TV fodder, despite the serious glances they sometimes gives the camera. "Liam Barrett's father has confirmed that his son was JI2 positive. His body was taken to St. Paul's Hospital shortly after where the so-called jitterbug video was taken."

FeeFeesFeed: jitterbug?

Jayhey04: its gone viral now, check it out

Another link then, with over twelve million hits. This video is clearer, a still point of reference rather than the jerky-cam style on the boat. No audio. It shows a clinical-looking room, bright lights that flare, blanking the image with white. There's the same kid laid out on a steel table. The curly hair and still, pale face. It takes me a moment to understand. He's dead, and this is his autopsy.

The camera trained on him wobbles. Someone must be holding it.

Jayhey04: u watching?

How could this be posted? Notifications flash at the bottom of the screen, more comments. The views are racking up.

Then I see it: his right leg has begun to hop. It's barely noticeable at first, the way your leg might twitch if you had a bad spasm. "Shhh …" says a voice. "There it is. It's happening again." A blurry hand appears in front of the lens, pointing. A moment later Liam Barrett's left leg jumps. Then his whole body starts to rock as if he's having a fit.

*Jesus Jesus Jesus.* My heart is beating wildly. What am I watching?

FeeFeesFeed: what is it??

Jayhey04: CBC says its some sort of lazarus reflex but who knows?

I type "JI2" and "lazarus reflex" into my search bar, my hands shaking. The first page in my feed is a *Globe and Mail* article from an hour ago.

## PHAC denies that JI2 is linked to
## post-mortem tremors

TORONTO – Vancouver's deputy chief medical health officer said yesterday the province was investigating protocols after an anonymous video taken by a nurse was released of a boy's body suffering what have been called post-mortem tremors.

Liam Barrett, aged twelve, was diagnosed two months ago with Juvenile Idiopathic Immunodeficiency Syndrome (JI2). His is the fourth confirmed death to be labelled as an accident in recent weeks. The case is being investigated by the Public Health Agency of Canada (PHAC)'s National Microbiology Laboratory in Winnipeg but officials deny there is a link to JI2.

Most doctors attribute the strange phenomenon to the so-called Lazarus reflex, which causes brain-dead patients to briefly raise their arms. Barrett, they believe, may have been improperly confirmed as deceased. The phenomenon is named after the biblical figure Lazarus of Bethany, whom Jesus allegedly raised from the dead in the Gospel of John.

But others have suggested a different explanation.

Dr. Eliseo Gilabert, the coroner who certified Barrett's death, said: "Liam Barrett was clinically dead, yet his body showed signs of enough cellular energy for certain genes to become active. All we can say is that JI2 seems to be inducing biological processes we still don't fully understand. It's time the medical community started talking about this openly."

I try to digest this. Has Mom seen it? Aunt Irene?

I switch off the tablet. I don't want to see any more videos or hear Jaina's crazy theories, not when it's my sister who's sick. I swing myself down from the bed. Kira is still asleep, hair mussed. I crouch down next to her and touch her shoulder. After a moment she stirs, pushes my hand away. One sleepy eye opens.

"What's wrong?" she grouses. It's even colder in here at night. I can see the goosebumps on her exposed arm.

"Nothing." I want to bundle her up in my arms.

"You're making a worried face."

"No, I'm not." I pinch her, an old reflex from when she was healthy and didn't bruise so badly. But she squeals, tries to tickle me back though I can keep her arms pinned to the pillow without much effort.

"Soff, don't!" she says in that voice that always used to mean, yes, keep going. "I'll kick your butt!" But after a second or two she scowls. "Just stop, okay?" She slumps back and pulls the covers up around her neck.

# 3

It's clear from the nervous energy in the house the next morning that Mom and Aunt Irene have both heard about Liam Barrett. When I leave Kira asleep upstairs I find Mom curled up on the couch with her sketchpad, fingers blackened with charcoal, drawing meaningless patterns on the page. Something about the shape of them reminds me of *The Yellow Wallpaper*.

*Up and down and sideways they crawl, and those absurd, unblinking eyes are everywhere.*

Aunt Irene is near the refrigerator, sniffing at a carton of milk. "Power went off again," she says, lips curled. "This is no good. Happy with toast?"

The bread is stale and neither of us trusts the butter not to have spoiled so we have the toast plain, both of us standing close to the stove. The heat is enough to keep the small space warm despite the chill rolling off the river.

"Leave her for now," Aunt Irene says when my gaze

drifts back to the sitting room. "She doesn't want to talk to anyone. She's pretty upset."

I shrug, try on an adult tone: "Kira's okay, though. She'll be fine." I can hear my own false confidence.

Aunt Irene wipes the crumbs from the counter into her hand. "Your mum wants to take her in to the Centre today."

I munch on the dry toast, swallow then ask, "Will you tell her? Kira, I mean? About the video?"

"Should we?"

I let the thought roll around in my mind. Liam Barrett on the table, his skin pale and bloodless. Then the twitch of his nerveless muscles. The image fills my mind like a dark cloud.

"I don't think it would help much, would it? You know how irritable she can get. There's no point in scaring her."

Aunt Irene nods slowly. "Do you want to come with me today? I can show you around the university. It'll be good for you. I don't want to leave you here by yourself."

"It's just a Lazarus effect, right?"

Her eyes drift toward the living room, settling on Mom's half-finished mug of tea. Mom's charcoals make a scratching sound, like an animal scrabbling to get out. "Try not to worry too much," my aunt says, the same thing everyone has been saying for ages. "It's no good for you either."

• • •

The pestilence which first began in the land inhabited by the Saracens, grew so strong that it visited every place…"

One of Aunt Irene's undergraduates is reading to her, rapid-fire. I can see him from where I'm sitting in the hall outside her office. He's a year or two older than me, gawky and skittish. On his nose sit thick Harry Potter glasses, which he pushes up as he looks over his paper. "Robert of Avesbury writes that the Black Death began in England in the county of Dorset. Those marked for death, he tells us, were scarcely permitted to live longer than three or four days."

"That's enough, Martin, thank you," Aunt Irene says. "Have you looked at the spread of the plague to York in 1373? Thomas Stubbs, a Dominican friar, wrote that following Christmas the River Ouse flooded and burst its banks. The sickness raged until the feast of St. James the Apostle, which would be, let me see, late July? So, six months then…"

It turned out Aunt Irene had forgotten she had scheduled a catch-up tutorial with one of her students. She's a bit like that sometimes, lost in her own head. Waiting isn't too bad though. I've curled up in a chair outside her office with a copy of *The Hobbit*. But I barely pay attention to it, my focus shifting back to their conversation.

"It was the same confluence of events back then," Aunt Irene says, "the changing weather patterns and shifts in the climate. For a long time scholars thought the plague was spread predominantly by rats carrying fleas but the story's more complicated than that. Black rats were rare in northern Europe yet those regions were still devastated by the second outbreak. There's evidence now that warmer temperatures were spreading diseases such as malaria and dengue."

"So as the climate changed, so did the transmission of all those diseases?"

"That was part of it, certainly, but scientists can't agree why. Perhaps it's that the shifts in the climate had already weakened the population. An unusually heavy rain in the spring of 1315, followed by harsh winters and cold summers, meant that most of the crops failed. It took more than five years for Europe to recover, and in the meantime there was widespread famine. Children were often orphaned and left to fend for themselves. Remember the story of Hansel and Gretel?"

The student, Martin, gulps, his sharp Adam's apple bobbing. Aunt Irene must see the look on his face as well because her tone softens. "All right, then," she says. "That should be enough to go forward with. I want you to do some reading on rainfall patterns in the north of England. Shall we meet again once term picks up?"

"I've got—" He frowns and glances at the doorway, me beyond it, but doesn't finish. "I'll find a way to make it work. I appreciate you seeing me early since I missed so much before Christmas." He stuffs his books into a leather satchel, then stops, pushes his glasses up his nose again. "I'm sorry, it's

just that I had some bad news this week. From the hospital."
I can hear a familiar jingling noise. He's pulling back his
sleeve to show Aunt Irene something: a medical ID bracelet,
just like Kira's. "I've just been diagnosed. I mean, the tests
came back positive." He's red-faced now. "My clinician says I
don't need to worry. Not yet. But there were complications
back in December … I wanted you to know so you didn't
think I was an utter incompetent."

"Oh, Martin, I had no idea. You shouldn't have come
in. This essay can wait. How are things at home?" I can't quite
make out Aunt Irene's face.

"My parents died two years ago. It's just my big sister
Cath and me now but she's clever. She's handling it really well."

Aunt Irene catches me staring and she stands to close
the door the rest of the way, muffling their conversation.
Embarrassed at being caught eavesdropping, I pretend to be
reading but can't concentrate. A few minutes later the door
opens again and out comes the student. He wipes at his nose
with his sleeve, glances at me.

"That's a good one." He nods at the book, trying out a
smile and I return it. He stands there, looking a little bit lost.
Is he waiting to be dismissed by me as well? Part of me wants
to hug him but I don't. Of course I don't.

"Sophie, you can come in now," Aunt Irene calls. He
hoists his satchel over his shoulder and with the barest lifting
of two fingers in a wave, he disappears. "Sorry, sweetie," my

aunt says when the door is closed behind me. "You shouldn't have had to listen to that."

"It's fine," I say, though it's her who looks more upset. I wonder if this is the first time a student has told her they have JI2.

I glance around, looking for a way to distract her. I've never been in her office before, which in many ways feels like an extension of the house. The smell of old paper, musty but comforting. Her desk is the opposite of Dr. Varghese's, cluttered with papers, receipts, a cheap vase with no flowers. Two enormous maps take up most of the north wall, one of them a replica of the Hereford Mappa Mundi that dates to the thirteenth century. I can spot the word *Ierusalem* in barely legible script at the centre. There—the British Isles sits in the bottom corner. Dotting the map are sketches of plants and animals, exotic birds, headless monsters with eyes glowing in their chests, minotaurs, phoenixes, camels and elephants. The second is a modern survey map of England with various pins and flags sticking out with labels bearing her spiky handwriting.

"So tell me about what you're doing here."

"What…" She shakes her head as if it's a radio set to the wrong channel. "It's a map of abandoned villages. Places where people used to live until disease struck, mostly the Black Death."

"It happened in 1349, right? That's what you and Martin were talking about."

"Top marks, niece of mine."

"You don't find it morbid working on this? I mean, now of all times?" *Morbid* is Mom's word for it, the word she uses when Aunt Irene isn't around.

She smiles faintly. "Morbid … well, maybe. When I was younger, I was fascinated by disasters. I used to keep newspaper clippings. Bits from museum brochures, whatever I could find. It was the really strange bits that I loved best." She stares at the pins on her map, then casually ruffles the curls of paper attached to them. "I remember reading that during the Black Death in some places there weren't enough churchyards to deal with the dead. So they laid all the bodies on top of one another. A macabre lasagna—that's how a monk from Florence described it. I couldn't conceive of a disaster that large. I knew it had happened but it seemed so far removed from my own safe life. There wasn't anything in my experience that helped me understand it."

Her neck flushes hotly when she sees my look.

"Mom doesn't like talking about stuff like this. She says we need to stay positive. No bad thoughts, you know?"

"Bad thoughts, well. That's one way of looking at it."

I can tell from her tone that she doesn't approve. "So how do you look at it then?"

"How much do you know about the spread of diseases?" she asks.

"Not much, I guess. Not enough." I feel embarrassed,

like I've been caught out not doing my homework.

"Shall we go for a wander?" She gathers up some papers from her desk and slides them under her arm, gesturing me out into the hall. New College is like a palace. Even the undergraduate residence wings are roofed with golden spires. But for all that it's beautiful it doesn't feel like a happy place. More like everyone's holding their breath, the students and faculty.

While she leads me through a series of arched corridors, she tells me about her work. "Disease shaped our development, not just at a superficial level, but our biology as well. Our genome is riddled with the debris of ancient viruses, invaders, colonizers who inserted their genes into our own. They *changed* us, and we changed them in return. We twisted them to our own uses. These things, these fossils, they come alive while we are beginning to form in the womb. They defend our cells from infection, and guide us in our growth."

She leads me out into a quadrangle lit up by the pale January light.

"But diseases have a history as well," she says. "That's what I'm interested in. Think about this: it was only when people began to gather in larger communities, during the Neolithic period, that the opportunities for diseases to spread increased dramatically. Diseases require people to be in close proximity to one another, to domesticated animals. That's when they become endemic, or perpetually present."

"So disease is the price we pay for being close to one another."

"That's a good way of looking at it, yes." Aunt Irene wears her interests so plainly it seems almost embarrassing at times—but wonderful too. She isn't afraid of people knowing what she cares about, unlike most of the girls I knew back home. "Disease presents us with the worst picture of humanity we can imagine. It shows us our fallibility, our mortality. At a basic level it makes us fear for our lives, for our communities, and that fear can be a powerful incentive for violence. But in times of plague there are also stories of great kindness, generosity and heroism. It's the testing ground of a civilization."

She pauses while a group of undergraduates rush past us, forcing us to one side. One of them offers a wave of apology to Aunt Irene. He has fine features, dark wavy hair and a slight widow's peak that reminds me of the portrait of Lord Byron in my *Selected Poems*. I feel a pang of longing that he's part of this place, part of her life here.

"I'm not upsetting you, am I? Talking about it like this?" Aunt Irene asks.

I hesitate. Seeing the close knots of students here reminds me of back home, Jaina and I waiting in line at school while nurses took blood samples. I was freaking out, and worried about Kira, but I didn't want to show it. Some of my other friends began acting weird after Kira's diagnosis. They never said anything, not directly, but they stopped coming over to the house and they got obsessive about smearing on disinfectant whenever I was around. It just made things worse, their fake sympathy and their silence.

"No," I tell Irene softly. "It's good to talk about it."

"Come on. Let's get you something to eat."


We hole up in the Senior Common Room, which is a bit like a private club for professors. I'm the youngest person here by decades. The couches are covered with blue and gold fabric that reminds me of chintzy hotel wallpaper. My aunt heaps my plate with cheese, crackers and a giant slice of chocolate cake.

It's only when she sits me down opposite her and her face goes serious that I realize maybe there's more to this visit than I thought.

"What is it?" I ask, stomach sinking.

She stares for a minute longer and then shakes her head, smiling ruefully. "You're smart as a whip, aren't you?" When I start to push the cake away from me she holds up her hands. "It's nothing bad, I promise. Or at least I don't think so. It's just—I'm involved in a project that might be interesting for you."

"For me?" My eyebrows inch up.

"I don't like to go on about my work too much."

"Because of Kira?"

She makes a noise but doesn't answer properly.

"Please. I want to know, really."

"You must be wondering about what's happening. After the news last night." A faint look of distaste crosses her face.

"What you're studying has something to do with that?"

She takes a deep breath and smooths back her hair. "Everyone is searching for precedents for what we're seeing, anything that might help pin down the mode of transmission or help us to understand the disease cycle. Diseases don't spontaneously generate. Like I was saying, they have a history, they *come* from something."

"From what exactly?"

She slices off a hunk of cake with her fork and smiles. "Sorry. This stuff is always on offer but I can't bear to take a whole slice for myself. Mind sharing?"

I don't feel that hungry anyway.

"Did you know that most of the quads in the College used to be burial pits for plague victims?" she asks after a minute.

"There are bodies underneath us right now?"

"There was a team of microbiologists that did studies on the plague victims to see whether there was a bacterium— *Yersinia pestis*—or something else, something we haven't discovered yet. My research has to do with that—the potential links between JI2 and earlier epidemics."

"But, c'mon," I say half-jokingly, "it can't be as bad as the Black Death."

She takes another bite of the cake, not saying anything. In the lull, a sudden wave of homesickness hits me, a longing for normal conversation.

"The issue isn't just scale. We've been processing samples of tooth pulp tissue taken from victims buried in plague pits in the Middle Ages, and earlier. Our original plan was to confirm previous findings, that the bacterium which caused the Black Death was present at those sites. But we found something else. Traces of altered DNA, evidence of a hormone they've detected in patients who have JI2."

I try to work through the implications of this. "You think they had it?"

She looks at me steadily. "Some of them, maybe. What if the bubonic plague wasn't the only cause of death? What if there were two outbreaks happening at the same time? Think about what JI2 causes: a weakened immune system, which makes victims more susceptible to other diseases. Almost half the population of Europe died in the plague and we still don't know for sure why it was so devastating."

"But what about the…" It feels strange to say the words, even comical. "The jitterbug. The Lazarus effect? Do the doctors at the Centre have any idea what it is?"

"That's what we need to find out. The Centre has decided to fund a project of mine. They've offered me a lab at the hospital, space to complete some of my work." She glances away almost shyly now, as if she's worried about overstepping.

"I thought you might help me with the background research. It's transcribing notes, mostly, and admin work. But if you really are interested, it would be a chance to learn more. There's a small pot of money for it."

"You'd really let me help?"

She nods, a slow smile spreading across her face. For a moment I can glimpse another person there, someone younger. The girl who would clip stories from the newspaper, searching for clues as to why things turned out the way they did. "Sometimes the dead are our only way of finding answers."

"Even now?"

"Especially now, niece of mine."

# 4

As the week stretches on, Mom won't let Aunt Irene turn on the TV, in case Kira hears about Liam Barrett on the news. She puts an Internet lock on Kira's tablet too, which leads to Kira pleading with me to let her use mine, just for ten minutes. She whines when I say no.

On Thursday we're supposed to hear back about Kira's blood work but no one calls. Friday, nothing. Mom's nervous about how much Kira is sleeping these days, nervous about the way she seems to blank out for ten to fifteen seconds at a time.

On Saturday morning, the winter sky is drab and dusky. A dull light shines through the kitchen window while the radio calls out gale warnings for all areas except Biscay, Trafalgar and FitzRoy. A fishing boat with a crew of eighteen is foundering somewhere in the Channel. High winds will batter Dover. There are fears that sea walls in London and Devon might falter. Maybe this time, maybe next time. No one knows for sure.

"God, a real tempest is brewing out there," Mom says.

She's making pancakes for breakfast while listening to the shipping forecast, one of the things she missed most after she moved to Toronto. Kira isn't up yet but it was cold enough in the bedroom to send me downstairs shortly after I woke. Even though I've put on my aunt's thick padded slippers, my toes are still chilly.

"Has Aunt Irene already left?" I pour myself a mug of coffee, then return to the book she left on the counter for me to read. When Mom's eyes skate over it her hand freezes. I can see her mouthing the title: *The Black Death: A Personal History*.

There have been intense whispered conversations between Mom and Aunt Irene since I went to New College with her, the words "A-levels" and "her education" flung back and forth between them.

"It's nice to see you up and looking so scholarly on a Saturday." There's a faint edge to her words, which she tries to soften with a smile. She turns back to the pancakes so I can't see her face. "Your aunt wanted to put in a couple of hours at work. She'll be back by lunch, I think."

I push my luck, hoping to coax a little enthusiasm.

"It's pretty great that she wants me to help. It's better than that co-op I did at Toronto East General Hospital, that was nothing but filing paperwork in an office. At least this makes me feel useful. It *means* something, you know?"

She looks as if she wants to object, but instead she says: "If it'll help with your history A-levels…"

"I've been reading about this little town up north called Eyam."

"Am I going to like this story?"

"It's not so bad. In the seventeenth century, a bunch of villagers there realized they were getting sick. They set up a circle of boundary stones, which no one was supposed to cross."

"A quarantine?"

"Uh huh. They bored holes in the rocks where they left coins soaked in vinegar to pay for bundles of food from their neighbours."

"Why vinegar?"

"They thought it would disinfect the coins and keep everyone safe. The thing is, mostly the system worked. The quarantine, I mean." The steam from my coffee makes a pleasant column of warmth over the cup. I take a sip. It's bitter and burnt tasting—delicious. "They had a pretty rough time of it in Eyam, but at least the plague didn't spread."

Now Mom's scooping up the pancakes and laying them out for me alongside thick rashers of bacon. "That was good of them," she says.

"It wasn't like all those apocalypse movies, you know? No fighting, or pillaging or anything. They didn't all suddenly become lawless barbarians. In fact, they probably saved a lot of lives by figuring out how to take care of themselves. It's nice to remember that people aren't *always* completely savage when they're abandoned in a bad situation. They made a decision for themselves."

She sighs and settles herself down on the seat next to me. "Just don't get too caught up in it, okay, sweetheart?"

"Aunt Irene says I can use it as an independent project," I reply defensively. "I've been making notes."

When I hold up my notebook, a tense look passes over her face, a tightening of her jaw. "Your aunt used to do the same thing when she was younger."

"She told me. I thought it sounded like a good idea to have a record of all this. What's happening."

"But why do you *need* something like that? Don't you just want to focus on other things? You're so young, Feef, I don't want you to worry about this. When I was your age—well. Let's just say I had my mind on other things. Other *people*."

Like Dad.

"I want to understand, that's all." I trace the spiral edge of the notebook. "Remember what it was like when Grammy got sick?"

It had happened when I was little. She and Dad's mom had always been close, even when things were rough between them. When Grammy was diagnosed with pancreatic cancer Mom had a hard time coping until Dad converted the basement into a studio. He was good back then but I wonder if that was the beginning of the end, the severing of one last tie between them. Not that I thought about that much at the time. I remember I used to go down sometimes and watch her. She'd create huge collages using hundreds of images from magazines. She'd cut out the pictures, faces mostly, and layer them on top of each other until they took on a new shape, almost three-dimensional. Additive magic, she used to call it.

She made one of Grammy just before she died, when she lost her hair and her face had that gaunt, yellowish sheen. She used all sorts of old pictures, making duplicates of the ones she could find in the old albums. Mom's collage dignified her, gave her depth—it showed something about who she had been, the part of her the disease never touched.

"Okay," Mom says at last, relenting. "If you think it'll help."

The collages didn't come with us to England. As far as I know, Dad still has them in the basement in Toronto, wrapped in plastic sheets like mummies waiting to be discovered.

"Pancakes!" Kira shrieks when she finally comes down the stairs, still rubbing the sleep from her eyes. "Soff, you should've come and got me."

"And you should've got up when I poked you an hour ago."

"I was tired." She slides into the chair across from me and leans on her elbows.

"How tired were you, Kiki?" Mom asks, faux-casual.

"Just *tired*. I don't know the number for how tired I was."

But then that strange look is in Kira's eyes again. When Mom takes Kira's plate from the oven she won't touch it. "I don't want bacon like this. Why can't we have bacon like it was back home?"

"That's just the way they do things here." I make a grab for her plate, which she yanks away. "C'mon, if you're not going to eat it then I will."

"Leave my bacon alone!" This is where we'd normally break into a comfortable sibling squabble, me poking at her, trying to tickle her sides, but the trill of the phone ringing stops us.

"Hello?" Mom's voice changes when she answers. It's Dr. Varghese, then. Kira glares at her plate while Mom disappears into the other room.

"Don't touch me, Soff," she says, "I don't like it."

"Sorry," I tell her, faintly ashamed. A fog of old bruises dots her arm, the webbing of veins visible beneath. Some days her skin seems nearly translucent, like those cave fish used to darkness.

"What is it?" I ask when Mom reappears but she doesn't answer me. She turns to Kira who's just finished scraping her mostly untouched breakfast into the compost bin.

"Sweetheart, can you come here for a minute?"

Kira doesn't look up. Her hands move mechanically.

She puts the plate on the counter next to the sink and starts running the water.

"That was Dr. Varghese on the phone. She's just been looking at the blood work we sent in and she's noticed a problem. She wants you to come in for observation overnight. I know it's a pain."

My chest tightens.

"I don't want to." Kira's voice is tense as a loaded spring.

"This isn't about wanting, baby girl. We need to keep you healthy."

There's relief in Mom's voice. Nothing definitive then, just more testing. Not that Kira is happy about it.

"I don't *care!*" With a fierce swipe, Kira sends her plate crashing into the floor. She stares at the pieces on the ground. "I'm not ever going to get better. We all know that. We just keep pretending."

Mom draws in a slow breath. Ceramic shards skitter away from me as I grab Kira's arm.

"Don't talk like that to Mom," I warn her. "You just have to…" I don't know. Her eyes are glossy with unshed tears. I tell myself I can fix this, I know I can. But this is the kid who used to do one-handed cartwheels in the backyard. She used to fly down the soccer pitch, the best player on her team. Everything she used to love is being stripped away from her.

"Let me take her out, okay? She just needs to get out of

the house," I tell Mom. Before I know it I've begun bundling Kira up into her waterproof jacket.

"Where are you going?" Mom demands. She won't look at Kira, who is furiously tugging on her boots.

"Not far, I promise. We'll come back if she gets tired. But I can get her calmed down. Just let me—"

BANG!

The door has slammed shut behind Kira. Mom's hand wanders to her throat. "I'm sorry," she whispers, "tell her that, Feef? I don't want this anymore than she does."

"I know, Mom. She knows too. She just forgets sometimes."

"Hey, come back!" Kira's fast but I'm faster.

"I don't want to talk to you."

When I grab her hand, she spins around, huffing, out of breath. "I'm not five," she says, "I can be outside on my own."

I hate the look of strain on her face, the dark smudges beneath her eyes. "Let me come with you. Just so Mom won't worry."

In a small, repentant voice, she asks: "Aren't you mad at me? I broke a plate."

"I'm not mad."

"I didn't mean what I said."

"It's hard for all of us, Kiki," I tell her.

"I keep scaring everyone. I'm so sick of it! And now it's just gonna get worse, isn't it? What happened to Liam Barrett's probably gonna happen to me too."

"How do you know about that?" I ask sharply.

She looks away. "I stole your tablet."

"You know the password?"

She shrugs.

"Kira, it doesn't mean anything. No one thinks it means anything."

"Jaina does. I saw her messages."

Jesus. I take a deep breath.

"Jaina's just being stupid. Remember when she told you that you could catch herpes from going to the toilet after Meg Cavendish? It's the same thing. It's just people getting scared and then doing the thing they always do when they get scared. Making stuff up to scare other people."

She kicks at a rock and sends it skittering over the side of the bank. "Why do people do that?"

"Because it's easier when everyone else is scared too, okay?" After she's wiped the tears from her eyes, I ask her, "D'you want to go back?" Near the horizon rain clouds stipple the sky. I remember the shipping forecast and that storm in the Channel.

"Nuh," she says, wiping her nose with her sleeve. "Let's go on a bit more."

I know why she doesn't want to go back. Being outside

feels good. It makes it easier to let the anger and resentment slip away. I don't want to go back either, not to the endless hospital appointments, to Mom's worry—not yet.

We follow the Thames along Fiddler's Island, a narrow strip of land between the river and the runoff ditch. Mud sucks at our heels and green streamers of vine and thorn cling to the knotted trunks of the willows. On either side of us the waters run high, squeezing us between bank and ditch and sending off a clear, bluish spray that tastes like sweat when the wind catches it. Black clouds are starting to bully the horizon, lit from beneath with a soft, sickening yellow.

We're a stone's throw from the footbridge to Port Meadow when Kira stops and pulls hard on my hand.

"You okay?" For a second I think she's stuck in the mud, maybe, or has snagged her clothes on thorns, but it isn't that. She looks as if she's concentrating intensely, listening for something. That blank expression, which Mom said might be a microseizure. The start of an episode. "Kira?"

Her palm is icy. Her jacket snaps as the breeze ripples across it. She doesn't move.

And then all at once it's as if we're trapped inside a diving bell. In thirty seconds we're drenched. The rain pours down in a sheet and our only shelter is the thin tunnel of arching branches overhead. The wind keens and hurls scoops of soapy foam against the banks on either side of the dissolving river path.

"We can't stay here." If we can make it over the footbridge we'll reach the turnoff onto the street. It'll be easier to find shelter there until the storm passes.

"I don't want to go." Her voice seems to belong to someone else. I barely recognize it.

"Come on! It's pouring out here." I haul her toward the metal footbridge. We're both shivering, blinded by the water.

"I *said* I don't wanna, Soff! You can't make me ..."

The air snatches away her words. The noise has become deafening, great crashes of thunder that rattle my teeth. Kira screeches and pushes at me, trying to loosen my grip, clawing at my wrist. I grab for the sleeve of her jacket, but she's left it unzipped, and it tears away from her, her arm swinging free. I latch onto her wrist.

"Please," I shout to her. "This way."

"Let go, Soff!" Her eyes glint with a look close to hatred. Her wrist slips out of my hands. She's five steps away from me, ten. The fury is gone and there's a strange, sleepy smile on her face. The white flares of lightning make a halo of her hair.

"Kira! Come back!"

And she tries to take a step. Toward me, toward the bridge, toward safety. Then her ankle goes sideways on the riverbank, made slick by the rain.

Frozen, I watch her fall. Her knee digs into the bank, leaving an imprint the shape of a doll's head. Her hands rake deep channels into the earth, but it crumbles around her. The current yanks off one boot and sucks at her ankles. She doesn't scream. Her lips are bloodless, the whites of her eyes shining like crescent moons.

I lunge for her but she slips from the bank completely.

# 5

At first I think Kira will be okay.

The emergency service people pack towels around me, under me. They wrap a foil blanket around my shoulders. My teeth are chattering but I don't feel the cold.

Kira regains consciousness in the ambulance where the smell of the river is everywhere, earthy and vegetable. Mom is there too, telling her, "you'll be fine, I know it, you're fine, baby girl, please," over and over again. I don't know how we got here. I don't remember much beyond screaming for help but it doesn't seem to matter. Mom and I are both so happy to see Kira's eyes open that we're hugging each other. We're crying in each other's arms, hanging on for dear life.

When the paramedics rush Kira into the hospital she's still awake, talking even. But her body looks so skinny on the gurney. A clutch of wet hair is slung across her forehead. No one will let me touch her.

"What's that?" she whispers in a hoarse voice as they wheel her away from me.

"What, Kiki?" I ask.

"On my stomach?"

"What?"

"It's my hand!" She stares at it like it isn't a part of her.

Hours later, I learn she's dead.

I'm huddled in the waiting room with Mom and Aunt Irene next to a coffee machine that doesn't work properly and a vending machine that does. Aunt Irene was here when we arrived. She'd been working in her lab at the Centre when she got Mom's call. I can't look at either of them. I'm covered in crumbs. My breath smells of cheesy onion chips that have left a slick of scuzzy grease on my tongue. I can't seem to stop eating them.

Her surgeon introduces himself by his first name. David. The same name as Dad though the two of them couldn't look any more different. Dad sports a fluff of light hair he tries to use to mask his receding hairline but his face is young, his eyes bright and alert. This man is almost grandfatherly. His hands have great purplish veins that tremble when he flexes them.

"I'm so sorry," he tells us. "We did everything we could."

Cold lights, pale green floor. My ears swim as if the air pressure is shifting.

"There were complications. Hypoxemia, which triggered cardiac arrest."

I don't know what I'm supposed to do or say. My body feels nerveless. It sounds like he's talking gibberish. There's another man with him, taller with wiry glasses. He introduces himself as Dr. Lane Ballard, the director of the Centre. He's polite on the surface but barely makes eye contact, even when he touches Aunt Irene's arm like he knows her, which, I guess, he must.

"I'm so sorry for your family's loss," he's saying, and I realize this is just the beginning. There will be more of this, an endless stream of strangers telling us how sorry they are and I hate him for it. He was supposed to *help* her.

Then I spot two police officers a pace or two behind him. There is something obscene about their appearance. Like they've all lined up to see us: a sideshow attraction.

"Irene, I tried to tell them we didn't need to do this but they insisted," says Dr. Ballard. The older of the two cops steps forward. His hair is closely shorn, like a monk's, and now I'm supposed to explain to him what happened but I don't know how to explain it.

"I was screaming for help. Someone heard me." My lips are thick and rubbery, face bloated from crying. I tell him how there was a jogger downstream. He spotted Kira in the river and managed to fish her out.

"I'm not saying it's your fault," says the officer as if he's talking to himself, as if Mom and Aunt Irene and his partner aren't taking up space in this hallway too, "but we're trying to understand how this happened."

I can't think of a response. He keeps his gaze trained on me until eventually his partner nudges him. "Don't you read the news?" she says to him. "They do it sometimes. The kids who... you know. They say it's an accident but..." He looks thoughtful as he places his notepad back in his pocket. "Come on," she mutters. "There are others we have to get to."

I feel so relieved when they turn away that I want to be sick.

After the officers are gone Dr. Varghese brings us into her office. She looks like she's been crying too, which strikes me as strange at first. She only knew Kira for a few weeks. But when she hugs Mom it seems like more than just a doctor comforting a grieving parent. She *cared* about Kira.

"I'm so sorry," she says, "Kira was special. Clever and funny. Everyone here adored her. She was..." Her words roll around me, water channelled around a dam. There are other things that she says but I don't hear them. It's only when she calls my eyes up to meet hers that I realize she's speaking to me. "You should understand, Sophie—your mother and I have to make some difficult decisions right now."

"What's going to happen to my sister's body?" I ask. Something is breaking apart inside of me. This is all my fault.

Dr. Varghese glances at Mom but she doesn't say

anything. I don't even know if she's heard any of the conversation. I take Mom's hand and it's moist, inert. Aunt Irene is silent.

"There are things we have to discuss because of your sister's condition. I was saying that the government has decided that burial isn't an option. Kira's body will need to be examined by our pathologists. Then she'll be cremated."

"Cremated?" My voice is hoarse and the sound of it surprises me.

"It's for the best, Sophie—"

"But I've been watching the news," I break in, head swimming. "People with JI2—no one really knows what's happening to them. Isn't there a chance…"

"Your sister is dead," Dr. Varghese says softly. "You need to understand that. We've observed the cessation of vital functions, her heartbeat and respiration. She's gone."

I feel panicky. My mouth keeps running. "But what does that mean now? Liam Barrett was moving. They said there was a burst of cellular activity. That his death might have been misdiagnosed or…"

"Sophie, she's dead," Mom whispers.

"But so was Liam Barrett!"

It makes me angry that she's so tentative, that she isn't asking these questions herself. That no one seems to be asking them.

Dr. Varghese's tone is quiet, controlled. "The

post-mortem anomalies are, as far as we can tell, meaningless. Your sister—she isn't alive anymore."

"As far as you know. I want to see her, I want to…" She was awake in the ambulance. She was talking to me.

"When the brain has been deprived of blood and oxygen, the cells begin to die. Until those cells die there may still be a burst of brain activity. Movement even—what they're calling the Lazarus effect. But it doesn't mean she's alive. Your sister can't talk to you. She can't respond in any meaningful way. What we're talking about is her body, not *her*."

"Sophie," Aunt Irene whispers. "There isn't anything we can do for Kira now."

Dr. Varghese's voice is kind. "I know you don't want to hear this, particularly with what's on the news right now. But you need to know that in every way that matters Kira is gone."

*Kira is gone.* I squeeze my eyes shut and try to focus on what she's saying. Dr. Varghese is looking at Mom again. She's staring out the window and her lips are moving ever so slightly but she's still not making a sound.

"Cremation is mandatory. We don't have a choice. I know this must seem terrible but until we understand JI2 better we need to take every precaution to minimize the risks of it spreading."

Mom won't agree to this. She won't let go of Kira.

"We need to—"

"Sophie." One word is all it takes. When Mom turns to Dr. Varghese I can tell something has cracked inside of her too. Her voice seems to come from very far away even though she's still right next to me. "When will it happen?"

"I can't say exactly. I'm sorry, I know this is difficult, but it's important that her body be examined for anything that might help."

"You can't do this." I hate the whine in my voice. It slices through any authority I have.

Mom's eyes lock on mine and I can tell I've lost. She says wearily, "Sophie, I need you to wait for us outside. We need to get through this. We don't have a choice. Your sister isn't alive anymore. She's…"

Her voice breaks and Aunt Irene gathers her up into her arms. She's falling apart and I should be helping her. I need to be strong for her, for both of them. For Kira too— but all I feel is weak. Powerless. I have no choice but to do what she says.

I wander back toward the ER, unable to stand still. My body buzzes with useless adrenaline, broadcasting calamity. Moving helps. If I don't move I might punch a hole through the concrete.

The hospital is a maze of bright lights and dim corridors. A knock-off underworld. I can see how tired the nurses are, how overstretched they must be, understaffed, wrung out. "Code green," I hear over the announcement system. Minutes later a covered stretcher passes me in the hallway. I recognize it from my time at Toronto East General. They're transporting a body. I can't follow that thought, can't hold it in my head. My grief is like a vast and smothering wave. Salt on my cheek, my tongue, my chin. No sound, too much sound, magnified in the hollow circles of my inner ear.

Then my phone is in my hand and I punch in Dad's number. *He should have been here.* He's the only person I can think of who might be able to help. So easily I've forgiven him those final days in Toronto, his strained smile as he told us he wasn't coming with us to England. The way Kira twisted into me, hiding her face. Him, saying: "You have to understand how difficult it is for us. It's complicated between your mom and me, there are complications and maybe time apart will help."

Kira's heart was hammering so hard I could feel the pulse of it in her neck. Mom had told us not to cry because he wouldn't be able to talk to us if we were crying. Soon Kira had shoved her fist into her mouth so her teeth pressed into her skin. That was when I snapped at him: "Enough, okay? Enough, Dad! We get it."

Something shifted in his face—guilt, maybe, breaking through the rehearsed words. I hope so. I hated him for betraying her—all three of us—so easily.

My finger hovers uncertainly over the screen, wishing desperately for the way things used to be. Remembering how it was before, when I was four and he used to read *The Paper Bag Princess* to me over and over again before bed while Mom tidied up after dinner. I had felt how much he loved me then, him squeaking the girl parts in a high-pitched falsetto, as Princess Elizabeth told Prince Ronald he looked like a bum. "The moral," Dad would always tell me after, "is that sometimes the princess has to save herself. You remember that, Feef, okay?" Then he'd chuck me under my chin and kiss my nose.

Right now he exists in another universe, one where Kira hasn't died. I could let him stay there, untouched by what has happened here, at least for a little longer. Do I really want to take away his happiness?

I miss him, I can't help it. I need someone—anyone— to talk to. I dial his number.

"Hey, you can't use that in here."

Someone in a blue smock is waving at me, a volunteer, maybe a couple of years older than me. A distant, inaccessible part of me registers how good-looking he is. Muscular and dark, bronze-coloured hair. But his mouth is tight with frustration, as if I'm a child who is misbehaving.

"What're you staring at, freakazoid?" I snap. A spasm of rage, like a muscle seizing up. I end the call before Dad can answer.

Instantly his eyes drop.

"Sorry," I try to tell him, embarrassed, "my sister, she died…"

I turn away from him. My face is blood hot, my fists are clenched. The adrenaline and the anger drain away. I was too weak to save her. And now it's too late.

# 6

I live at the thin edge of madness for the next three days.

I tie knots in my memories, make a rope out of them to keep me sane. When I wake up there are these precious pockets of time when I forget what happened. Sleep transports me to a better world. Kira recovered. A Kira who didn't fall. When I'm awake, it's the slackness of her jaw, blue eyes, blue veins, so much blue. I want to see it reversed. Mended. The world as it should be.

When I remember it's like losing her all over again. The scene plays over and over. Her gurney is here. She has a thermal blanket pulled over her to keep her warm. I tell her everything will be okay and I'm sorry, I'm so sorry, I'm sorry I ever let her get hurt in the first place.

She says to me: "It's okay, Soff. I'm fine now, see? I'm not hurt at all." It doesn't feel like a hallucination. It's more like I've gained a special form of vision.

So I read to myself, anything I can find. Sing songs under my breath. I pinch my arm when I start to nod off.

And life goes on. On the first day, Aunt Irene tells me

they don't know when we'll be able to get Kira's ashes. The hospital is holding Kira's body in the morgue for the examination. They don't know how long they'll take.

"What do they think they'll see?" The subject is off limits but I try anyway.

"That's just the procedure right now," Aunt Irene tells me. "But we've decided to go ahead with the funeral. Or a memorial. I don't really know what you call it." She presses her fingers to her temples. "They say it will help. With closure. That we shouldn't wait. Your mother needs that, Feef. I think we all do."

I don't look at Mom. I know she took the car out last night. She spent all night in the hospital parking lot. I heard her downstairs telling my aunt how she wanted to be close to Kira. Maybe Aunt Irene's right. Maybe a funeral will help stop the pain.

On the second day I learn that Dad isn't coming because overseas flights are all grounded.

"What do you mean, grounded?" Mom whispers into the phone while Aunt Irene fishes from the oven a cottage pie the College staff brought over. We only seem to eat in the kitchen. Congregating, Aunt Irene calls it. It has that feeling of ritual, standing against the counter with cooling plates. Bland grief food.

The storm that drowned Kira has swept out to sea where it's gathering new strength. Something about this feels right, the sense of all that energy massing on the horizon. An unstoppable force that could sweep everything away.

Mom has put Dad on hold and is speaking to Aunt Irene, ignoring me. "He says it's out of his control. But he'll send money. Whatever we need right now." I wish I could hug her but I can't. "He wants us back in Toronto after. With Kira gone, there's no reason to stay in England." Aunt Irene reaches over and squeezes her hand. Mom hasn't touched her cottage pie. Has she eaten anything today? I can't remember.

"You can stay as long as you like," Aunt Irene says.

"He wants us to bring the ashes. So we can all scatter them together. As a family."

"He wants us to go home?" I ask, clocking what she's been saying too slowly.

Aunt Irene looks hurt. A moment later the phone is in my hands.

Dad says: "Sophie, baby, how are you doing?"

I stare at my plate dumbly. "Okay."

"I love you, sweetheart," he's saying. "I want you and your mother to come home. We'll be able to get you back into school. You'll be with your friends again, and, and—god, I never should have let you go but your mother said—"

"Don't, Dad. I don't care." And then, without thinking: "I don't want to go home."

Aunt Irene jerks her head up but it's Mom I want to look at me. I want her to know she made the right decision.

That this wasn't her fault. It was mine. I should have looked after Kira. I should've held on to her.

"You don't have to decide right now. It's too early. You're still hurting."

I remind myself tomorrow will be worse than this. I'm glad he won't be there for the funeral. He would only make it harder for Mom. All at once I feel exhausted, utterly drained. I don't care about his feelings right now. I don't want to try to help him through this.

"I just keep remembering you as a little girl. How open to the world you were. I know how much you loved your sister but you mustn't let this change you." *It's not your fault*, he doesn't say. *You weren't responsible.*

I make my silence into a wall, a cloud, a thick, vanquishing force.

Grammy Josephine used to bounce me on her knee when I was little and feed me round toffees from her purse. I was twelve when she died. We were all at the breakfast table when Dad got the news. "Fried eggs for Soff!" Kira kept shouting, banging a metal mixing bowl with her spoon.

Throughout the call Dad was perfectly calm. He kept turning the eggs so the whites would harden, just like Kira liked them. "I see," he said, and "okay, that's fine, I'll take care of it." But then he turned to us. There was sweat on his upper lip. He wiped at it, his eyes glazed. "My mother just died." His voice rose at the end like it was a question.

Everyone came out for the funeral. Cousins and half-cousins, old family friends, Dad's six older brothers and Aunt Sally with her kisses, her faux French. Kira was five then. She spent most of the wake hidden under a table covered in wineglasses. I found her there, tugging at her black dress. She kept saying how much it itched and couldn't she just go home now? I sat with her and tried to explain to her. We had to stay for Dad. He needed us.

"Because Grammy died?" she asked me.

"Yeah."

Kira spotted his shiny shoes from beneath the table and I poked his ankle. "Do you want to go home now?" I asked when he bent down. "You could take me home if you want. I could be sick."

Dad could always tell when I was being sneaky. Back then he seemed like a different person: kinder, less obsessed by all the parts of the world that weren't us. He crawled under the table to sit with us, breath heavy with whisky, that harsh peaty tang. He was too big to fit but he squeezed his arms around his knees.

"Dad?" I asked. It was the first time I had seen an adult like this. Weak. It scared me.

His eyes wandered over both of us and then he pulled us into an awkward half-hug. His jacket smelled of mothballs but I snuggled in close anyway. "It's all right, Fee-fi-fo-fum," he told me. "It's a bad day. But it's good to know how much she was loved."

Sometimes memory is a noose. It loops back on itself, pulling tight round your throat.

And now Kira's funeral.

The church has gravitas: the smell of ancient stone and mouldering earth. It's a *nice* service. *Nice* flowers. But the church is mostly empty. Just me, Aunt Irene and Mom in the front pew and a few of Aunt Irene's work colleagues behind us. Dr. Varghese isn't here. I guess if she went to every patient's funeral she'd have no time for her work.

I want to touch Kira and take her hand. Brush the soft curls around her face. But there's no body to touch because Kira is still under observation at the morgue.

The light filters through a gorgeous stained-glass window, reflecting blue, rose, red, pale yellow. The rented casket gleams like an expensive old car. A showpiece, a display model. Adult-sized, so big it would've dwarfed her.

"For the things which are seen are temporary," says the celebrant in a soft voice. "But the things which are not seen are eternal."

Eternal things? He means her spirit, her soul. Some part of her will live on after. The idea is supposed to comfort me, but it doesn't. It makes me faintly sick, the thought of some part of her trapped inside her body, a witness to everything.

"Everything born passes away."

The rose window shows the Annunciation, an angel in a white robe come to tell Mary how she's destined to give birth to our Lord and Saviour. Mary's face is happy, a picture of delight. But the angel? The angel doesn't look happy. The angel looks bored rigid by the whole mess, the angel has seen it all: the culling of firstborns, the slaughter of the innocents.

The angel doesn't care. Mortality isn't his bag.

# 7

After the funeral Aunt Irene drives us home.

The dense cloud cover hides the stars. The smell of rain is in the air, more of it coming. Sandbags line the river but why we're still fighting the water I don't understand. We should abandon the city and move to higher ground: Cumbria, Northumberland, the Scottish islands. Except there won't be enough room, will there? Not for everyone.

Inside the house, Aunt Irene drops her keys in the bowl on the table and pours herself a glass of water from the tap. Doesn't drink it, just brings it to her lips, breathes out and places it carefully back on the counter. Mom fishes a bottle of pills out of the top cupboard where she keeps the medication. Then she climbs the stairs to her room.

"Sophie … " begins Aunt Irene. Like Dad. Like everyone. I'm getting sick of my own name.

"You don't have to say anything to me." I take off my dress shoes. The hardwood floor is cold against my bare feet. A moment later the heater boils to life, steam banging in the pipes. "I don't want to talk. I just want to sleep. Please."

She stares at me, exhaustion carving into her face. "Okay." She grazes my shoulder with her hand as she passes. "I'll be in my office. Whistle if you need me. Promise?" She holds my gaze until I do.

Upstairs I run a bath for myself. The extractor fan is broken so Aunt Irene has left the window open a crack. Still, black mould edges the cracks between the tiles. It's so chilly in here that steam rises in a cloud from the tub, and gooseflesh spreads all over my arms and legs. I unzip my black dress and it pools at my feet.

Waiting for the tub to fill, I check my phone. Forty-three notifications. A link to a memorial page someone put up online. Dad? The words are cliché, filled with stock phrases. The brief gift of time Kira was given on this earth, how she touched the lives of her family. Markeys Ellison whom I kissed in ninth grade has posted a response: *my condolencs on ur loss*. His profile picture: tousled hair and a crooked smile, a Titans basketball uniform glued to his lanky, muscular frame. Our kiss feels like ages ago, a different lifetime.

I thumb off the phone and step gingerly into the water. Hot enough to scald me. Good, good. That's how I want it.

I stare at my hands until they look utterly alien—thin blue veins, skin lined at the knuckles, mounds of bone. I remember holding Kira hours after she was born. Her hands were so tiny, her crescent moon fingernails. She gripped my finger and I laughed at the look on her face. That monkey *O* of surprise her lips made. When she took her first steps a year later, she walked from Mom straight into my arms.

The water is too hot but I don't care. I like how each of my nerves feels bright and electric whenever I shift. The heat creeps up my neck, touches the tip of my ears. I could go lower, lower. How long can I hold my breath? Thirty seconds? Forty? Forty-five? And then what? For a moment it's tempting. I drift, drowsy from the heat until suddenly I've had enough. I tug on the chain and the bath gurgles as it drains out.

My phone dings with another notification and I wish that I'd turned the stupid thing off. Still, naked in the tub and half-boiled, I can't resist plucking it off the mat and reading what it says:

Jayhey04: just heard oh god

A long pause. I wipe the condensation from the screen.

FeeFeesFeed: yeah

Jayhey04: u wanna talk?

A veil of steam shimmers above my arms and I stagger, almost slipping, to my feet. I wrap myself in a large burgundy towel and sit down on the closed lid of the toilet, staring at the screen.

Jayhey04: soff? U okay?
Jayhey04: promised myself I wldn't ask that
Jayhey04: but still
Jayhey04: u there?

FeeFeesFeed: yeah

Jayhey04: mom says u should talk

At the top of the feed is the link she sent me, a tiny thumbnail of Liam Barrett's body. The starburst of light flashing off the cold metal table.

FeeFeesFeed: maybe later ok

Jayhey04: u sure?

FeeFeesFeed: yeah im with my family right now

Jayhey04: ok
Jayhey04: luv and hugs
Jayhey04: talk soon

I go to turn off the phone but my thumb hovers where it is. I click on the link and the video box pops up on my screen but an error appears in the box: *Sorry, this video does not exist.* A quick search shows a bunch of proxy links but each one of those has the same error message when I try to follow it.

A stab of anger dulls when I think, how would I feel if it were Kira?

I wrap the towel around me tightly and head to my bedroom, slip into my flannel pyjamas, climb up the ladder and beneath the sheets. Then, after a moment, I straighten up and open my tablet. I log into one of the forums Jaina showed me. I've never seen reports of anything like this in the mainstream news before now—but if it's true there has to be more out there.

There are hundreds more posts than the last time I looked, mostly from usernames I don't recognize. All of the new threads are about Liam Barrett. I open one at random. The first couple of comments are all about whether the video is real or not. A comment from "corrosivetransfer" says if you look at the twelve-second mark you can clearly see a disruption in the feed, which means it was doctored. A flood of messages afterward tear this theory apart.

No one can agree on what's happening, what it might mean.

Someone claiming to be a scientist working for the

CDC in Atlanta thinks the Lazarus effect theory might be right and the whole thing is being blown out of proportion. It isn't a sign of something else, a spark of life.

"MumbaiBB" says that Liam Barrett isn't the first. He's seen others, seen their bodies begin to move. I trawl through his user profile to track some of his other posts and find a couple about cremation pyres in a place named Varanasi on the banks of the Ganges. People are dying there, loads of them. The pyres are running every day but they can't keep up with the demand so people have begun to dump children's bodies into the river at night. They've washed up in the shallows downriver. He has pictures. Bodies tangled together with brightly coloured sheets, red, magenta, orange and indigo. *There are over a hundred of these,* he writes. *It is worse now that the Ganges has shifted its course. Sometimes they begin to shake and thrash around. No body will touch them, not even to dispose of them.* In another browser I try to find more references to what's happening in India but I can't. The earliest mention is in a long-form article in *National Geographic* from several years ago but all it says is that the practice of cremating the dead beside the Ganges is thousands of years old, and is believed to bring the spirits of the departed closer to some sort of release. *The Hindu attitude to death is not one of loss,* it says. *The body is shed just as one might throw away clothes that are too worn-out to wear.*

I scrub at my eyes. A thought is growing in my head

like an invasive weed. If I pay attention to it then I think I might just go crazy. So I read on instead, jotting down usernames, odd comments, in the spiral notebook Aunt Irene bought for my research. It's comforting to know the words won't vanish when there's a power outage.

Another thread follows an interview with Liam Barrett's father. He is fighting the court-mandated cremation order. He wants his son's body to be released to him. *What's happening now is a miracle,* he told a local reporter, *it's just that nobody can seem to see it.* Christian groups are beginning to lobby on his behalf.

*We dont know everything. how can we trust what they're telling us?* writes "JoshuaReturns" and below that is a large chunk of Bible verse: *Mark 16 says as they entered the tomb they saw a man dressed in a white robe and they were alarmed. don't be alarmed he said he has risen! He is not here. See the place where they laid him. But go tell his disciples he is going ahead of you into Galilee. you'll see him just as he told you.*

From there the chain of messages spins off into even stranger fantasies of locusts and plagues, the burning of the unbelievers. They are grasping after something, all of them. The hope of the dead rising, life returning.

I can hear Aunt Irene moving restlessly in her office downstairs. Her chair scraping along the floor, her desk drawer clicking shut. A moment later there's a soft rapping on my door before it opens a crack. "Sophie? I saw your light on."

"I'm okay." My voice is hoarse. I hate the way it sounds.

"Can I get you a glass of water?" She comes closer. I see that she's red-eyed just as I am. She forces a smile. "It was a hard day."

"Yeah."

She sees the notebook in my hand. "You're not trying to work, are you?"

"I'm just…" I stare at the notes I've written, a collection of thoughts and feelings with no direction. It reminds me of an E. E. Cummings poem I read last year for a project on Buffalo Bill:

> and what i want to
> know is
> how do you like your blueeyed boy
> Mister Death

"I'm just … writing it down," I tell her. "What happened today."

Her eyebrows form two delicate *V*'s. "Maybe that's a good idea," she says but I can't tell from her voice if she thinks it is or not. "Get some sleep, will you? Try, anyway." She reaches out and lightly touches my forehead, the same gesture Kira used to make when she was younger. It surprises both of us.

I feel a sudden rush of affection for her as she slips out

the door again. She's the sort of person I would like to be one day: strong, sure, but also full of kindness. Full of hope. *Sometimes the dead are our only way of finding answers.* We both like to write things down. What did she say? Bodies stacked like a macabre lasagna.

When I volunteered at Toronto East General I learned the weight of a man's cremated remains is about seven pounds. A woman's is five pounds. Sometimes the nurses would joke about it, gallows humour. "Death is the best weight loss remedy I can think of," my supervisor told me once.

After they scrape the bone dust Kira will weigh about three pounds. And it's this thought that sets the tears loose at last. Three pounds is nothing at all. It isn't a person.

I should try to sleep like Aunt Irene says, maybe take a pill or two to help with the edge, but I don't want to. I think about Mom in the hospital parking lot that awful first night, hoping Kira wouldn't feel alone.

Except Kira isn't supposed to feel anything anymore. That's what Dr. Varghese told us.

But I have questions. So many of them. I can't answer them though, not today, not tonight. I had to see her empty coffin, had to sit quietly while the priest talked about the survival of the spirit beyond all things, beyond darkness, beyond death.

It's as if all of my life has been funnelling me toward this single point, this decision. Do I let it go? Do I let *her*

go? And I can't, I know I can't. I stare down at the final lines
I've written:

> *Things return to us.*
> *Maybe. Maybe.*
> *Please.*

# 8

Mom and Aunt Irene have gone to bed. I slip down from the ladder and dig out jeans and a grey sweater from my closet—comfortable, invisible clothes. My hands shake as I scrub my face. The girl I see in the bathroom mirror is like a wraith.

My nerves tingle the way they do before a big test. My feet prickle with sweat, excitement thrumming through me. I try smiling at the mirror, a trick Jaina taught me. Smile and you can trick your body into believing it. But the grin in the glass is jagged and unsettling. *This is crazy. What am I doing?*

When I squeeze my eyes shut I'm convinced I'll climb the ladder up to my bed. Like Dorothy in Oz clicking her heels together. *There's no place like home, there's no place like…*

But something tugs at me, a singing in the blood. It's hypnotic. My movements are dreamlike and slow. I open my eyes and I'm in the kitchen. The jangling mass of Aunt Irene's key ring is in my hand. House keys, university keys, hospital security chits. Most I don't recognize but one is familiar. Five minutes later it fits snugly into the Renault's starter. My fingers shake with adrenaline. *Sweet, sweet, sweet* whispers my body.

For the first time since Kira died I feel strangely excited. Almost happy.


The road to the JR Hospital is deserted at this time of night but I take it slowly anyway, watching the streets grow less and less familiar further from the city centre. The view through the windshield looks all wrong from the driver's seat on the right side, a weird sense of dislocation. I haven't practiced driving since I got here. The car nudges over too far, the centre line a thick blur as the night rushes by like water.

There are more scattered cars than I would've thought outside the trauma ward. I park about fifty metres from the entrance, in the gloom of a broken overhead light.

Inside the foyer the glare of lights blinds me. I pass by orderlies moving supplies and more than a couple of volunteers who look dazed by the late hour. It's strange that they're here but the more I wander the more I get the sense of the scale of the crisis. The patient bays are mostly full and more people are trickling in, clutching snotty kids complaining of bad stomach aches. One father grabs an orderly by the arm. "For Christ's sake, my daughter won't stop bleeding," he's shouting. His shirt is stained with red.

I follow a long hallway past the triage station. Head

tucked down, dodging the glance of the on-duty nurse. The chaos helps. No one stops me.

At East General the morgue was in an unmarked room in the basement. The philosophy was that no patient wants to be reminded of unpleasant possibilities. From the hall you'd see a door that led to an office like any other— except several metres down was a large metal slide door leading to the adjoining fridge where the bodies could be wheeled in. All I have to do is watch, wait, listen for the hospital codes. At Toronto General, code black meant a death on the ward. But the meaning would be different here. I have a hazy memory of the ER after Kira's death— code green, the covered stretcher.

It's easy to be a ghost here: thin, insubstantial. I float through the hallways, keeping close to public toilets where I can slip in if someone looks at me too closely.

I check out the exits. It'll be difficult to get past the waiting rooms near the trauma ward without being seen. The hospital map shows nothing but the outlines of buildings. No help at all, so I range through the corridors furthest from the outpatient areas and head down the stairs. The traffic is lighter here, good. I'm near the Resonance Imaging Department when a tinny voice announces over the PA system: "Attention, code green, bay four."

I freeze and glance around. This is my chance.

The back elevators are largely unattended. Only a few

orderlies in drab uniforms and the odd nurse. Restlessly I circle the area until I see someone wheeling a stretcher with a white sheet draped over a bulky form.

The orderly is a few years older than me, nut-coloured hair tied back loosely. She hardly glances at me as she passes by, one wheel of the stretcher squeaking. What's one more ghost in a place like this?

I follow about twenty paces behind her, tracking her when she turns corners by the sound of that squeaking wheel. She arrives at a sliding metal door, waves a plastic chit across the sensor pad and carefully hauls up the door. A cold breeze wafts into the hallway and the hairs on my arms prick up.

After a few minutes she's back in the corridor, *sans* stretcher. She closes the sliding door behind her, then pauses to stretch the muscles in her back. It looks like it's been the longest day of her life. Then she's gone.

The hallway is empty. I pull out Aunt Irene's keys again and work my way through the plastic security chits. Most of them are emblazoned with the university's blue coat of arms but there's a chit here without any markings on it at all. I take a breath. If I swipe this chit and nothing happens then I'm done. And standing here in the hallway, nostrils sharp with the faint whiff of disinfectant, I almost want to fail. At least then it would be over, just like Dr. Varghese said.

I do it and wait. One second passes, two. Relief floods my system. That's it then. Fine.

Then a faint *snick* startles me. The light on the pad flashes green.

I lift the door, duck inside and carefully lower it behind me. The morgue feels slightly warmer than a meat locker. Its ceilings and walls are covered in galvanized steel. Cold bites the inside of my nostrils, my lungs. I remember a news story in Canada about a toddler leaving her house on a frigid winter night, being found the next morning frozen nearly solid. But she was resuscitated, brought back to life. For dead flesh a place like this would be protective. Decomposition slows as the fluids in the body begin to gel and eventually harden but it doesn't stop. I can still smell rot mixed with formaldehyde: vinegary, like day-old wine, spoiled meat.

Two of the walls are filled with steel drawers, and there is a closed door and clouded glass window leading into what I assume to be the office. The orderly's stretcher sits in the middle of the room. Several sets of portable mortuary racks, heavy duty shelves on wheels for extra body storage. A quick tally shows me there are close to thirty bodies here. Each is bound in shiny black vinyl with three straps tightened against the chest, the waist, and the thighs.

I examine each bag for a label that says KIRA PERELLA. It takes me a minute to find it. Her age and date of death have been noted in blue pen.

With numb fingers I unbuckle the straps. Start to tug the zipper along the J-shaped path. Then a sound comes from the office. *Oh no, Jesus.* I crouch down beside the rack and glance toward the window. Someone has entered the office from the other side. A lab technician? The shape lingers and I will it not to enter the morgue. "Go on," I whisper. My breath is a bright cloud of white. "Go back the way you came."

At last the figure does head back into the hallway. I slip into the office, desperate for the heat. There's a lab coat on a hook and I put it on, rolling back the too-long sleeves.

Then I head back to the fridge. Staring at the mortuary racks, the flesh on my arms goosebumped. My grief has hardened into a thick, immobile mass: *I can do this.*

Her body bag is light, so much lighter than I expected. It reminds me of Jaina's thirteenth birthday party. We'd stood around her chanting "light as a feather, stiff as a board, light as a feather, stiff as a board" while we tried to raise her up with nothing but our fingertips. It didn't work. Of course it didn't work. But Kira is weightless. I wrestle her onto the orderly's stretcher and cover her with a sheet. *There.*

It isn't enough. What if they notice her body is missing?

CHRISTINA VASCO is the name on the bag beside Kira's. Aged nine, died the same day as her. She looks roughly the same size too. She must have been tall for her age.

There is a set of small shears on a shelf. I snip off the identification tags and tie Kira's information to Christina's bag, tucking her label into my pocket. Let them ask about Christina Vasco. Let them wonder what happened to her, if

they ask anything at all. As many new people as there are
here, and with the increasing number of JI2 diagnoses, it
could be days before anyone notices.

I lift up the sliding door and peek out into the
hallway. Bright lights and clean, pastel colours. Empty. I
gently pull the stretcher through the door, pausing as the
wheel lets out a long, vicious *k–k–kreeeeeeeech*. My stomach
drops but I quietly lower the door and push the stretcher
through the hallway.

The blue line marked PARKING guides me through the
maze of corridors back toward the trauma exit. There must be
back ways for the movement of bodies, but I don't know them.
People whisk past me and I keep my head down, hope no one
can see how badly I'm shivering.

The double doors are visible at the end of the hallway.
I'm almost there, almost there, when—WHAM!—a heavy
mass slams into me.

"Sorry, bloody hell, sorry!" he murmurs.

I'm yanked up by the arm. Staring face-to-face with a
volunteer, maybe a couple of years older than me. His dark
eyes blink slowly with concern.

*No no no…*

He takes in my sneakers, jeans, the oversized lab coat,
my face. I watch the recognition travel through his synapses.
"You…"

*What're you staring at, freakazoid?*

I squeeze the hand that's pulling me up, squeeze it hard. "Please. She's my sister."

His mouth opens. He seems to be listening to some voice that isn't mine, a voice far away. Then, very slowly, he nods.

He points down a turn-off to the right. "That way," he whispers, "no one uses that exit at this time of night."

I don't know what to say to him.

"Go on. Hurry!"

I'm shaking but I turn right again, then left. Walking as fast as I can. The stretcher squeaks past signs for the Co-operative Childcare and the Eye Hospital. He was right. This wing is mostly empty.

There—the exit leads out to a bus parking lot. I keep to the far edge where the street lamps don't cast their light. I manoeuvre the stretcher under the parking gate, then I head around to the back to the lot where I left the Renault. I wrestle the plastic sheeting into the back. Tears slide down my cheeks, the wetness cool on my skin. The lot is empty.

Except there, watching me. A silhouette standing outside the trauma exit. I recognize his face, his broad shoulders. It's him. His fingers rise as the Renault glides by, a partial salute which I don't take the time to acknowledge.

# 9

The road outside Oxford is dark, a handful of stars piercing the night sky. The car is thick with a gamy, animal smell, a whiff of storm-rain. Hot air shoots out through the Renault's vents while the Common Misfits spill out over the speaker. *Ooooh, baby, baby, where'd it all go so wrong? Nothing's as good as it used to be.*

I've got the music blasting so I can't hear the noises—if there are any. From the back.

Exhilaration skates along my nerves. Through the front windshield I can see the two-hundred-foot chimney of the cement works silhouetted against the pearl-edged clouds. It's halfway medieval in the gloom. Signs everywhere say KEEP OUT and NO TRESPASSING. But there's nothing but a rusted padlock on the front gate. I stop the car, get out and bash off the lock with a chunk of concrete the size of a softball. Drag open the gate.

The Renault shudders along a shoddy gravel road, pitted and broken up, toward the cement works. Great tranches of water reflect the moonlight like giant silver platters. It takes time to navigate the car around deep potholes. I glance at the nearby buildings for something I can use, snatching glimpses of burnt-out silos with rotted doors. *No good, no good.* They're all too exposed to the elements. But something about this place feels right: maybe just the wildness of it, the look of abandonment. No one will find her here. She'll be safe.

Rainwater has lengthened the quarry lake, feeding into a labyrinth of ditches. The headlights shimmer on the bottle-green surface of the lake, tingeing it with an electric glow, and thick mist hovers over the water. I can make out a building the shape of a boot, an ancient conveyor belt and a flooded pit. There are jagged arches that look like an ancient Roman bathhouse.

This place reminds me of all those fairy tales I used to read her in bed. *Be bold, be bold, but not too bold.*

I'm out of the car and into the darkness, the body bag in my arms. Pressing my back against the rusted metal door. The hinges resist. I keep pushing and pushing and pushing. Finally the door creaks open. I have to struggle with her now, aware of the fungal softness of her body beneath the vinyl. My arms are rubbery with fatigue. I lower her to the ground and drag the bag inside, leaving a deep muddy groove behind me.

Inside the building there's only a thin wedge of light from the car. The tower telescopes toward an open roof.

*I can do this. I have to do this.*

When I touch the zipper it isn't cold anymore. I tug it most of the way down—there! The gleam of the shaved head, pale as an eggshell. Her skin is glazed and nacreous. She still looks like my sister. Her lips, her chin, the slight snub nose. Her eyes are closed.

*Soff, am I playing dead?*

*No, Kiki-bird, the dead don't talk.*

Tiny tremors ripple though her muscles. I lean forward. Is this it then? Is this what I wanted to happen? A gust of cool, yeasty air escapes her lips. It happens again. And again. The smell is unfamiliar, faintly sickening.

What have I done?

I scrabble to my feet, my heart racing, numbness crawling across my skin. Kira's body has begun to shake violently. The smell of decay. The noise of her limbs shuffling against plastic *skritch skritch skritch*. The sound of something coming awake, trying to free itself.

*Oh god.*

I thought I could handle this. That I would be strong enough. *What is she?*

Now I'm running through the door of the tower, slamming it shut behind me. Climbing into the driver's seat of the Renault.

My foot slams the accelerator and the tires squeal. The headlights explode the cement works into blocky shapes, a strange geometry of angles and curves. I crack my head viciously against the window as one of the front tires drops into a gash in the broken concrete. My vision swims but I don't slow down. I speed through the open gate.

Trees flash by as the car sails up Bunkers Hill. Mud gums up the tires, making the wheel jerk in my hand. I'm fighting for control now. I need to be careful. I need to *concentrate*.

There's a drop on the left of the road. Not a cliff, I remember, but a thirty-foot tumble through partial woodland. No safety rails, no shoulder, and the slick runoff makes it hard to stay in control. The Renault's back end keeps fishtailing. Then the rear tires hit gravel, making an awful sound.

My fists clench as I try to wrestle the car back under control. *Focus.* The road curves, shoots up and then dips as the Renault crests the hill.

And all at once the fear drops away, transmuted into something else. A giddy, slaphappy high. I could loosen my grip on the wheel. And what? Disaster? The feeling is amazing. Adrenaline rattles my nerves but it heightens my senses too. Shadows peel away from one another beyond the circle of my headlights. A shiver slides along my spine, a watery feeling in my stomach. The thought of something moving out there, of Kira moving.

My eyes flick to the rear-view mirror. The tower has been swallowed by the forest and darkness. The beams of my headlights catch the thick bars of tree trunks as branches whip against the side of the car. My heart is pounding. The Common Misfits croon, *Why can't it be like it was, sweet baby? I would have stayed like that forever...*

Then the wheel skitters in my hands. I have a drunk's sluggish sense of things spiralling out of control. Headlights coming my way, so bright I'm blinded. Left is the edge of the road. Left is the thirty-foot drop. *Veer right, I have to veer right ...* I don't veer right—instead, I let go of the wheel. The car lurches into the trees like a rampaging animal. I *should* be terrified, but I'm not, not even a little bit. As branches splinter against the windshield and the night fragments into a spiderweb of cracks, my body lights up with a feeling close to joy.

# 10

Consciousness hits me like a bucket of cold water.

"Hold still, my love," croons the voice of a woman I don't recognize. The bitter smell of hospital-grade disinfectant stings my nostrils. A twinge of pain in my left wrist makes me squirm, but my arms lie awkward and heavy. "Can you tell me your name?"

"Sophie." The words stick in my throat. "Sophie. Um. Perella."

"Good, Sophie. You've had a nasty bang-up, but just a moment longer and I'll have you sorted." Darkness creeps across my vision. Heavy and claustrophobic against a bright fluorescent glare.

My brain goes soft and crackly. The low whine of a heart monitor bleeds out nearby.

"Take a deep breath now, that's it."

When I come to again, she's next to me, face drawn and tired, deep grooves of sadness around her mouth, but she smiles when she sees me staring at her. "You're at the John Radcliffe Hospital. My name is Nurse Rew. Dr. Perig asked me to handle this for him, but don't worry. I'll have you stitched up right fast, love."

The tip of her tongue touches her lips as she concentrates on a cut that runs across the underside of my arm. The skin around it is abraded, red like hamburger meat. "I told you not to look," she says with a grimace. "You won't like what you see here, now will you?" She cleans the wound carefully and then prepares to suture it closed. Nurse Rew's fingers are heavily calloused but they move daintily as she works. The anaesthetic must have kicked in because I feel nothing but the pressure as she tugs at a curved steel needle. She ties off the knot and snips the thread with surgical scissors. "There you go. All better."

My thoughts are loosely coiled. I don't want to think about where I am, what I've done. I don't know what I'll say if she asks me.

"Listen. There's something I must speak to you about, my love. We haven't been able to locate your medical records so I sent a blood sample in for testing." She touches my forehead with the kind of casual ownership you take over the body of someone you're tending.

"You didn't need to do that." A long pause as I try to bring my sluggish brain to bear on the problem. "I was tested back in Toronto. A few months ago. They said I was negative."

"Just to be sure then. With things as they are we tiptoe round the grave." I can't help looking down at her handiwork. Little black stitches zipper up a length of about four inches. She dabs them with a cloth to get rid of the blood. There's more of it than I would have expected. She wraps a white gauze bandage over the stitches, tapes it in place.

"We'll keep you for a few hours for observation." I want her to take my hand again. The craving for contact is so powerful that I can feel pressure mounting behind my eyes. "With any luck, you'll be just fine."

I don't believe her wavering smile. The blood is leaking through the bandage.

"Please," I whisper, "can you call my mom?"

I've slipped into an almost trance-like state of waiting, but now a tense conversation beyond the privacy curtain jolts me awake.

"Where's my daughter? I need to see her right now."

"She's just through here. But it's important I speak with you for a moment first. Her blood wasn't coagulating properly …"

"God, let me see her, will you?"

A moment later Mom teeters at the edge of the curtained area. Mascara from the day before darkens the creases beneath her eyes. She glances from monitor to monitor, then she comes to the side of my cot. "Sophie," she says. "Oh god, Sophie. You're okay. When the hospital called, I thought. I thought…" Her gaze snags on the bandage, the bright smear of blood on the sheet. The yellowy cloud of bruises near my collarbone where my body slammed against the seatbelt. "What were you doing?"

"I just couldn't sleep. I wanted to take a drive."

She stares at me. "Sophie…"

"I know it was stupid."

"You shouldn't be doing that. You haven't passed your test. You shouldn't be…" Her voice is dopey and leaden. I remember she took something, a sleeping pill. But despite that her eyes are two bright dots of panic. "You could have died."

I know she's right. I look around at the machines cast like a constellation around my bed. I wish I could hide. The monitors spill my secrets to the world: blood pressure too high, my heart is galloping.

I'm not okay, not by a long shot.


"Try to focus, Sophie. Please."

Dr. Varghese touches me lightly on the shoulder, trying to be comforting. Mom is standing in the far corner, dull-eyed now and not talking. She has heard all of this before. We both have. The medical ID bracelet the nurse gave me feels unpleasant and alien around my wrist.

"I know we've talked about how JI2 operates, but it's important that you understand, that you *really* understand, what this means for you…"

*We tiptoe round the grave.* Dr. Varghese's doing that, isn't she? She's tiptoeing, trying not to scare me too much, not right away.

"Sometimes your blood might not clot properly. Or you might experience arrhythmia, your heart beating too fast. Most of the time these symptoms are benign and your body manages to sort itself out but if you're under stress the symptoms could get worse." Her eyes skim over my arm. A rusty smear has crystallized beneath the tape.

"How much worse?"

"I know what happened to your sister was terrible." She touches my hand again but I pull it away. "Her case was different. You're older, Sophie, and you're healthy. Your body should be able to handle the condition better and we're learning more about it every day."

"You mean, you might have a cure?"

"We're doing everything we possibly can to grapple with this." A thoughtful expression crosses her face but it quickly disappears. "I'll be with you every step of the way. But there are some things we should talk about it. We're beginning to understand the effect JI2 might have on your brain chemistry better." She sounds uncertain here. "There's a chance it might affect your judgment, your emotions. Bear with me for a moment: Have you ever heard of the parasite *Toxoplasma gondii?*"

My gaze wanders, focuses on the chewed pen cap in her pocket. The stray threads on her sleeve.

"It's not a bug exactly, but a parasite that causes changes in animal behaviour," Dr. Varghese says. "The parasite is excreted by cats in their feces. After several days it matures and becomes pathogenic. Mice who consume it become more active, more likely to venture out into open spaces when in the presence of predators. Their reaction times are delayed. In essence, the parasite tricks the mouse into making itself vulnerable so it becomes easy prey for the cat." She swallows. "We think that JI2 might have a similar sort of effect. It can change your response to frightening situations so you don't get scared the way you should. You might feel exhilarated, or even happy in some cases. Reckless. We've learned that now."

"We never had cats," I tell her. "Just a dog. He died when I was younger." I want to understand what she's telling me about the mice. The mice who aren't afraid of cats. Is that what happened to Kira?

That strange glint in her eyes, I saw it. Time and again I saw it but I didn't know what it meant.

"Would my sister have felt the same thing?" A sick hiccup of laughter bursts out of me. I thought I was responsible for what happened to her. Mom glances up and there's a terrible look on her face, a mixture of anxiety and shock.

"It's possible," Dr. Varghese concedes. "Kira sometimes talked to me about feeling different. Like she knew how she was supposed to feel. How people expected her to feel. But the extent of the changes seems to be different for every patient. With some, the symptoms are more severe but others may not notice anything different than, say, the shifts in mood you experience during your period."

I've already felt the effects, haven't I? That glowing sense of glee as my fingers slipped away from the steering wheel. It felt *good* to let go. The same way I felt when I decided to leave the house to get Kira.

"We'll have regular sessions to monitor your condition and if there are any changes we can tackle them together."

"You didn't know all this before," I say, wanting to provoke a rise. "And Kira ... she died because of it. Maybe if you'd known then she'd still be alive. What else don't you know?"

Mom makes a noise deep in her chest, a sort of *nyehh-urggh* like an engine starting up in January. "Please," says Mom and now she's talking to me. "I can't do this. Not now. I'm so sorry, Sophie, but I can't go through this again." She's staring at me. "You're old enough, right? You can hear this on your own? You'll be all right?"

"Charlotte, you should stay for her." Dr. Varghese holds the clipboard in front of her like a shield. For the first time she's flustered, but Mom is staggering to her feet.

"I just—can't," she says. Then she spins and vanishes beyond the privacy curtain.

Dr. Varghese thumbs a strand of dark hair behind her ear. Does it again.

"Tell me what happens after." My voice is hard.

She blinks twice before she speaks. "It's too early to have that discussion." She can't look me in the eye.

"I need to know." Hot tears blur my vision. "What's really going to happen to me after I die?"

"Let me be honest with you," she says. Her voice has lost its professional polish. She sounds raw and uncertain. "Sophie, this condition doesn't react the way a typical disease does. We still don't know the full extent of the symptoms. But the post-mortem anomalies…" She sucks in a breath and shakes her head. "You need to know that it isn't you. Whatever happens after it won't be you anymore. It's something else."

"How do you know?" I ask.

"You have to trust me," she says. Which isn't an answer at all. Beneath the sympathetic exterior is a hard kernel of fear. She knows it isn't just a Lazarus effect. She knows something is happening to them and whatever it is, it scares her. And I remember Kira's body last night, her muscles beginning to twitch. My own wild hope. As far as I know Kira is still there, alone, but what if Dr. Varghese is right? What if it isn't *her* coming back but something else?

"You couldn't help Kira," I say. I want to sound angry but my voice comes out small and frightened. What have I done?

"That doesn't mean we can't help you."

# 11

After Dr. Varghese leaves me a nurse comes by with a sedative that sends me into a long, dreamless sleep. Hours later, when I wake, Aunt Irene is in the room with me, quietly reading a book.

"Sophie?" she says as I start to stir. She rushes forward and gathers me into an awkward hug, practically lifting me off the bed. I'm so glad to see her it makes me teary. All the frozen parts of me begin to thaw and I let myself take the comfort she's offering. Soon I'm sobbing into her chest while she holds me. "Oh, my darling child," she says in a voice I've never heard her use before. She gently rubs my back. "I'm so glad you're all right."

I try to respond but I'm still groggy and wrung out. She releases me and pulls away to look me over. "I'm not all right," I tell her, holding up my wrist so she can see the medical ID tag. The fear and anxiety rush back.

"Charlotte told me," she says quietly. "I'm so sorry, sweetheart. It's not enough, I know it's not enough—but I'll do whatever I can to help you with this. Both of us will. It doesn't have to be like—"

"Kira."

"What happened was an accident. It was just an awful, stupid accident. You understand that, don't you? And Dr. Varghese is *very* good. The research she's doing could really help people like you. If you're careful then there isn't any reason you can't go to Cherwell College and take your A-level exams like you were planning."

For a moment I let myself believe what she's saying. Maybe she's right, maybe it doesn't have to be so bad. I could get past this, I could be safe, or safe enough, if I just listen to her and Dr. Varghese and Mom.

"Where's Mom?"

The smile disappears. "She had—there was…" A pause. "Someone from the Centre called about an hour ago. They're going to release the body to the Barton crematorium later today. She has to go pick up the ashes." I look at her in surprise but Aunt Irene goes on. "After what they told us I thought it could be weeks, months even, but it's better like this."

Panic squeezes my lungs but I force myself to relax. They haven't discovered she's missing yet. They'd have to tell us, wouldn't they? Or maybe this is just their way of hiding the mistake.

"Will Mom—could I go too? Could I see Kira?"

"That's not a good idea. They won't let anyone see her body. There are protocols in place. It just isn't—not while the condition is still active. Things are different now. They're taking precautions." A pause before she presses on. "We can scatter her ashes somewhere really beautiful, somewhere she would have loved. Port Meadow, maybe, or we could take a trip to the south coast—Bournemouth or Dorset."

"But Dad wanted us to go home."

"No one's thinking about you going back to Toronto. Not while you're sick."

"Does he know?" I ask sharply.

Aunt Irene squeezes my hand. "He agrees. The best place for you is here. But listen—maybe this is too much, too fast. You don't have to think about it right now. For now let's just get you home."

———

Outside, the sky is streaked gunmetal grey. Milky puddles line either side of the road, broken branches garnish the lawns. The rental car smells like pine-scented air fresheners. It reminds me that there are other things to talk about, practical consequences for what I did.

"I shouldn't have taken your car last night. I'm really sorry. It was a stupid thing to do."

"You're okay, Sophie, that's the most important thing. It could've been much worse. These country roads aren't lit very well and most of them haven't been properly maintained. You're just lucky there was someone around to find you. You could've been stuck in the car for hours. You might've…"

*Died*, she doesn't say but I can tell she's thinking it, because I'm thinking it too.

"I know. My head wasn't screwed on straight." This has the ring of truth, at least.

"Believe it or not, I understand how you must've been feeling. Blindsided and angry and ... well, however it was you were feeling. It was ... *our* fault for not taking better care of you. So where you went, how you handled your grief, I understand. But you can't take risks like that, not now."

I manage a shrug.

"Better things will come. I promise. We'll get you a bicycle so you can get around on your own." The car lumbers awkwardly through a roundabout. "We should have done that earlier but there was just so much to get organized when you first arrived. But you'll need one, particularly once you start school. Then you'll be able to see your friends more easily." She's trying to distract me, I think, trying to make me feel better. "You had one at home, didn't you? Or I suppose you just took transit—but everyone rides here. You'll need a helmet, of course."

When we pull up in front of the house, the sandbags are still there beside the Thames, but now the men in fluorescent vests are struggling with unwieldy sacks. No more *Hulloo, me durrck*! And then I realize they aren't sandbags at all. As they lift, the damp canvas briefly reveals a human form: hips, knees, shoulders, the faint bulge of a head. They're fishing bodies from the river.

There were others then, drawn to the flood like Kira was. Caught up in the locks and weirs or tangled in weeds.

"I can't come in with you. It's the start of term and they need me at the university," Aunt Irene says. "Will you be okay for a little while? Your mom should be there."

She isn't saying anything about the bodies. The hiss of the Thames sounds monstrous in my ears—a terrible, blank static.

"I'll be fine."

"I know you will." A pause. "One more thing. The nurse gave me this." She hands me a HemaPen. "You know how to use it?"

"Yeah," I tell her, hating it. The dull, dead weight in my hand.

The council's notice beside the door to Aunt Irene's house, already dog-eared and etched in dirt, lists the number of registered inhabitants in case of a flood evacuation. Now it's in need of updating.

Inside, a grey smear of light falls across the entrance. The first thing I see is a sympathy bouquet from the Dean of New College—white roses, anthuria and orchids in a crystal vase next to the sink. And another made up of lilies and purple larkspur. The flowers are beautiful, but the sight of the cut stems annoys me. They're already dead. This is just the pretense of life.

A noise from one of the bedrooms startles me and for a moment I have a mad thought that it's Kira come home from the cement works. I close my eyes and the shuffling sound becomes footsteps, barely audible. Everyone has a unique set of sounds, I've discovered. When you live with someone, share a bedroom with them, you can identify their breath by rhythm, texture and pitch. Each exhalation is distinctive. I open my eyes, walk as silently as I can up the second flight. Upstairs, I press my ear to our bedroom door, but whatever I heard has vanished. No movement.

The noise sounds again from behind me and I cross the hallway. A thin slice of light bleeds out from beneath the entrance to Mom's bedroom. I raise my hand to knock.

*She must have heard me come in. She must know I'm out here.*

I stare at the door, willing myself to move. A series of sharp gasps, ragged half-sobs come from inside. Then a shadow cuts the light beneath the door into uneven wedges and my skin prickles. The door wobbles briefly, but it's an old house, it breathes with the wind. Sometimes the foundations creak and the bathroom door flies open when you think you're alone. You'd think the house was haunted. If you were the kind of person who believed in ghosts. As I rest my forehead against the smooth grain of the mullion, the latch bolt catches the door from swinging open. I hear a faint *snick*.

Inside, someone has turned the lock. A ward has been set against unwanted guests.

My exhaustion is too much. I know there are things to do, that Kira is out there. In the back of my mind is a faint whispering, *go, go on* … but every part of me aches. *Go on yourself, I'm wrung out, I'm beaten.*

In the bedroom, too tired to make it up the ladder, I collapse onto Kira's bed. It still smells of her: sweet, milky and slightly stale. For a moment I let the familiarity of it surround me. This is the Kira I want, the way she was before it all went wrong. As I lie there breathing in and out, remembering her, sleep slips a dark sack over my head and ties it tight.

# 12

I open my eyes to daylight. It's nearly two in the afternoon but the air in the bedroom is so chilly I feel sheathed in ice. "It's the river," Aunt Irene told me when we arrived, "that's why it's so cold. I have to wear gloves if I want to get any work done in here. It can get colder in here than it is outside."

The river—of course, it's the river.

I go to the bathroom cabinet looking for some painkillers but I don't recognize any of the labels. None of the brands are the same as they were in Canada. Paracetamol? Anadol? I take two and hope for the best.

The house is quiet. I wonder if Mom has already left for the crematorium. If she has, this may be my best chance.

I dress quickly, head downstairs and shrug on the green wool coat Aunt Irene bought me for Christmas and a jersey knit hat. I sling a cloth satchel filled with cereal bars and two bottles of Coke over my shoulder as my stomach flip-flops between hunger and nausea. I start to write a note, get about halfway through before I crumple it up and shove it into my pocket. What am I going to say, anyway? What would make sense?

Outside, the January air mists my face with light drizzle. Above me, the clouds huddle close to the peaked roofs of the terrace houses, creating an endless sky. Pure white without detail or shading. I walk to the centre of town where I find a double-decker bus headed north. "Oy," says the driver. "In or out?"

It's an unspoken rule that young people go to the top level, and leave the bottom for the elderly. But as I grab my ticket, he nudges the gas. I stumble forward. I can't risk the narrow stairwell, not with my arm aching like it is from the accident, so I sink into one of the plastic seats on the bottom level.

An old woman with pearl-white hair glances at me. "I don't see what you're sitting down here for," she says. "Someone will be needing that seat." I feign deafness. The bus is sparsely populated but she doesn't want me here. I rub self-consciously at my medical ID bracelet and pull my sleeve down to cover it.

"Are you listening, child?" the woman insists, her voice low and querulous. She pokes my foot hard with her cane. "Go on then."

I don't answer and she doesn't try again but I can feel her gaze on me. Doesn't she know that I'm scared too? That I have no idea why any of this is happening? That I didn't want it? Maybe death frightens her, but her body is understandable, its decline is slow and predictable. But me? I may as well be another species.

The bus takes me as far as Shipton-on-Cherwell, a tiny village north of Oxford, and I have to do the rest of the journey on foot. An hour later, I find myself hobbling beside the drainage ditch that borders the road a couple of miles from the cement works. The runoff is foamy, the colour of snail shells, creating a treacherous layer of muck.

But the long walk has loosened up some of the stiffness in my muscles. There's still a nip to the air but the clouds have dispersed enough for the sun to chase the chill from my skin. Green-checkered fields and gently rolling hills surround me, hard limestone beneath. I pass signs for the Oxford Airport but the sky is empty of planes.

Soon I'm climbing steadily up Bunkers Hill. The air is heavy with woodsmoke and the loamy smell of rotting leaves. When I find the place where I went off the road, I can make out streaks of black rubber on the pavement. Shattered windshield sparkles like crystal. There: a trace of the Renault's paint is lodged in a furrow in the bark of a yew tree. I trace it with a finger and the silver flecks crumble off easily.

Below me, past the tree line, I can see a broken vista of the cement works: trashed offices, gutted clinker silos, a pump house and a rusted water tower perched on the edges of a lake. And that massive two-hundred-foot chimney where I left Kira.

Is she still there? Do I still want her to be there?

When I close my eyes I want to pretend the whole thing has been a bad dream. That I'll open them to find time has gone backwards. It's the three of us walking out here, Aunt Irene promising to take us to see castles in Warwickshire when the weather warms up.

But it's not a dream. Soon they'll burn up another girl in Kira's place. Someone's sister, someone's daughter. And what will they tell her family?

This is my responsibility. Mine alone.

I abandon the road entirely, push through the line of trees toward the tower while I still have my nerve. I lose my footing almost immediately on the steep decline, slide through the muck until my fingers snag around a gnarled root of an oak tree. A dozen yards from me is the fence. I find a gap and dig my elbows into puddles of water as I make myself small enough to crawl under. Sheared metal whispers and snags my coat, then I push free.

Soon I'm pressing my palms against the rusted metal door of the chimney. The hinges resist but I keep pushing.

The door creaks open and light spills through, the colour of honey.

When I step inside there are three things I notice.

The first, a sound like rustling.

The second, a figure, tiny and pale—Kira—a barely recognizable muddle of limbs and shadow.

But it's the third thing that stops me dead in my tracks: *she's not alone.*


Who *is* he? How did he find her?

Fear burns a bright tang on my tongue. There's an electric shimmer to the air, the same tingling on my skin. My body explodes into the gap between him and Kira and I swing my satchel, still full with two glass bottles of Coke, into his back. I slam into him.

Warm breath bursts from his lungs as the two of us crash into the concrete wall of the tower. He's bigger than me, stronger too. I grab him, or try to, but he twists, easily, pinning my shoulders against his chest. His heart hammers like it could leap out of his body and into mine.

"Hey," he says, "hey now. You don't need to—" His lips are close to my ear. I smash my head backwards into his chin. A hot crescent of pain surfaces where his teeth make contact with my skull. He grunts and loosens his grip enough for me to slip away.

One step, two steps. I spin around to look at him.

"You…"

I know his face, even in the shadows. That wide forehead, almost hidden in curls, those dark eyes.

"I won't let you take her."

He takes a step back, afraid of me. Good. I'll take him apart if he moves again.

His voice is low. "I just wanted to help."

"Help? Help how?"

He touches his face and his hand comes away bloody. I've split his lip. "I followed you from the hospital. You don't remember?"

"You were there," I say slowly. There are gaps in my memory after the accident. I try to fit him into one of them. "Out on Bunkers Hill."

"You nearly hit me. When you—after your car went into the trees you were in and out of consciousness. Talking about her. How you left her here." His eyes are wide. He takes a step toward me.

"Don't move."

He stops, hands in the air. "However you want it."

*Fuck. What to do now?*

Keeping an eye on him I kneel down next to Kira and gather her up in my arms. I recognize the sharp joint of her elbow, the way she curls her feet against me. But her lightness reminds me of china teacups, how delicate their arms are, how easily they break. She's breathing still, and I feel her heart thudding, the blood travelling through her thawed veins and there's a sweet leaping feeling inside my chest. Hope. I was right then. Somewhere inside, my sister might still be alive.

"When you left her here—"

"Shut up, would you?" I tell him. "I just need to figure this out."

"You better let go of her. Please." He wipes his lip on the sleeve of his coat, leaving a smear of blood. "You'll snap her bones if you don't leave off."

I touch the back of her hand, damp, slightly tacky, and her knuckles flex and release. The air goes out of my lungs. How long have I been holding my breath? I lay her carefully back down onto the ground but she's left a trace of something thick, glutinous and stinking on my palms.

"She listens at last," he mutters.

"If you come near me I'll scream."

"For all the good it will do you. Do you think anybody would hear?"

"I—" A movement from Kira distracts me from finishing. Her hand knocks against my knee gently: sleepy, somnambulant, at once recognizable and utterly foreign.

"Her muscles are breaking down," he says. "I don't think you should touch her. She also looks as if she's lost bone mass. A fair bit."

I stare at her, trying to decide on my next move.

*Where are you, Kira?*

She cranes her head toward me, and her neck stretches and elongates. Thin silver lines radiate across her temple where the skin has already been stretched. Her eyes are larger than I remember. A corona of white circles the pupil. The amber rim of her iris is dappled with specks of grey-blue, glossy as oil, as if the pigmentation is beginning to break down. A small fold of tissue has grown into the outer corners of her eye. As she stares back at me, it shutters horizontally across her pupil with the speed of a switchblade and I jerk back.

*It won't be you anymore*, Dr. Varghese had told me. *It will be something else.* A horrible thought: maybe I shouldn't have taken her. Maybe it would have hurt her less to burn.

He's close enough to help me up and I let him. "You're bleeding," he says. "We need to take care of that." He's right. The bandage over my stitches is gluey with blood. I try not to think about infection and septicemia, hemophilia, strokes. All the ways Dr. Varghese said my body might betray me.

Every decision is a doorway and I always seem to be stuck on the wrong side. Should I trust him? The weight of his arms around me, the smell of sweat, smoky and sweet at the same time. Human, at least, and alive. So. Which side of the door do I want to be on?

## 13

Outside the tower I can see him properly: dark hair, brown, melancholy eyes. He's wearing an old donkey jacket, the kind used by labourers, bunched at the sleeves and unbuttoned down the front. Blood on the collar now, thanks to me.

"Tell me your name."

He rubs a knuckle against his eyebrow. "Names," he says. "Right. Bryan Taite."

"I'm Sophie," I offer warily.

"And her?" That classic English awkwardness has taken over.

"Kira."

"I don't know if it matters." He sits down slowly on a large concrete block. I stay where I am, close to the door to the chimney. "Her name, that is. But it's good to know."

"It *does* matter. She was my sister. She isn't just some … thing."

"Sorry," he says, not quite meeting my eyes. "That was an idiot thing to say." He takes off his jacket even though a chilly breeze has begun to lace its way through the wreckage of the cement works. Grimacing, he stretches his arms, rubs at the spot between his shoulders where I hit him. "What was in that bag?"

"A couple of Cokes."

"Any of them still going?"

Inside my satchel, the bottles are still intact. I hand him one, then back away a pace to open my own. Coke fizzes over my hands. I catch him grinning at me. "Let me look at your arm," he says. A peace offering?

"Are you a doctor then?" I snipe.

"I saw the accident. I saw the blood. I…" He pauses. "Wasn't sure if you were going to make it, to be honest."

"Yeah."

"But I'm pleased you did. Make it. Anyway, my mum's a nurse. So let's have a look." Reluctantly, I peel back my sleeve and he lifts the gauze. The stitches are still holding, but the skin looks raw and ragged. He doesn't say anything about my medical ID bracelet. "Hold on a mo." He pulls a sealed package the size of a teabag out of his back pocket and presses it into my hand. An alcohol prep pad. "Clean your hands first." I tear it open with my teeth.

"Do you think they are…" I don't know how to say this. "Infectious? Is that how it spreads?"

That half-shrug again. "Whatever is happening to your sister, you can bet you oughtn't to be mucking about with it."

"What do you know about them?" I ask him. "The ones like Kira?"

"I don't. *Know* very much, that is. I've only seen pictures before and even then it's not the same. It's just…" He shakes his head. "That smell, yeah? Acetone. Anorexics have the same smell. It's called starvation ketosis. The body breaks down fats and turns them into acids that can be used for energy. That's what's happening to her—or at least I think it is. You can feel how light she is."

"You touched her?"

"No, I just…" He puts up his hands defensively. "I wanted to make sure she was all right. But her bones? Soon they'll be like the bones in tinned salmon. Soft like that. I didn't know if she would…" He runs his hand through his hair.

"If she would what?"

"Survive the night," he spits out. "So I came back. To see how she was and maybe help." He leads me to his truck, which he has parked out of sight behind one of the gutted buildings. There's a blue plastic tarpaulin hanging over the back. "I thought maybe I'd try to rig up some sort of shelter, keep the elements off her. Who knows what might affect the nymphs?"

"Nymphs?"

"That's what they call them at the Centre."

"Like from the Greek myths? The ones who were always being chased by fauns?" I try to make sense of this.

"Not exactly. It's more technical than that. A nymph is a stage in the process of metamorphosis, I guess. Something that changes into something else."

I shake my head. "The doctors at the Centre *know* this? And they still insist on cremating them?"

"Think about it. It's nightmare stuff, yeah? They don't know what's happening, only that people with JI2 are dying—but when they do, biologically, the bodies keep going, they keep—"

"Changing."

He grimaces unhappily. "What does that remind you of?"

All those horror films I watched with Jaina, giggling while the undead lurched their way out of their coffins and onto the streets. It doesn't seem so funny now.

"Cremation's the best way of stopping it while they figure things out. Clean, efficient—and people don't ask too many questions." He takes a swig of his Coke and when he's finished his expression has settled again. "I thought you must've known this. If you didn't know then why'd you bring her here in the first place?"

I'm still trying to work through the implications of what he's said, what it means for Kira. "I didn't know all this. Some of it, maybe, I guess." I tell him how Kira died and what Dr. Varghese said to us in the hospital. "I saw the look in Kira's eyes. Something was driving her toward the river. But if what you're saying is true, maybe there's more to it. Maybe some part of me knew already that I was infected and wanted to understand how it happened." He keeps quiet throughout, studying me with a steady gaze. "I didn't think about what would happen next."

I turn away. The stark shape of the chimney draws my eye: dense concrete, pitted by time, the pale blue of the door frame, spotted by rust. The remnants of a metal ladder climb the left-hand side, broken and twisted in places. The light refracts from the sheared metal. The sky above is reddening, the clouds textured like herringbone in peach and gold as the sun begins its descent behind the treeline.

"What you did was really brave," he says after a while. "I never would have had the guts."

"How do you know all this stuff about them? The— nymphs."

"I've been volunteering at the hospital. My mum, right? She thought it would be a good idea. For me to feel useful." He glances away from me, doesn't meet my eyes. "It's mostly been cleaning duty, easy stuff I can't mess up. When I saw you pushing that stretcher, I knew that you shouldn't be there. I wondered what you were doing. Maybe that's why I followed you out here. I was—"

"What?"

"Jealous."

I laugh. I can't help it.

"You aren't the only one who wants to know what's happening," he says roughly. "I lost someone. Her name was Astrid. We were going to get married." Then he shakes his head, clamps it down. "And so when I saw you…"

"What?"

"I suppose there was a part of me that wished I'd known enough back then to get her out. They cremated her body."

"Did she have JI2?"

"Yeah, she did. I know that now." He startles me with how close he is, close enough he could touch me if he wanted to. The expression in his eyes is too complicated for me to parse. "I won't tell anyone," he says.

Warmth rises in my cheeks. "Thank you," I tell him. "For last night. For your help. You might have saved my life."

He shrugs.

"And thank you for coming back. For Kira." After a moment: "What's going to happen to her?"

"I only know a little," he says, "not enough. At the beginning, the hospitals were still performing autopsies. My mum is an autopsy nurse. She was involved in some of the early ones, when the doctors thought JI2 was caused by a parasite. When the Centre was officially set up specialists were brought in so she hasn't had much contact since. But I've been looking into what she learned. In tropical forests, there's this type of fungus. A zombie fungus, called cordyceps. It infects ants. I found an old nature documentary about it. You can see the fungus taking control until eventually it bursts from the ant's head like a radio antenna. So these doctors thought it might be like that: a foreign body had invaded the host and was hijacking its nervous system."

"Which caused the tremors," I say.

"That was their theory. But they haven't been able to find any foreign elements in the bodies. No parasites, no bacteria. Not at the earliest stages. Or later, even, after they realized the hosts weren't entirely dead. The host suffers brain death but something happens after. First the tremors, then they sink into a sort of stasis."

"Then what?"

"Most places cremate the bodies. But there are other options. You can donate your body to science. They say it'll help people." His body has begun to shake, deep shivers at the level of muscle. But he doesn't stop talking. I don't know if he recognizes that it's even happening.

"What if you're still alive? What if some part of you can sense what's happening?"

"It's what I've done," he shoots back. "That way if I die at least I can still do some good. Mum and I talked it over. She said I wouldn't feel anything, they'd make sure of that. If it even is me inside, which no one seems to know for sure."

"You're sick too?"

He holds up his right hand and pulls the cuff of his shirt back. I can see the metal tag with his patient ID number on it. "It's why I'm on cleaning duty. They don't want me working with patients. You?"

"I was just diagnosed."

His eyes widen a fraction of inch. "Welcome to the monster club."

# 14

In the amber light of the sunset, Bryan helps me to rig up a tarpaulin to keep the rain off Kira. I still feel terrible about leaving her here but it's late and I have to get home.

"Good night, Kiki," I whisper. She has curled herself up, knees tucked awkwardly beneath her body. A slow susurration of tremors steals across her muscles. "Stay safe. I'll be back as soon as I can."

After I come outside, Bryan fastens a chain around the door of the chimney, and snaps a sturdy-looking lock on it.

"It's the best we can do for now." Rather than pocketing the key, he buries it in the damp soil beneath a loose brick. "That way you can find it if you need to get in." The anxious energy I sensed in him earlier has dissipated, replaced by a friendly reserve. We're on the same side, yes, but the same side of what exactly?

A wave of wooziness hits me. Phantom lights flash in the corner of my field of vision and the ground seems to tilt. Suddenly I'm staring up at the winter twilight.

"Hey." Bryan kneels down beside me.

My stomach heaves. I turn away from him, coughing up a sick, syrupy froth.

"We need to get you home."

He grabs hold of my arm, and gently helps me to my feet. Then he half-walks, half-carries me toward his truck.

The drive home is a monotony of dusky field and hills, and the sound of Bryan's breathing. Twenty minutes, half an hour, we drive.

I ask him to drop me off near the railway station so at least I don't have another thing to explain to Mom. "Take care of yourself," he says, "and have someone look at your arm again." It's only then I notice the blood I've left on his shirt where he held me against him.

I make my way carefully along East Street, which is eerily dark. Another power outage, I guess. The line of terrace houses is quiet. There are vacant properties, more than you'd expect in a good area. The town is emptying out, as if some mass migration is already underway. All I can hear is the low murmur of the swollen Thames moving beside me.

A light winks at me from the downstairs window of Aunt Irene's house.

"Sophie?" Mom calls when I slip inside. There are two candles lit in the hallway, which flicker wildly as I open the door. I kick off my mud-caked shoes.

She is sitting at the kitchen table between a hurricane lantern and the bouquet of lilies. One of the flowers has been stripped down to a pale green stem. Shredded white petals litter the table top, her lap, the floor. Beyond them sits a sealed cardboard box with a small, print-out label of the kind I'm used to seeing in the school office: KIRA PERELLA.

Another wave of nausea hits me at seeing that. Those are the ashes of a stranger.

"I'm sorry I'm…" I begin, but she has spotted the bloodstains on my clothes. The petals fall from her lap as she stands suddenly, moving toward me, a hand half-raised toward my arm. "Thank god you're home," she says and she hugs me so tightly I can feel her bones through the unhealthy looseness of her skin.

"You didn't have to worry, Mom. I'm fine, really." I gently extract myself.

I expect the interrogation to begin but instead Mom clutches at my hand. "Help me to bed, will you, Feef?"

The words slur together. A shudder runs through me when she touches me again, seeing her like this. There are dark, clay-coloured smudges under her eyes. Her hair hangs limply around her face, unwashed. I lead her with my good arm, holding the wounded one away from her. We must look like two drunks, both of us swaying on our feet as I blow out the candles in the hall, as the stairs creak beneath us.

Inside her bedroom, she slips off her dressing gown and

climbs under the sheets. As she pulls the covers up around her neck, she whispers, "You shouldn't have to do this. I should be able to do it on my own." And then after a long sigh: "Shut off the light. I can't sleep with the light on."

I do and close the door gently behind me.

Then I stumble toward the bathroom where I vomit into the toilet bowl. I sink to the floor and the tiles are cool beneath me, comforting, the door to the hallway still open. A noise in the hallway stirs me and I rinse my mouth out from the tap, then I peel off my jacket, roll up my sleeve, and rinse away the blood that has leaked out from the bandage and smeared across my skin. The soft sting of heat is pleasant and pink-tinged water swirls down the drain.

"You're back then, are you?" Aunt Irene rounds the door frame, looking tired. "Has your mum gone to bed? She was waiting up for you. She took something but she wouldn't tell me what." She runs her hand through the tangle of her hair. She doesn't say anything when she sees my jacket on the floor, just reaches for it and then pulls her hand away when she sees the blood. "I thought you might be getting hungry," she says but her eyes are lingering on the stain. She bends over again, this time taking the jacket and hanging it over the side of the bathtub. "Can I make you dinner? We don't have anything much in the house, I'm afraid, but I could fry some potatoes."

Suddenly I'm starving.

Downstairs, she relights the lamp then sets about peeling and chopping. Since the power still hasn't returned, she has to start the gas stove with a match. "How are you?" she asks. "Are you okay?"

I glance at her. "I don't think I know how to tell if I'm okay anymore. I don't know what that means. Is that weird?"

"I just meant, is there anything I can do for you?"

For a moment I want to tell her everything. Sink back into being a child again, when I could trust the grown-ups around me to look out for me. "The potatoes are all I need," I say instead.

She smiles, looking pleased to be able to do something. Soon the aroma of fresh rosemary and grease fills the kitchen. I tuck my feet beneath the kitchen chair, fidget with flower petals that dot the tablecloth like snowfall.

"So will you tell me where you went today? Your mum didn't know." She lays a plate heaped with oily, crisp-edged potatoes in front of me.

"I just needed to get out of the house. All of Kira's stuff is still in the room. I hated seeing it, having it there around me."

She purses her lips. "You need to tell your mother or me where you're going. Especially now."

"I didn't want to disturb her."

Aunt Irene gives me a look but I keep my head down, shovel the potatoes into my mouth. Eventually she nods very slightly, relenting. "We'll need to do something about her things, I suppose. You should take my room in the meantime."

"I can handle it. I mean, I feel better."

She watches me push the potatoes around the plate with my fork. As hungry as I am, there is a faint sourness to them that puts me off. Then after a moment she makes a move to leave me to it.

"You don't have to go," I say, surprisingly myself. But when she sinks down beside me, I find I still can't look at her.

Instead I look at the box carrying the ashes of a girl I never knew. Have they told the family what happened or have they covered their tracks? Maybe it's just that there's enough bone ash to go around.

"Do you believe in heaven?" I ask Aunt Irene suddenly.

She picks up the container as if she's only just become aware of it, then sets it down again. "I don't," she says. "You know—I once was pregnant. The baby was a girl but she died in hospital a few days after she was born. It was a terrible time for me. My daughter would have been close to Kira's age now if she had lived. A year older."

Aunt Irene goes quiet. I don't know what to say.

"When your sister came into the world, she looked exactly how I imagined my daughter would have been. I visited for the summer. Your mum was so happy—and I was happy for her. I loved you and your sister so much. But sometimes that happiness felt like a mirage, something I was holding onto so I didn't have to deal with what had happened. Kira wasn't my little girl. Sometimes it would feel like she was, but then I'd remember. It would hurt all over again. I needed time by myself. Time to put things to rest. For a while I tried to lose myself in my work. I got promotions, I became a professor here."

I look at her carefully, her face a harder version of Mom's. But younger too. I forget that.

"Maybe it is a bit grisly," she says, "studying the dead the way that I do. But I've always had a sense that disaster should be understandable. That it must *mean* something— or else it's all such a waste, isn't it? As a student, I spent a summer travelling around Italy and Greece. I visited Pompeii, Akrotiri, and Delos. All the ancient sites, or what remains of them. I remember seeing a collection of burial stelae in Athens. Fascinating things, these great carved slabs of stone, each thousands of years old but perfectly preserved. I was drawn to those images. One showed a girl standing in profile with her head bowed. And she was young, very young, you could tell, but her face was strong and serene. And she was holding two doves, one nestled in the crook of her arm, the other perched on her hand. There were others like it. Each of the carvings had a similar image, a young girl clutching a bird, or offering it. Daughters to their mothers. Sisters to one another. Doves were symbols of Aphrodite. It was believed they could journey to the underworld and back. The archaeologists discovered bird bones in the graves." She shakes her head as if she has lost her train of thought.

"I suppose what I'm trying to say is that there are things we do when we're mourning the deaths of people we love. There are things we come to believe to try to help us deal with the pain. The ancient Greeks did it, we still do it now. But loss is loss. The only way through grief is *through* it. And you have to find your own way. So, no. I don't believe in heaven. But I don't believe the universe is senseless either."

The way she has opened up to me makes me want to do the same. Trust her the way she has trusted me. But the words lodge in my throat. Is what I'm doing just a way of trying to ward off the pain of Kira dying? Is that how she'd see it?

Eventually Aunt Irene stands up, the soft fabric of her skirt rustling. "I should let you sleep, honey. You look exhausted."

"Yeah." Sleep feels terribly distant. "I just don't really know how to do this."

"Anything worth doing is worth doing badly until you know how to do it well. That goes for living, too." She wipes her eyes. "You're strong, Sophie, and you're smart. But I should've been there for you. When you were growing up—and last night. But I'm worried about your mum. How fragile she is right now." She shakes her head. "You shouldn't have to be this strong. She relies on you so much."

I think about her going back to her office. How she has surrounded herself with the dead there, countless records of them.

"It's okay," I tell her, touched by this display of tenderness. "I'll survive."

# 15

But sleep doesn't come easily.

In the early hours of the morning, the moon has come and gone, the clouds have dissolved to reveal a handful of stars. It's close to three in the morning when I hear the creak of Mom's door opening, the sound of her telltale shuffle heading downstairs. Another door opens from the other side of the hallway. The noise must have woken Aunt Irene.

I get out of bed and crawl carefully down the ladder, pull a blanket over my shoulders to keep off the chill and pad to the landing.

"I couldn't sleep," I hear Mom murmuring to Aunt Irene. "I thought maybe a hot drink would help." Dull yellow light spills out into the lower hallway. I sit down next to the banister, still mostly in shadow.

"It's okay, Char. Let me help you." The soft thud of the drawers opening and closing and then silence, then the sound of chairs moving, the two of them settling in.

Mom's voice again. "I couldn't stand being in the

hospital with Sophie. I've spent the last few months terrified. And I thought that the terror would be an inoculation. If anything ever did happen I'd be prepared for it. I'd imagined it so many times already."

"There isn't a way to be ready. Not for something like this."

"I gave up David, and then I lost Kira. You'd think I wouldn't be so damn careless with the things I love."

The hardwood floor is cold against my bum. A deep chill is setting in. There are tears on my face and I pull the blanket closer around me.

"Did it stop hurting for you?" Mom asks after a little while.

"No. Not ever. But I made peace with what happened. After my daughter died I was a wreck, Char, you remember that. But slowly I came out of it."

"It was easier when Mum and Dad died. I know you did most of the work, clearing up the house and taking care of the arrangements—but that's not what I mean. There's a wrongness to this."

The kettle whistles.

"Take some time, Char." A sharp breath. "Really, if that's what you need, then go away and put yourself back together. You could head north—Dad's sister lives up there still, near Warwick. We've kept in touch on and off. You remember Jacklyn and her boys?"

"Cousin Jackie…"

"She has a patch of farmland where the kids stay, the grandchildren too. It's beautiful. She's asked me over before but I've been so busy lately and I thought we'd take the girls."

"I can't do that. Not now."

"Think about it. I can take care of Sophie for a little while."

The silence stretches on and after a while I can hear the sound of crying, little gasps for breath. I don't want to hear any more of this. The anger I felt at Mom leaving me in the hospital has leeched away. What's left is guilt—and a deep sense of regret. I wish I could help her but I don't know how.

I head back to my bedroom. Shrugging off the blanket, I stare out the window: a perfect view of sky, dusky rooftops, the stippled surface of the Thames, reflecting streetlamps and starlight, bounded by a line of slack, wind-snapped sandbags. I pick out constellations I recognize from when Dad used to take us to the outskirts of Toronto to watch the Perseid meteor shower in August. Orion's Belt, his top shoulder marked by a bright reddish star and his bottom foot by another of silver-white. The cluster of pinpricks that make up the Seven Sisters.

Will Mom leave like Aunt Irene said? Do I want her to?

*The only way through grief is through it.* I've begun to find my own way but she doesn't know what I know. She doesn't have any hope. Maybe her leaving for a while would make it easier for me to see through what I've started with Kira.

On the bedside table is an old storybook we used to read together. A fragment of Kira's favourite story floats into my mind. It described a time when the world was underwater—no land to be found anywhere, just endless ocean and endless sky. And birds—hundreds of them, thousands of them, filling up the empty space with their song. Birds like smoke, birds like weather. Among them was a lark. When her mother died, there was nowhere to bury her body. No earth, only water. And so the lark lived in grief, idly circling. Her path was a knot of sorrow. On the third day she buried her mother in the back of her head.

I always loved the simplicity of that image, the clear blue of the waters, the endless horizon. I can picture it as a kind of heaven—the memory of what you loved, kept safe inside you. But how do I keep Kira safe?

Time is an arrow without a target, hurtling into the unknown. What will happen to me if Mom goes away? To our family? Kira's death has changed us all. And we're still changing, everything still in motion, nothing coming to rest. Stars, cities, sisters.

How much does Kira still feel? Has she locked away some memory of me within that strange, new form? Does she know where all this is going? Does she have a mind? A soul?

I suppose it isn't just her I'm thinking about, but me.

How *I* should've done all this first so she'd know the way. So she wouldn't be alone. How for once she is going to reach the end of something before I do.

I'm afraid of being left behind. I guess that hurts too.

# TWO

CATERYN MADDYNGLEY
JANE MADDYNGLEY
AMEE MADDYNGLEY

(names of the dead scrawled near the front door of
Church of All Saints and St. Andrew in Kingston,
Cambridgeshire, during the outbreak of 1515)

# 16

In the days that follow Mom struggles to take care of me, to keep our family intact. She wants to be strong but it isn't easy. Aunt Irene helps her sort through the unsparing paperwork that follows a child's death. There are phone calls to Dad: some terse and businesslike, others that explode into anger and tears. She still can't sleep at night, she says, so she goes for long walks in the evening. When that doesn't work she takes pills that leave her movements slow and narcotized. It scares me to see her like that.

It's only when Aunt Irene finds her collapsed from exhaustion in the middle of the day that the decision is made. "I've already spoken to Jackie," my aunt says. "She's expecting you, Char. Take as long as you need out there."

The next day I walk her to the train station. We sit together on a bench, sipping coffee and eating the last two soggy croissants for sale at the kiosk. There are families camped out here with piles of suitcases, everything they can carry.

"This will be good for me." She sounds as if she's still

trying to convince herself. I squeeze her hand as she stares at the departures sign. The routes to the south are still cancelled, the tracks mostly underwater.

"How long will you be gone?" I ask.

She glances at me guiltily. "I'll only be an hour away. You'll let me know if you need me? Sophie?"

I promise her I will. That I'll be okay without her.

After that we don't talk much, not about Kira, not about anything that has happened. When the departure for York is announced, everyone struggles to haul their baggage through the gates at once.

The truth is, I'm glad she's leaving. Relieved. I don't know how to take care of both of us right now. I need her to find her own way.

Her spine is rigid when she hugs me goodbye, her "I love you" almost formal but when I hold her a second or two longer she relaxes. Her smile when she pulls away is brittle but it's there at least.

"I love you too, Mom."

My life settles into a new routine.

I keep a log of my symptoms, tracking changes in my body, looking for symptoms: joint pain or stiffness, weakness or fatigue, problems with my cycle. Any of these could be a signal that my condition is worsening. I touch the HemaPen to my index finger and wait for the prick of pain that tells me a sample has been taken. Aunt Irene keeps an eye on me but her work at the Centre leaves her less and less time. I assist with her project when I can, making notes on medieval tax records, church rolls, wills and contracts—tracing names and dates, births and deaths, first English translations and then increasingly in Latin as my skills develop. They're different from the chronicles she had me reading at first, more like debris, the flotsam and jetsam of daily life. But they're something I can focus on, something that gives me a sense of control.

January turns to February, February to March and nothing changes. Mom stays north with Aunt Jackie and her family, sending me sketches from time to time: acres of stunted peach trees, a portrait of Stephen, the youngest of the lot, barely five now. My favourite is a charcoal drawing of Warwick Castle that I decide to tape to the wall above my bed. When I run my fingers over it I discover traces of lettering, a message to herself she never intended me to read:

*where did she go? Sometimes I think I hear her.*

I sleep when I can, and when I sleep I dream. Odd dreams of darkness and light, moving bodies that glitter like textured pearl. Someone urgently calling my name. The words a silver cord hooked into my stomach, pulling me up and up and upward toward …

Morning.

Cherwell College takes up the rest of my time, with tutorials starting at nine in the morning and homework in the afternoons when I can be bothered. It's difficult to concentrate or really care about the work. Today, we're making our way through the A-level exam syllabus. Post-war writers, doom and gloom stuff. George Orwell and John Wyndham. It's sweltering in the classroom even though it's only March.

Outside, we can hear the frantic clicking of wings, tiny bodies confused by the glass. Flying ants, Bryan told me. Once a year they grow wings, all of them, so they can take to the air in search of a new colony. It happens after a heavy rainfall in the summer when the weather turns muggy and humid. But now the days are getting hotter earlier in the year. The seasons are out of joint and the ants are confused by the heat. The changing weather patterns. By nightfall they'll have shed their wings. All over England this is happening.

"So, what's the commonality between these writers?" Mr. Coomes is waving a copy of *The Day of the Triffids* but mostly I've tuned out, scanning the growing swarms outside. I can see the ants landing on the pane, skittering along the edges.

Next to me a girl named Lilee MacGilrea with a bog of rusty hair is sliding a safety pin through the first layer of skin on her thumb. Her lips are chewed, patchy with scabs. She wears her JI2 ID bracelet without a trace of self-consciousness.

It's the two of us at the back, quarantined together, staring at the backs of the other kids. Evie Chudwell with her too-pink lipstick and Nate Peverill in his neoprene bomber jacket, which he isn't supposed to wear over his uniform. I hate them, just a bit.

"Apocalypse. From the Greek, meaning, literally, an uncovering," Mr. Coomes says. He's creeping toward sixty, creases under his eyes and heavy yellowish earlobes. "A vision of heavenly secrets that can make sense of earthly realities. When St. John was writing the book of Revelation he wasn't just writing about the end of the world. He was peeling back the surface of reality. Does anyone know the Latin root of 'revelation'?"

"*Revelare*," I murmur under my breath, "to lay bare. From *velare*, to clothe or conceal." My work with Aunt Irene is paying off.

"Sophie?" he asks, arching an eyebrow. "You have something to contribute?"

I'm used to him trying to draw me into the conversation, but it's easier if I don't give the up-front kids a reason to turn around and stare at me. So I pretend to search my notebook where I've copied out fragments of text from my research.

*In the same year, a remarkable thing was noticed for the first time: that everyone born after the pestilence had two fewer teeth than people had had before.*

But Evie turns to look at me anyway, her eyes filled with disdain.

"Sorry, sir. I don't know."

"This is important." His voice has an edge of irritation. "When writers imagine apocalyptic futures they're trying to illuminate what's already embedded in their own society beneath the surface. Both Wyndham and Orwell lived through war-ridden times."

I slide lower in my chair, hating it when his eyes slide away from me even though it's what I wanted.

Lilee flashes me a brief smile in sympathy, but we don't speak to each other. She brushes a flake of dead skin from her thumb and turns back to the sharp point of the pin. She stabs it in and lets out a sharp intake of breath. Blood wells up, staining her nail.

"Um, Mr. Coomes," says Evie when she spots what's happened a minute or two later, "could you maybe fetch Lilee a plaster? I'm not squeamish or anything but…"

He scowls. "All right you," he says, "go clean yourself up."

Nate and Evie hide smirks under their hands. Their eyes are varnished with amused distaste. They still believe this won't happen to them. I glance down again, underlining my notes:

*these bands processed through towns and villages*
*along their way, chanting in unison and whipping*

*themselves and each other until the blood ran freely down their back and shoulders. It was said that many had died in a state of ecstasy from their beatings. Where they went hundreds flocked to join them, and thousands welcomed them into their communities, singing with them the flagellants' hymn and hoping that their abasement and suffering would ensure their town or village exemption from God's pitiless scourge.*

I glance out the window at the cloud of things moving in the sunlight. *Larva.* From the Latin meaning a disembodied spirit, or ghost. They're ephemeral, forced to search out a new home for themselves. No one knows if they'll make it.

The flare of the sky after the dull classroom lights is blinding.

Spring has made Oxford beautiful. The grass is a lush carpet dotted with ox-eye daisies, dandelions and meadowsweet, their blossoms gorged on sunlight. I always loved spring in Toronto, the strange delight that seized hold of everyone once the snow began to melt. We'd wear short skirts even though our legs were still goosepimpled with the chill, and all the boys would stare as if they'd forgotten what naked skin looked like.

It's the same here but now I find it unsettling. The men who live in the houseboats along South Street strip off their shirts to enjoy the heat, lying on the bank beside the Thames. Women in string bikinis dip themselves up to their thighs. The floodwaters have receded and winter is barely a memory for these people. The papers report our thinning numbers but no one seems to care. There are still late-night hen parties at the pub across the road, still shops selling confetti and cheap champagne as the end of term approaches—the pop and crackle of fireworks after dusk. They just want to forget.

I pick up my bike from the racks, careful to keep clear of Evie and Nate, the nastiest bullies. That lot are all healthy looking, their arms slim and muscled, reddening in the new sun. They congregate on Paradise Street, cackling and sniping, swatting each other's books from their hands. I've heard they know a pub that'll serve them but no one's told me where it is.

Not that I'd want to go, not with them. I'm speeding past when Nate fakes a run at me and I swerve. "Slow down, Perella," he calls after me, "you fucking nearly took my head off." I keep my mouth closed, squinting against the droning swarms as Evie squeals, picking ants from her hair.

It's a long ride to the cement works where Bryan will be waiting for me, the same as he does every day he can get away from the hospital.

• • •

Forty-five minutes later, I lean my bike against the warm concrete of the tower. My muscles are tired and I'm out of breath but I've got stronger—despite everything. The afternoon light suffuses everything in a warm, saffron haze. The foot-high grass, the profiles of trees, Bryan himself, a hand shading his eyes. He tilts his head slightly, and we communicate wordlessly. *Yes, she's still alive. Yes, I'm fine.*

When I open the door to the tower she's exactly how I left her yesterday. I fill a bucket of water and begin the slow process of cleaning her. Her skin has toughened into a hard layer of keratin. It's pale and lustrous, lacquered like the inside of a conch shell. Dark shapes are visible beneath the surface: her bones shifting slowly. Her ribcage, the thick ridge of her sternum. Her fingers have shortened and fused. Her lower jawbone juts out like the prow of a ship.

The tremors have passed now, but for weeks she has barely moved. Her legs have thinned down to the width of saplings. There was a time when she could beat me to the end of the block and back even though I towered over her, even though she had to work double time, two strides for every one of mine—there she would be, huffing away, red-faced and grinning madly, waiting for me to catch up. "Did I do good, Soff?" she would ask me. "You did good, Kiki-bird," I'd tell her, "you beat me fair and square."

The keratin shell is beginning to flake away. She's trapped in a kind of stasis, Bryan told me. But as I run the damp cloth across the hard line of her mouth, lips receded to reveal a serrated, chitinous edge beneath, I wonder: what is she turning into?

I dump the sponge back into the bucket when I'm finished and dive into the opening of *Peter Pan*. "When the first baby laughed for the first time," I read to her, "its laugh broke into a thousand pieces, and they all went skipping about, and that was the beginning of fairies." We get as far as Wendy's flight to Neverland before I dog-ear the page and head outside to join Bryan.

He hands me a beer from the cooler we keep stashed in the bushes, as he settles himself down on a blanket. We have a pact not to speak of this ritual, of Kira, to anyone. Some nights I still wake in a cold sweat, certain someone has discovered her. Bryan says she'll be cremated if they find her, but the more I see of what's happening to Kira, I don't understand how they could.

I sit down next to him, close but not too close, trying to let my mind go blank, just soak up the sunlight—the few free hours before dinner time when Aunt Irene gets home. She's worried for me all the time now, trying to keep track of the things Mom always did for Kira. My general whereabouts, my appointments at the Centre, the new curfew rules for ages eight to eighteen. The Thames Valley

Authorities introduced them in February to tackle "antisocial behaviour": the rising levels of drunkenness, vandalism, and disturbances caused by so-called disaffected youths. The unrest is a natural reaction in areas threatened by disease, Aunt Irene says. But we've reached an agreement. While my blood work is stable I can do what I like, but I carry my phone, which has a GPS tracker turned on at all times, and a tube of fibrin sealing glue in case of bleeding.

"I won't be out here tomorrow," I tell him.

He glances up.

"I've got an appointment at the Centre. Another." It's my second this month. "Then I'm heading out of town." Aunt Irene has been planning this research trip for weeks but she's had to put it off several times because of emergency meetings at the university or last minute phone calls with her colleagues on site at digs in Sheffield and Lincolnshire.

"I can look after her," he says without me needing to ask. "Don't worry. I'll let you know if there's any change."

"Thanks," I say slowly but Bryan just shrugs like it's not a big deal. He makes a show of flipping through one of the ancient issues of *New Scientist* his dad used to collect and holds up a spread to show me. It advertises one Major de Seversky's ion-propelled aircraft: a gas lantern attached to a giant overhead circle of metal. *Come see the incredible magic carpet of the future!* reads the headline. "In five years," he reads aloud, "the ionic drive will prove more efficient than either propeller or jet as a method of aircraft propulsion."

"When was that exactly?" I put down my project notes and crack open the can, swallowing a mouthful of warmish beer. The fizz burns my sinuses.

"Nineteen sixty-four. So much for progress."

I sing a line from the Common Misfits. "Nothing's as *goo-ood* as it used to be."

He lets the issue fall open on his chest. "My da loved all this. Figuring out how things worked, building stuff himself." I smile.

Bryan sports a burnished tan below the rolled-up sleeves of his jacket. During these afternoons, bit by bit, I've come to know him better. He isn't like Markeys Ellison or any of the boys I hung out with back home. He's quieter, more restrained. Funny at odd times in a dry, sarcastic sort of way. I still keep at a distance from him. I remember what Aunt Irene told me, about mirages and false comforts, and I wonder if I look like the girl he lost, Astrid. He hasn't brought her up again and I haven't asked.

"You think you could build something like that?"

He snorts. "Sure. And a rocket ship too."

When he isn't volunteering at the hospital—or here— he spends most weekdays as an assistant at the Orinoco scrap store even though his mom, he says, has been begging him to quit the job. Just until his nineteenth birthday, just for *this* year.

But he's methodical and very good with his hands. He's replaced the temporary tarpaulin he rigged up over Kira with a sturdier structure built from old two-by-fours. He wove a line of battery-operated fairy lights around it that glitter in the darkness. Sometimes he brings odd projects like this old ham radio that used to belong to his dad. It crackled with snippets of French, German and Portuguese when he finally got it working. The inner workings of diesel engines and electric motors fascinate him. The only time he really settles is when he has a set of blueprints, tracing the faint lines, understanding how they come together to create their own particular kind of magic.

It helps pass the time. Neither of us knows exactly what we're waiting for, only that Kira continues to change.

Today I'm feeling a bit on edge. The BBC has been reporting on two bodies discovered in one of the subterranean tunnels that drains off at Christ Church Meadow. Brother and sister, twelve and fifteen years old. An awful state of decomposition, they reported, but there were no pictures. No one knows what the boy and girl were doing down there, only that their parents had lost their council-owned house in one of the early floods. The newspapers say they've been cremated.

Thinking about it makes me finish the first beer fast. It sits unpleasantly in my stomach. Still, I take another one from the cooler. Bryan watches me. Only when I return for a third does he comment: "Steady on."

"Don't be an asshole," I say, rolling my eyes. I'm being brattish, I know, but I can't help it. Now he watches as I crush the can between my hands. *Twist and crunch, twist and crunch.* I don't really want another, but I don't want to stop drinking either. Bryan coughs. "If you're planning on getting plastered, we probably should've picked up more supplies."

"I'm not planning on getting plastered."

"Right."

His eyes turn back to his magazine and he flips idly through the pages. For some reason this makes me angry. I make to stand but the ground tilts precariously beneath me. Stumbling, I shake my head, then stagger to my feet. His eyes follow me.

"Sophie?" he says.

"What?"

"Are you—okay?" He looks away, as if asking something personal is deeply unpleasant. I rest my hand against the wall of the tower. The hot stone reminds me of the heat of Kira's body beneath my gloved fingers. Even out here there are traces of her body's bitter smell underneath the cherry blossoms and loam. My eyes fill with tears.

*Please don't let Bryan look at me.*

But now he's beside me, not quite touching, and I can't hide. He waits until I wipe my eyes on my sleeve, as if crying is something that can't be interfered with. He squints. "Will you let me try something?"

"What?"

"Just let me…" I flinch away from him at first, but then he rests his hands on my shoulders and they feel warm and soothing. He has his own particular smell—musky and sweet. Hot sand, paraffin wax, sweat. He guides me to the entrance of the chimney and unchains the door.

"I don't want to go in there again."

"Trust me. Please?"

The chain slides through his hand into the dirt. Then he's holding my shoulders again, his mouth close to my ear. "Okay," he whispers and guides me through. His breathing is uneven, uneasy, puffs of air brush the small hairs on the back of my neck. There are no other sounds.

Dust and crumbled flecks of keratin dance in the angled light streaming through the open top. It reminds me of the old-fashioned kaleidoscopes we got for Christmas one year, the world of brightly spinning colours we saw when we pressed our eyes to them.

The dust moves around the structure Bryan has built in a slow spiral. Underneath it, Kira has tucked her knees beneath her, foreshortened arms hunched around them. Hundreds of thousands of years of evolution whisper to me: *This is dangerous. Monster.* I can't tamp down the tug-of-war inside me whenever I see her new, alien body—I keep hoping I'll catch a glimpse of my sister in there but the suspicion has been growing in my mind that whatever is happening, she isn't coming back to me.

"Hold still," Bryan tells me. Carefully, he places his palms over my eyes. Heat spreads through my cheeks. "There now. Can you see anything?"

"Nothing." They put blinders on horses, I remember, to keep them from being spooked. Is that what he thinks, that I'm scared of her? Maybe I am, a little.

"Good. Then look properly."

"Your hands—"

"I know," he says. "That's the point. Try to see her as you used to see her."

Some part of me resists. "I don't want to."

"Why not?"

"I hate remembering." I breathe in and out fiercely. "It just makes it worse. She looks—broken now." I push him away, my chest boiling with an anger I don't entirely recognize.

"Hey," he says. A look comes over his face: frustration, apology, pain. "It was just a trick I learned from my mum. When my da was really sick. It helped. I don't know why. I needed to remember the way he was before. That he wasn't a stranger."

"It's like someone has taken her away. Locked her up. I catch glimpses but it's as if she's a long way off, hidden. And then I wonder if maybe I'm just imagining my sister is still in there."

"At least she's isn't alone."

His breath is warm. His body is warm. I lean into him. His hand circles my waist. I don't know what this is exactly, only that it's good to touch him.

"Bryan?"

But he pulls back.

"Sorry," he says, "I didn't mean—"

"No, I know." I try to seem casual but I'm stung by his withdrawal.

He's heading out the door now, digging around for the key to the padlock. I throw one last look toward Kira. I wonder if she even knows we're here at all.

But then she *does* move, ever so slightly. She glances up. Her pupils glow a dull red in the low light like an animal's at dusk. They follow me carefully.

"Kira?" I whisper.

A membranous film flicks over her eyes.

"Is it you?"

They don't open again. Her body settles once more into the slow rhythms of sleep.

# 17

I sleep badly that night, dreading the appointment, and by the time it comes my skin feels itchy and feverish. I can't tell if it's nerves or some new development in my condition.

In Dr. Varghese's office, I stare at the only personal thing in the room, a framed photograph sitting on top of her filing cabinet. In the picture she is a teenager, in hiking gear, baggy, pocketed trousers that seem to dwarf her slim frame, and behind her the waterfall cascades down a gorgeous, tiered set of rocks. "It's from Lakhaniya Dari, near where I grew up," she tells me when I ask about it. "In the rainy season the waters are furious. Amazing." I wonder how far it is from Varanasi where the bodies are abandoned in the river, what she's heard about what's happening where she grew up. But I don't ask.

Even though she's been trying to help me relax, our relationship still feels too formal—too one-sided, I guess—for that kind of intimacy. Sometimes she reminds me of a big sister, joking with me, telling me stories about her home—how she misses the smells of ginger and cumin, the taste of sweet milky tea on hot days. She's vague on the details but it's enough to encourage me to talk.

"What do you love about Toronto?" she asks me and I have to think about it for a bit.

"How clean the air feels before it frosts over," I say, at last. "I miss seeing the ice on the trees, thick enough that the branches sparkle like they're made of glass. I remember last year it got so cold my mascara froze on my way to school. When I got inside, it melted down my face. My friend Jaina had to help my scrub it off before anyone saw."

"I've never even seen snow," she says with a tone of wonder.

Then she asks me about Kira, about how I'm doing emotionally. But thinking about Kira reminds me of what Dr. Varghese must know about the nymphs that she won't tell me. How she's keeping her own secrets. They must have seen what I've seen.

"And physically?" Dr. Varghese asks. "How are you doing? Appetite still good?"

"I could murder a pizza, if that's what you're asking."

"Sounds about right."

I try to peek over the top of the open folder and catch sight of a clipped school photograph from last year, when my hair was longer. I'd been trying to look like Antal Lila, the lead singer from Sleepy Jesus.

"Anything else I should know about? Any irregular bleeding? Mood swings?"

I shake my head, blushing faintly.

"The good news is that things are holding steady. No deterioration. No signs of immunodeficiency issues. You're healthy."

"Healthy-ish."

She jots something down in my file, pretending not to have heard me.

"I've been thinking a lot about what could happen. A friend of mine told me there were options. Cremation isn't the only choice."

She glances up. "You don't need to worry about that right now, Sophie."

"But I want you to tell me about it."

She sits up straighter. "It's just a bit complicated."

"Why?"

"Because of the state of the deceased. They can't be buried. Donation to science is an option but I'm going to be honest with you, it isn't a good one. We can't use the organs of someone with JI2 for transplant surgery. But in some cases, we can arrange for the Centre to make use of the body for a short period for medical research. After that time, it would still be disposed of."

"Disposed of?"

She shifts uncomfortably but doesn't say more.

"Does something happen to the bodies afterward?" I ask. "Is that why you want to observe them? I've heard there might be genetic changes … anomalies … not just the tremors."

"I can't tell you any more about that, Sophie. We're beginning to experiment with a drug called M-Plagge that could block the production of the juvenile hormone, but it may be some time before we know how effective it is."

"What does it do?"

"The theory is that the hormone interferes in the body's normal operations. It prevents your body from fighting infections and diseases, and interferes with the production of adrenaline, norepinephrine, dopamine and serotonin. If we can suppress the production of the hormone then we hope the body should reset. Begin to operate as normal. But I shouldn't really be talking about this with you. The tests are preliminary. It could be months before we know more. And for the moment you're healthy. Focus on your schoolwork. Your family. That's where your attention should be. You have to try to live a normal life."


"How was it?" Aunt Irene asks me as she gets up from the chair in the waiting room.

"Nothing much to report."

My energy is low. I just want to head back to the house to rest but Aunt Irene has other ideas. "We better get a move on if we're going to make Ashwell by noon."

"Now?"

"I've got that conference on virology in London all weekend. It's now or never, niece of mine."

I try to smile like she wants. I'd been looking forward to this trip before she delayed it, the idea of getting out of Oxford for a little while. But as I watch her packing her notes back into her tote bag I can't quiet the edge of frustration. How much does she know about what goes on in the Centre? Her research is connected to what they're doing but is the flow of information two-way? Whenever I ask she goes quiet and thoughtful. Kira's death has made her less sure of herself around me, more reticent about JI2. Sometimes I catch her watching me when she thinks I'm not looking, trying to suss out if I'm as fragile as Mom. If I need the same kid-glove treatment, after all.

We head toward the parking lot and I try to settle into the Renault, which was repaired after the accident. My phone beeps and there's a message from Jaina, though it's four days old. They still haven't managed to get the network to work properly, leaving us with constant power outages and dead spots in my reception. It's beginning to feel as if England has broken off from the rest of the world, is drifting further and further away. Dad's calls are broken up by static and delays. I can barely make out what he says most of the time, only that he's unhappy. He wishes we were with him. He hopes I'm doing better.

As we drive into the outskirts of the city, my gaze

drifts over the landscape. Distant farms and fields of early bluebells surround the motorway. Dilapidated barns that have been refurbished by the families moving inland. Makeshift accommodations. They resettled half of Somerset in places like this, places where the floods haven't been so bad.

We pass a church signboard.

**BEHOLD! I MAKE ALL THINGS NEW!**

There are emergency vehicles parked in front of it, the calamitous orange lights blinking in the distance. I've heard about this, that they're digging up the bodies of anyone who died within six months of the first recorded death, before the cremation policy took effect. Just in case. I crane my head to see what they're doing but we're heading past too quickly. On the side of the church someone has spray-painted the symbol of an insect. The jitterbug. Underneath it they've scrawled:

**HOW MUCH MORE CAN WE TAKE?**

It's midday when we turn off the A-1. Ashwell is a cozy village tucked on the River Cam, with medieval cottages and Tudor town houses lining the streets. Quaint, like the

Industrial Revolution never happened here.

"What do you think?" Aunt Irene parks the car outside a pub called The Bushel and Strike. Its garden is filled with picnic benches, families basking in the early March heat. A small child of three, maybe, stares up at me with wide eyes as she sucks her fingers. At the next table is her brother, fourteen by the look of him, with the same brown eyes and prominent nose. A smattering of acne on his chin. Even without the medical ID bracelet around his wrist, I would have known he was sick from his paleness, the wariness of his expression.

"Postcard pretty," I say, not sure if I mean it. One of Mom's phrases.

Aunt Irene smiles faintly. "She'll be home soon, sweetheart. Any day now she said. She and Jackie are finishing up with the spring preplanting."

It's the parish church we've come for. Inside it are chalk-painted arcades and a roof of coal-black timber. There are a few tables stocked with knitting and jam jars, a jumble sale to raise money for repairs to the south aisle and transept roofs. Chipper women wrapped in modest sundresses gossip and chuckle with one another, brooding hens.

We skirt the edges of the crowd to get a closer look at the building itself. Separating the nave from the chancel is a decrepit rood screen, a series of old wooden slats fixed together to form a semi-circle. It depicts the sounding of the last trumpet on Judgment Day. At the bottom cower the souls of the dead, naked, some being ushered by the heavenly host toward the alabaster halls of paradise while the others are forced toward a great burning city. A sketchily drawn Christ sits above in robes of faded red while around him swirl dark shapes, black-bodied angels with bat-like wings locked in an endless battle.

Aunt Irene stops in front of it. "It's beautiful, isn't it? This is old, mid-fifteenth century. See how the colours are so bright? There are only a few examples like this left from the period. Most of them were destroyed in the Reformation and the civil war, but this one survived."

My eye is drawn to the Devil who leers at the sinners, his mouth open and hungry. Near him, clay-coloured bodies with their hands stretched out in supplication climb from coffins whose lids have been carelessly overturned. Below the etiolated coat of arms is an inscription: *Let every soule submyt him selfe unto the authorytye of the hygher powers for there is no power but of God.*

I try to take the image in, try to see what she sees in it. "The priests in those times really hated the world, didn't they? *This* world, I mean. The world of flesh and blood. They were so fixed on what was coming afterward."

"I suppose their world must've seemed hellish to them. Bodies in the street, so many of their friends dead. Society was breaking down."

I cast a steadying glance toward the jumble fair, so

homely, so mundane. "How did they find a way to keep going? I mean, how many of them really thought they were going to heaven? For the rest—for *most* of them—the afterlife would've been the same nightmare they'd lived through. Only then it would last forever. I mean, at least when you strip away religion, there's a way out. If things get too bad, well. You know. But something like this—" I point at the painting, with its deathless faces, its tormented misshapen bodies. "There's no end to it. No escape."

Her brows furrow and I wonder if I'm surprising her a little with these dark thoughts but it's hard not to think about what death means now. Some of the figures look so much like Kira it makes me uneasy.

She takes my shoulders and turns me away from it, guiding me toward the north wall. "Here—look. This is what I wanted you to see."

"What?"

Aunt Irene draws my fingers to a set of deep grooves cut into the ancient stonework of the wall. "Think you can translate it?"

"The people who remain … *miseranda ferox* … wild and miserable?" I falter. Latin abbreviations can be so tricky even with Aunt Irene's help. "They are … um … *testis*."

"Wretched witnesses to the end. A strong wind is thundering over the whole earth. Written on Saint Maurus's day, 1361," she murmurs. "Someone carved those words ten years after the first outbreak of plague."

I had just read about this in one of the books she gave me recording the spread of the Black Death in the eastern counties. The villagers called it "the pestilence of boys" because all the young men died. That seemed unfair to me—women and girls were dying too. When I say this to Aunt Irene her laugh has an edge to it: "They never care about the girls and women, do they?"

A huge storm blew in from the north, flattening trees and houses, the mills and all the church towers. I feel a sudden chill despite the musty warmth of the church.

But Aunt Irene's face is alive with interest. "You see it, don't you?"

I think I do—the sickness and the storms. "It's like what's happening now, isn't it?"

She nods and digs through her tote. Out comes her own dog-eared notebook, a twin to mine. "The same patterns occurred in the Middle Ages. Changes in the seasons, terrible storms. There had been a string of volcanic eruptions that began in 1258. Here." She hands me her notebook. "See for yourself."

*Afterward, the north wind prevailed for several months ... scarcely a small rare flower or shooting germ appeared, whence the hope of harvest was uncertain.... Innumerable multitudes of poor people*

*died, and their bodies were found lying all about*
*swollen from want... . In London alone 15,000 of*
*the poor perished; in England and elsewhere*
*thousands died.*

Shivering, I hand it back to Aunt Irene, thinking about
the numbers. The papers suggest more than fifteen thousand
have now died from JI2, worldwide.

"There were over ten thousand skeletons found at
Spitalfields Market alone." She smooths the pages. "That
was where they buried the plague victims. But it wasn't just
that. In 536, there were three massive volcanic eruptions that
ushered in an earlier period of cooling. And it coincided with
one of the worst epidemics the Roman Empire had seen.
The plague of Justinian."

"But what's the link with volcanoes and storms?"

"The earth has always experienced natural fluctuations
in its temperature. The Middle Ages coincided with a period
of intense ecological change. The Little Ice Age. A terrible
stretch fell between 1290 to the late 1400s when plagues and
famines ravaged Europe and glaciers descended from the
Alps. Changes in the climate, droughts in the summer,
increased flooding of coastal regions."

"That sounds familiar."

She takes out a fresh sheet of paper and carefully rubs a
record of the Latin in charcoal, glancing at me before she speaks.

"The earth is a vast self-regulating system. But sometimes it doesn't work properly. Volcanic eruptions led to more dust in the air and less sunlight breaking through—but the problem is that what we're experiencing now is far more extreme. Some of the causes are the same, but add in human activity, greenhouse gases, and what we're seeing is a feedback loop. There has been more seismic activity, more eruptions as the melting of continental glaciers causes massive shifts in already geologically active regions. Storms and flooding here, droughts in Europe and across most of the Middle East. The scale of all this change is unprecedented. They're calling it the Anthropocene epoch. A period of dramatic human impact on the environment."

I watch the way the words seem to appear on the page out of nowhere as her hand moves over the paper. I've heard all this before in my environmental studies class but it never really sunk in before, not the way it does now. "You think that somehow relates to the spread of disease?"

"Maybe. There are some patterns. During the Black Death, coastal cities were hit hardest."

"Just like here."

She nods. "The theory was that the Black Death was spread by ships infested with rats docking in new harbours. But I don't think that explains everything. The areas with the highest mortality rates of JI2 have been China and the Philippines. Bangladesh. It hit earliest in places where there was massive flooding."

"So you think it might be in the water?"

"Not exactly. What if JI2 isn't a disease in the traditional sense?" She stops and turns to me.

"But what else could it be?" I ask.

"Think about it like this. What we know at present is that the condition we call JI2 can be identified by the presence of a specific hormone in the bloodstream. The juvenile hormone. That hormone seems to trigger a reaction that results in the host's death, followed by the beginning of some sort of new biological processes."

I swallow thickly. "You're talking about the jitters, aren't you?"

She nods. "Something happens to the bodies after death, something we don't entirely understand. But what interests me is the spread of the condition in the first place. It seemed to be responding to environmental triggers, triggers we saw then that we're seeing again now. The amount of carbon dioxide in the air. Or perhaps it had to do with the melting glaciers. Something in the water, like you said. Or the storm conditions."

"Does the Centre know about this?"

"I suppose they do," she says. "I send them regular updates on my work but I have no idea who reads them or what gets passed along. I know it takes at least a week for my contact to process most of what I report into bulletins—but even then links to the Black Death may still strike most of their medical researchers as … tangential to the main problem."

I wonder if she's stumbled on something Dr. Varghese doesn't know about yet.

"But you said traces of the hormone were found in the bodies of people who died from the Black Death. It had changed their DNA. But why? What kind of change is it?"

"I don't know, Sophie. I don't know why the body reacts the way it does—or what it means. I wish I did—and I'm trying. We're all trying." Disappointment squeezes the air from my lungs.

"But what if something of the host survives the changes?"

"There's no evidence of that."

"That you know of." An echo, me at the hospital, saying the same thing to Dr. Varghese.

Her voice is low. "Maybe, but my subjects have been deceased for too long. There's nothing I can learn about that. Besides, the problem isn't what happens after but why the condition is spreading so fast in the first place. That's how we'll figure out how to do something about it. The situation is serious, you know that, but I can't help thinking it's going to get worse. Much worse."

The noises in the church seem too loud and they echo weirdly off the stonework. I don't want to look at what Aunt Irene is scratching onto the page. The last trace of all that misery and death. "Is this it then? This could be the end?"

"Sometimes I think so." Desperation in her voice. "But then I try to remember this isn't the first time people have been sick. The Spanish flu killed millions. There was the AIDS crisis. Ebola. Zika. Your generation isn't the first to suffer, to feel alone and frightened. But I'm doing this for you, Sophie. You're the reason this matters so much to me." She touches my shoulder gently with her charcoal-blackened fingers. "That's why I wanted you to come here and see this place. These people are the children of survivors."

Trinkets and jams, scarves and cookies and lace. Harmless, petty objects of everyday life.

*The people who remain are driven wild and miserable. They are wretched witnesses to the end.*

"It's why we need to take precautions," she says. "Cremating the bodies. The curfew. I know you don't like it, Feef, but it's for your own good. We need to protect you." A pause. "I don't trust despair. It's selfish. It frees you of your responsibilities."

"But if it's as bad as you say…" I don't understand her sometimes. How can she look around at what's happening and keep going as if nothing has changed?

"Hope is the last—and best—form of resistance. Things change and we endure, we learn from what came before us. We can grow stronger because of it. That's how we survive." With a few more sweeps of the charcoal, she contemplates her work. "That's a good thing to learn, niece of mine. Remember it, okay?"

# 18

The next morning I wake up with a vice squeezing my temples and an ashy taste in my mouth. I wonder if this is how Kira felt, a constant drag on her energy, her nights filled with vivid, feverish dreams. The HemaPen is flashing beside me, waiting for another sample, but I hold off and try to gather my thoughts.

I was dreaming of Mom and the trip we took together with Kira to the Bay of Fundy last July. It's one of those magical places where the rules of nature are rewritten. Twice a day an unimaginable flood of water drowns the seabed and the tides are as high as five-story buildings. She had always wanted us to go.

It was before Kira's diagnosis. She was still stable, still herself. But tensions were high at home between Mom and Dad. Mom thought it would help for us to get away together, just the girls. Without him it felt strange, as if we'd been cast loose.

We arrived at Burntcoat Head later in the day than we planned. From the first landing we could spot the rock formations: islands as if on stilts, their heads shaped like flowerpots. But already the ranger was herding tourists off the red mud flats to safety, warning us the tide would be turning any moment now.

We descended down the iron stairs, found the next viewing point, but ended up in the middle of a crowd of tourists going the opposite direction. After they'd passed, Kira was gone. Mom panicked. White-faced, she searched the shoreline.

"Don't worry, Mom," I tried to tell her even though I was anxious too. "You know how she is."

"Your dad—what if something happens? I only took my eyes off her for a moment, just a moment!"

The ranger was a bearded man with wind-chapped skin. He listened patiently as Mom described Kira. Within a minute the radio crackled with news that she was found. I spotted her waving from the lookout tower.

In the dream though, it happened differently. Bright colours and too sharp smells. The salt of the Atlantic stinging our nostrils, our arms greased with sunscreen. There were no crowds—Mom and I were alone on a seashore where the water seemed to hiss and the elevated islands cast bulbous shadows over the mud and sand. "She's down there, Sophie. She's down there, but I can't see her." Mom gripped the railing of the lookout, staring. Slowly, the water spread across the seabed, thick and viscous and sepia-coloured. She didn't move, and neither did I. We couldn't do anything to stop it. Mom was terrified, but she didn't budge as the ocean rushed toward us. "Go on," she whispered, "go with her."

"I don't want to," I told her, but she wouldn't listen.

She didn't look at me. "Of course, you want to. Go on then. Go."

I heard Kira, yelling: "Come with me, Sophie!"

Now as I touch the HemaPen to my finger and wait for it to work its magic, I can hear Aunt Irene moving in her bedroom, drawers opening and closing as she packs up the last of her things for her conference. I roll over onto my back, trying to shake off the feeling of guilt and anxiety brought on by the dream. One of Mom's sketches is pinned above my headboard. I can make out the smudged charcoal outline of Warwick Castle.

She'll be coming home soon. She's been gone for weeks.

On the bedside table, my half-charged phone winks at me. There's a new message from Bryan: *St. Ebbe's Church. 2:00.*


Black has gone out of fashion—no one wears it, no one touches it so funerals have a new dress code. We take out our summer clothes early, dress in bright floral prints, wide hats and sunglasses as if we're going to the beach. Which means

I don't look out of place at a funeral in St. Ebbe's wearing a petal print sundress, seated in a pew next to Bryan who fidgets with the hem of his parakeet green shirt.

I didn't know James Catter, the deceased. Bryan told me they'd gone to grammar school together. "He died from a brain hemorrhage," he murmurs when I ask him about it, which is code for JI2. Any unusual medical symptoms in a young person is code for JI2.

An elderly priest in violet vestments speaks with fervent authority: "Behold, I tell you a mystery. We shall all indeed rise again: but we shall not all be changed. In a moment, in the twinkling of an eye, the last trumpet shall sound and the dead shall rise again incorruptible."

The scent of flowers suffuses the church hall. Dim lights. The congregation shimmers with restless movement like a breeze grazing the surface of a still pond. Bryan is straining forward in his seat to listen. His chin juts out, lips slightly parted. His knee brushes mine with a soft thump, like a bumblebee bouncing against a screen door. Why did he invite me here?

A lump of anxiety sits in my gut. The dream: *Go on*, Mom had whispered to me. *I don't want to*, I had told her. I didn't take her hand. *Of course, you want to. Go on then. Go.*

"For the corruptible one must put on incorruption, and the mortal one must put on immortality," says the priest, his voice rising to a fever pitch. The look on his ancient face is almost ecstatic. As if he has been waiting for this all his life, the end of days.

When service is over, someone opens the doors at the back of the hall, allowing the breeze to whisper through the church. A wide beam of light cuts through the shadows and touches the last row of the pews where already the congregation is rising. We've been released.

But as Bryan and I file out through the pews, a shoulder jostles me from behind: an old woman, her legs unsteady. The movement alarms me and I almost shout at her. I'm not used to crowds anymore. At last, we're outside. "Should we take the bus?" I ask Bryan. I want to flee, let it just be the two of us, him and me out at the cement works. I want to see Kira.

"Hold up a mo," he says.

There's a circle of people our age standing in what looks like a smokers' huddle, foreheads down. No one's speaking much. When Bryan approaches they open up to admit him.

"Howya?" one of them greets him in a lilting Irish drawl. He has a sculpted face, dark curls, thin lips. Hipbones that jut out beneath a narrow waist.

Bryan shrugs. "Just grand."

"Oh, aye, grand indeed." The Irishman laughs a little too loudly and I can smell whisky on his breath. "Come to raise the parting glass with us?" A silver flash glints in his hand. He twists off the cap and takes a quick swig. "Here's to dear Jamie. May the heavens receive his ashes. Much more of this and we'll have snow in July."

"Enough, Reddy," mutters the girl next to him. She's a little older than me and infinitely prettier in a sleek, silky dress the colour of champagne.

"Leave off," echoes another boy, slim with wiry glasses that keep slipping off his nose. I feel a flash of recognition—I saw him in Aunt Irene's office. He cocks his head slightly, then smiles as if he remembers me too. What was his name? Michael? Melvin? "You can ignore him," he says. "The rest of us do. I'm Martin. Martin Paisley."

He offers his hand gently. His palm is warm but oddly dry after being in the humid church.

"It's not enough. Not by half it isn't," the one named Reddy says quietly. "And what about you, Bryan? Where have you been keeping yourself hidden away?" Then his eyes fall on me and his lips curve in a smirk. "One mystery solved at least."

My face goes hot.

"This is…" Bryan stumbles, "Sophie Perella. She's just a friend." Hotter still at that. "Be gentle, Redmond."

"He isn't one for gentleness," says the woman. Her face is angular with high cheekbones and very red lipstick. She has a French accent, crisp syllables and unexpected hesitations. "My name is Liv." Her voice inflects upward as if this is a question. I smile awkwardly, suddenly feeling young in my floral dress, childish and unsophisticated. But she returns the smile before glancing back to Bryan.

It's strange to see him with other people. A vague sense of protectiveness grips me. Possessiveness and discomfort. I'm on the outside—again.

Redmond snaps his fingers in distracted thought. "You look familiar, love … yes, that's torn it. Irene Mooney? I can spot the family resemblance—same eyes, same mouth, I think, and around the eyes, though I confess, untenured though you may be, you are much, *much* prettier."

"Let her be, Reddy!" says Martin.

"She's my aunt," I mumble.

"I was just talking about her, wasn't I? You were there, weren't you, Paisley?" Martin scuffs his feet. "Front row seats to watch your aunt eviscerate Professor Pace, at a seminar back in Michaelmas."

Martin shrugs and gives me a warm nothing-to-be-done look. "Old Pacey called her a storm-chaser, kept arguing she was reading the chronicles too literally."

"That's right! What was it? Warm winds blowing from the south, corrupted by the conjunction of Mars and Jupiter. Something like that. God, she was so angry!" He shakes his head, and takes another swig of his flask.

Martin murmurs: "She's been testing the bodies from the plague pits, hasn't she? Digging them up."

A hush falls over the group as they contemplate this before Redmond breaks in. "Enough of this doom and gloom stuff. At least for tonight, eh? Jamie's off, god keep him, and we should be too. And you, my lovelies, will you join us? Let's speak some wise words and drown our sorrows."

Liv touches Bryan's hand. "He would've liked it if you came. It's been too long. You keep to yourself too much."

But Bryan steps back. "We weren't close, Liv. Not like we used to be. But I wanted to be here for this, to say goodbye." He shakes his head in apology, glances at me. "Sophie and I—there's something we have to do."

Kira is waiting for us at the cement works but I feel so tired at the thought of facing her again, breathing in the sharp tang of her body, cleaning her, reading to her, waiting for some sort of response.

"What do *you* say?" Redmond turns to me. There was a time when I would have pined for someone like him, too charming for his own good, used to getting his own way. But I'm conscious of the cold circle of my medical ID band around my wrist.

"I…" Nothing comes out. His smile begins to collapse, just a little. But then Bryan nods his head and I follow his gaze, catch sight of the familiar wink of silver at Redmond's wrist. Liv's too.

That's when I think, *Yes.*

The word resounds loudly in my head.

*Yes.*

I won't go to Kira today. There will be tomorrow—tomorrow I'll go back there. But today I want this very badly. People. Friends. Something else but her. The illusion of a normal life.

I take a deep breath and meet Redmond's gaze. "What the hell," I say and Bryan grins.

# 19

The five of us end up as a sort of advance guard to set up for a party—a wake, more like it. It turns out that all of them are students at New College, which makes me a bit nervous. I've seen what it's like there, the kind of life they must be used to: the affluence and ease, the heady debates and disputes. They'll grow up to be politicians and lawyers, renowned scientists and artists. It's intimidating. But they don't treat me like a kid at all. They include me in their jokes and stories, Martin holding back to explain the bits I don't understand.

Redmond is in the lead. He takes us over Magdalen Bridge, where we can see the Cherwell floodwaters still lapping up the school playing fields. I hang toward the back as Redmond parts what's left of the tourist crowd.

It turns out this part of town's mostly cosmopolitan grunge, a lot like the Annex in Toronto where I used to live. The sticky sweet scents of curry and frying chips pour out of open shop doors and there's a heavy bass line coming from the speakers mounted over a vintage record shop. As evening starts to lay on, the street fills up with clutches of girls in stiletto heels and thigh-cut dresses heading out to the clubs. Only a couple of hours until curfew, but Redmond and his friends don't seem bothered, so I tamp down my worry.

"Call it a dispensation for those of us with special privileges," Martin tells me. "Sometimes the police show up to tell us off for being too loud but that's it. Say what you want about the university, but they look out for us. On College grounds we can mostly do what we like."

Some of the girls we pass have white paint smeared on their faces, not like Goths exactly, more like a Greek chorus—elegant, composed. Each of them has a little crystal skull winking in her ear. Liv has the same.

"What are those?" I ask her.

"These?" She tucks strands of sorrel-coloured hair behind her ears to show me. The skull, roughly cut, glitters and reflects the streetlights. "Just reminders. Some of us have started to wear them."

"It's a way of knowing death," Martin says. "Remembering that it's always close by."

"You don't want to forget?"

"We can't, can we?"

Redmond interrupts. "This'll be like the last days of Pompeii. We'll play at a bit of filthy hedonism, shall we? Eat, drink, and be merry—then—then—"

"Arrivederci, citizens," says Martin.

• • •

We head down a narrow footpath and eventually come to an old churchyard on private grounds belonging to Oriel College. Ahead of us looms Bartlemas Chapel, a fragment of the fourteenth century tucked away behind the busy main road. Its walls are the colour of parchment, adorned with slender arches.

"It was a leper hospital, would you believe it?" Martin says quietly while he pours wine for me into a plastic cup. He twists the bottle to prevent the last drop from catching, just like the waiters would at the fancy restaurants Dad sometimes took us to. It makes me laugh.

"Pilgrims came from miles around to touch the relics. Apparently, they have the comb of Edward the Confessor, which cures headaches. They've also got the crosses of St. Andrew and St. Philip, and a piece of skin from St. Bartholomew ... I saw them once when we went to mass here. I always thought it was strange what they did with the bodies of saints. Collecting the bits that were left over after these horrible things had happened."

The pale violet dusk is settling into indigo and there is a handful of early stars in the sky. The air is warm even now, redolent of grass and peat and old stone. Liv has laid out a felted blanket for us, settling in next to Redmond. Others have begun to filter into the clearing, faces I recognize from the funeral. More blankets appear and the gloom gives way to a party atmosphere, the sound of Redmond laughing as he uncorks another bottle. Bryan, sitting nearby, glances in my direction and I want to let some part of me lean against him. *What if?* But I don't. Instead, I smile, and he smiles back.

Martin passes us a bottle of thirty-year-old scotch that burns as it goes down. This helps. "That cost two-hundred quid," he moans as the liquid disappears, but no one seems to care.

"Enough of that now, Paisley." Redmond slaps him on the back. Martin looks back owlishly, but then he shrugs. Someone murmurs to me that his grandparents were landed gentry. I guess two hundred quid doesn't mean so much to him.

Bryan seems happy enough to be here but a bit uncomfortable too.

"It's just that they're *students*," he whispers to me when I ask him what's wrong. "It's all a bit posh, isn't it?"

This last makes me start to laugh until I realize he's serious. I'm still getting used to living in a city like Oxford where so much is controlled by the university and geared toward students. It must be hard for him, not being a part of that.

"So what am I doing here?"

"It's different for you. You're not from here. Your accent doesn't give you away, where you were born, who your parents were and how much money they had. You can be anything you want."

"And them?"

"They were Jamie's friends. And—Astrid's."

"She was a student?" I peer at him, surprised he's willing to talk about her. But the wine and Martin's scotch have left him relaxed.

"She started a year ago. With some of this lot. She was young for it but clever." A note of pride creeps into his voice. "Sorry," he says after a moment. "I don't mean to go on about her."

"We don't have to stay, not if—"

"It's fine. Jamie would've been glad for me to be here. And Astrid too." He touches my hand. "Besides, it's good to see you smile."

After another pass of the scotch, it seems as if we've all been friends for ages. Liv has us all playing a drinking game where we take a swig holding the bottle with our left hands. The rules are complicated, and anytime someone screws up we have to beat our fists against the dirt like maniacs as a penalty.

The world has gone bright around the edges. Redmond has taken a gulp with the wrong hand and now we're all crashing our palms into the ground and hollering loud enough to wake the dead.

Faces and bodies blur, and I remember parties in the Rosedale Ravine in Toronto, me and Jaina and the others laughing and drinking beneath the overpass. Time slows and I close my eyes, lean back against the chapel's wall. My body seems made up of a different composition than before. It floats and sinks.

Bryan nudges me awake. "It's not so bad," he whispers or maybe he doesn't. Maybe that's just what I'm thinking. A weird sense of déjà vu like all this has happened already.

"Remember how Jamie ran to the Porter's Lodge starkers in January?" Redmond has made a scarecrow of a nearby sapling with his jacket. "His cock had shrunk down to the size of a pencil stub and there was Rowena Higgs laughing her head off! Thought she was gonna piss herself! And Mysie Ardrey chasing him across the quad, screaming 'That's not how the French do it *at all!*'"

"Mysie Ardey!" Martin laughs. "Everyone told him she would be trouble."

"Aye, but Jamie was crazy for her. Serves him right."

"A fool in love, our poor James," says Liv.

Lit cigarette tips punctuate the darkness, as they trade stories back and forth. Their voices go softer, an incantation to call up the ghost of the dead boy.


The crowd has thinned out, about thirty or so left in small pockets, tangled together on blankets. Redmond croons a filthy song to a trio of dishevelled girls who add their own discordant *tooraloomaloomas* to the chorus. Bryan is lying near me, his head propped up on his elbow. "It's past curfew. Your aunt will be wondering where you've got to. I should get you home."

*Home.* The word has the mass and weight of a stone. "Soon. Not yet. Besides, she's gone for the weekend. No one's waiting for me."

Now Redmond has left off singing so he and Martin can join an animated argument with one of the girls, Caitlyn, a pug-nosed brunette sitting opposite them. "I swear it's the truth," she's saying. "All those tunnels beneath the Bodleian Library? They've emptied them out completely. They're being used for storage. *Body* storage."

"Nonsense." Martin pushes his glasses back up his nose. "How would you even *know?*"

"Terrence Arbon told me so. His brother, Westie, works in the archives. He used to fetch and carry the books they kept in storage. But he says they've cleared them all out."

"It could be just because it's a flood risk," he argues. "You know what it was like over the winter. All those tunnels? They must've moved the books somewhere above ground. Terry needn't have pretended it was anything so drastic."

"That's what *I* said, but *Terrence* said that Westie'd seen people. Not the library staff. And they had the old conveyance system up and running again, the one that was supposed to be used for carting around loads of books. Terrence said they were using it to move these bags, right? Like so." She sketches out her own height. "He said the whole place smelled like it had been scrubbed in vinegar."

"But they'd have to keep the bodies cold, wouldn't they? I don't understand how they could do that beneath the Bodleian. Besides, it'd be illegal."

"They have to keep them somewhere, don't they?" the pug-nosed girl retorts. "If they're *experimenting* on them."

One of the other girls breaks in. "Do you remember that study in bio?" I haven't caught her name but she reminds me of Jaina, the same bob haircut. "About the origins of certain hormones in insects, you know? These blood-sucking things. You remember, Liv, we did that tutorial on it together. What was it?"

"*Rhodnius prolixus*," Liv supplies.

"That's right. They cut off their heads with little bits of waxed thread. And then they did it with caterpillars too. And blowflies. To see where it was the hormone was coming from and what exactly it did. To see if the body would moult if the brain wasn't attached. Then they stitched them together, body to body, two bodies to one head. Just to see what triggered the changes." She shivers.

"You think the Centre is doing that legally? Come off it," Martin says.

"Enough now," Liv sniffs. She rests her head against Redmond's shoulder. "Of course they wouldn't. The Centre is taking samples for testing, that's all they'd be legally allowed to do."

"All I'm saying is that maybe it's good, that James, you know, that they cremated him."

A long silence falls until Liv breaks it. "I don't understand all of you."

"What?" says Redmond.

"You all walk so softly around this. *Death*."

As Liv speaks, we all lean in to listen.

"When I was a very small child," she says, her accent thickened with alcohol, "I developed rheumatic fever and I had to stay in bed for weeks. My father brought me a kitten to keep me company. She was very sweet, very soft, with grey fur like a cloud. I loved her. But just as I began to recover the kitten got sick. Eventually she died, but I didn't know. So I went looking for her—and then I found her."

A burst of laughter floats across the churchyard. A slim boy in an unbuttoned dress shirt struggles to keep his seat atop his friend's shoulders, as they charge toward another pair in the same position.

"I cried all day and all night too. Then my mother said to me, 'That's enough crying now. Your kitten has gone to heaven!' But my father didn't believe in God, so my mother had to tell me. 'Heaven is the place where everything is nice for the kitten. From now until forever it will be nice for the kitten, so don't cry.' I said to her, 'Forever? My kitten will wake up and it will be the same forever?' My mother didn't understand why I was so upset. But I was upset because I don't like forever, the idea of it. Tomorrow is good. Maybe I'll be happy or maybe I'll be sad. But being the same? All the time? I didn't want it to be forever for the kitten. Not even in heaven! I didn't like that idea, the attempt to turn death into something it wasn't. Death is simple, the end of one set of biological processes. Our bodies disappear and the cells that once we were made of decompose and feed new life. It seemed beautiful to me. So when I grew up, I followed my father not my mother. I didn't want to be bound by superstition. I wanted to be a scientist too, so I could understand why nothing in the world stays the same forever."

"What're you saying, Liv?" Martin asks. "Do you still think things are as simple as that?"

"Life, death—we've always thought those were fixed concepts. But what if they aren't? Biologically speaking perhaps they never were. Think of conception and childbirth. Energy transferred from thing to thing, the cellular material passed on from generation to generation, never truly dying. We privilege one form—*our* form—simply because we're hardwired that way. But science is always showing us the world is richer, more fantastic than we believed possible."

"They're like monsters," whispers the pug-nosed girl. She pushes herself upright, then stumbles to her knees. "I saw Clara Brewes. She died in College from a pulmonary embolism. I was the one who found her. She was shaking, just like that other boy."

"We can't be afraid all the time," Liv insists. "The world is changing and we have to find a way to adjust. This is how nature works. Progression, change, destruction—or self-preservation. One thing changes and another responds, again and again and again."

"Bullshit," Bryan interrupts. "What about the ones who die? What about James and all the others? Astrid? She was, what? Just debris? It doesn't matter that she died?"

A pained expression comes over Liv's face. Her voice is tender. "I don't know, Bryan. I wish I did. All I know is—"

But Bryan isn't listening anymore. No one is. Because Caitlyn has begun to scream.

# 20

Confusion in the field. Drunken bodies stumble to their feet, or try to. *Stay down*, I want to tell them. *Don't you feel it?*

Something very big is moving above us.

I raise my eyes. At first there's only darkness. An open sky lit by the slackening glow of a half-moon. A walloping sound. Then one by one the stars seem to go out. Fear slaps breath back into my lungs. Somehow my fingers have found Bryan's and his hand is clammy, cold as clay.

"Sophie," he whispers. My eyes trace the edge of the blackness. There: a massive shape, thrashing wildly in the sky, a spiralling flurry of muscle and slick feathers. Then it shrieks, a knife-edge of noise that slices across my nerves. The sound is familiar—tormented, yes, or perhaps not that at all. Exhilarated. Rapturous. It's so little like the soft burring noises that Kira now makes I wonder how my mind connects them. But it does.

*I know you.* The words hover on the edge of my lips.

The light seems to warp into rainbows around it, breaking apart the night, as its wings—*wings!*—unfurl like the sails of a ship, at least ten feet across. It glides above the peaked roof of the chapel, whipping up the air around it. A battering sensation drives thought from my brain.

All I can think is: *It's so beautiful.*

"Bloody hell," Bryan whispers.

My head whirs with strange images. Memories that don't belong to me flicker in front of my eyes with the speed of a zoetrope, hovering over my vision. First darkness, then two strange faces. A woman with hair like bright copper coils. Soft hands touching my face, my fist wrapped around a fat finger. I am tiny and the world is vast and incomprehensible. I don't understand my place. Only—*I am alive, I am born.* My skin as sensitive as if it had been scraped raw, every nerve new, and it's terrifying. She is—*mother.* A feeling more than a word, a warm buoyancy like floating in the ocean. She cradles me in her arms. This moment is perfect.

And then it ends.

A distant *pop.* It could be the sound of a firework going off. I expect a flare of light zipping across the sky, but there's nothing, only a vicious burst of pain in a body that isn't mine. *The nymph.* The signals transmit along an invisible umbilicus, and my own ribs hurt.

Then the connection snaps, leaving me adrift, reeling. Some crucial piece of knowledge has been snatched away from me.

The faces around me—Bryan, Liv, Martin,

Redmond—are wet with tears. It's as if we're all awaking from the same dream. As if we were all feeling it together.

Above us the creature loses control of its wings and it dips and tumbles. Its body slams against the peaked roof of the chapel, and there is a furious scratching. Slate tiles scatter off the edge of the roof.

I hear an anguished wail from nearby. I think it might be Liv. There is a second *pop*, and Bryan is the first of us to react. "Get down," he cries out as he pushes me face first to the ground. The smell of the dry loam overwhelms me, chalky and sweet. I struggle to breathe, try to flip over onto my side, but Bryan's weight keeps me pinned in place. Some part of me is still with the nymph. I can sense its panic, its horror, feel its chest convulse with pain. It swings its head from side to side. It sees so much more of the world than I can. The field shimmers with colours, awash in an almost electric glow I can't process.

Now Bryan rolls off me. Drunkenness makes me slow to move. He's so close to me that I think he might kiss me, but he doesn't kiss me—instead he shakes me hard enough to rattle my teeth. "Sophie," he says, "you have to go! You run, and you don't look back." His voice is grim and urgent. To the east of us, a squad car lights up the tree line with flashes of red and blue. "Get up!" My legs are leaden, entirely bloodless. Clumsy, clumsy. Bryan is yelling: "Go, go, run!"

The ground tilts underneath me, and after three steps

violence explodes around me. "Get back you," cries a police officer—where did he come from? There are howls of rage in response and the moonlight glints off lunatic faces, the same faces that were laughing a few minutes ago. I can feel it too—an electrifying jolt that goes beyond adrenalin. Something has wired us together, is urging us on.

A few feet away from me Martin is on the ground. He struggles to his feet but an elbow knocks him flying. His legs collapse at awkward angles. Without thinking, I take his hand in mine and yank him up. Strands of sweat-licked hair hang limply around his face—his glasses are nowhere to be seen, his pupils shrunk to pinpricks. He makes an animal noise deep in his throat and his fingernails sink into the skin of my wrist, tearing at the scar line and leaving deep gouges.

"Sorry," he whispers hoarsely. But his fist convulses again.

I feel in him a raw anger that shocks me. It's all I can do to make him let go, and a moment later he has vanished into the crowd.

More police in fluorescent vests are running at us, grabbing people, pinning them to the ground but there are not enough of them, not for us. I catch sight of Bryan rushing a cop, a young one with colossal shoulders.

"Why'd you have to shoot her down?" he screams. His parakeet green shirt is a map of sweat. I can almost feel the explosion of his breath as Bryan hurls himself toward the solid weight of the officer's torso. The man spins in a tight corkscrew and now Bryan's on the ground, and, oh god, I can see a boot coming down. Again. Again.

His hands are up over his face and I struggle to get to him, but I collide with someone with a meaty *thwack*. We both fall over. *I have to get up. I'll be trampled.*

"Stop," says a police officer. His voice is harsh, but his eyes are calm, sane.

He yanks me to my feet and twists me around. Bands of cool metal tighten around my wrists. Handcuffs, I realize. Then he hauls me up. My toes skim the grass and I struggle but he has me over his shoulder. There are wild noises around me, whoops and hollers, and blood pulses in my temples. I want to be out there with them, all of us—together. But at the same time I feel sick and heavy, and I stare at the ground as the cop carries me away from Bryan, from everyone.

Blood drips down the palm of my hand. Behind us, the field unspools into savagery.

# 21

The officer dumps me in the back of his squad car.

I twist in the seat, searching for Bryan out of the back window but I can't see him. Other police cars arrive. Pulsing red light stains the field beyond the window.

I don't know how much time passes before the officer opens the front door, settles into the driver's seat. "Okay," he says at last. "Okay, you don't say anything for a while. Got it?" I can only see a slice of his forehead in the rear-view mirror, a mottled and sweaty brow. I drop my gaze away from his reflection.

It takes him several minutes to edge through the disorder. We pass two ambulances and a pair of fatigued paramedics who are shuffling a covered stretcher into the back of one of them. *There weren't that many of us out there*, I think, *but now maybe there are fewer*. I cough up mucus into the sleeve. The gouge marks in my wrist leave a line of blood on my cheek. "Hey," he calls from the front. "Are you hurt?"

I shake my head, fighting back tears.

"Fucking hell," he mutters, turning and staring at me with big, hound dog eyes. And then: "You kids, just. Shite…"

The squad car crosses Magdalen Bridge and below us the river glimmers. I don't know where he's taking me. Am I under arrest for breaking curfew? Wouldn't he have to tell me? Maybe he doesn't.

I slump against the window, feeling relief, maybe. There are no choices to make here. That should scare me— but it doesn't. I replay the scene in my mind: the creature tumbling against the roof of the chapel. It was a nymph— it had to be! I'd felt a connection with it. Then Martin grabbing my wrist. And Bryan, hurling himself at the officer. I know how he felt, that little flame burning inside like a pilot light, ready to explode.

We drive silently through the city centre, passing the spires of St. Mary the Virgin, then the massive iron gates of the examination halls. We turn down St. Aldate's and head south. Is the station this way? As we cross the Thames, the squad car starts to slow. I don't know this area, which is deserted and rundown. Paper flyers stick to the light posts and doorways, slicked down by spring rains and pulped into unreadability. No one has bothered to put up new ones.

The officer stops the car, gets out, and then opens the door to the back. "Prepared to behave?"

All the fight has gone out of me, replaced by a dull ache in my temples. "Yeah."

"Good." He closes the door again, locking it, and heads down the street. The cuffs on my wrists chafe. Nothing to do but wait, and wonder if Bryan is bleeding out on a stretcher somewhere. I think about him pressed against me in the dirt.

*Please don't let him be dead.* A prayer whispered into the night. I can still see the image of the officer's boot coming down on him again and again. *Please let Bryan Taite be alive. Please don't let him leave me. Please.*

The officer is back. He stares at me through the window as he struggles to fit the key into the lock while keeping a hold on two take-away boxes. A draft of cool air bursts in when he manages it. I have to shuffle over, twisting with my bound hands so he can slide in next to me.

"I'm Police Constable Trefethen." He's calmer now, the gruffness smoothed out of his voice. He balances the two grease-laden boxes on his knee, fishes through his pockets for another set of smaller keys to release the cuffs. Watches me warily once he's done it.

"Hungry?"

I nod. He tears the lid off and hands one of the boxes of fish and chips to me. "Thanks," I manage.

Eating is more important than talking. My body is calorie starved, amped up with adrenaline.

"Thought you might need that. Thought your parents

might appreciate you coming back sober."

"You aren't going to take me in?"

He picks at one of the chips thoughtfully, as if he is surprised by it, by its existence, here in this car. "No," he says. "I'll take you home. Just this once."

"Why?"

He shifts on the seat. The firearm at his side seems like an uncomfortable weight, one he isn't used to. As if he doesn't like it very much. But he doesn't answer me.

"What happened to my friends?"

"The JR if they're hurt. Some of them may go to lock-up while they cool off. We can't hold them forever. Not enough space, but overnight, maybe. The Colleges will be after us if it's any more than that."

He stares at me and I realize from the glazed look that he's in shock. "You're young, aren't you?" he asks. "Young for the Colleges, I mean. For—what happened out there." Disgust in his voice now. "We never wanted to hurt any of you, but what were we to do? That thing in the sky … and then all of you lot, it was like you all went mad. Never seen anything like it, not here. You're supposed to be the best and brightest but you were damn near trying to rip us apart."

"We didn't mean it." He just blinks his eyes in disbelief. I wipe my lips on the back of my hand, return his stare. "*You* shot it down."

"Rubber bullets," he spits. "All this civil unrest, the

curfew, now they've issued us with fucking riot gear. We'd just heard about a gathering of you lot. Drunken kids, you know. But then it was—"

"It was a kid."

He stares at me in disbelief. "That was no child."

"It *was*," I insist. "Or it was, once."

He cradles his head in his hand, pressing his palm against his forehead. "Bloody hell." His hand spasms into a fist. "Bloody fucking monsters now. It wears a man out, watching this. The dead should stay dead."

"They aren't dead," I try to tell him but he doesn't seem to hear me.

"I lost me own. My boy was thirteen. I was teaching him football. Jesus fucking Christ. It was bad enough when he passed. It's no wonder they burn the lot of them up. Imagine looking up and seeing your own? It's *wrong*."

"We just don't understand it properly."

"What's there to understand, girl? This is madness. You all went mad out there, but I don't know if I blame you. Maybe the whole world has gone mad. Rotten at its core." Remembering where he is, who I am, a note of pleading creeps into his voice. "You weren't doing anything, were you? You were just scared. Can't lock you up for being scared, can I? So I'll bring you back to your mum and dad, safe and sound. Food in your stomach. And you're damn well going to mind what you do with yourself, understand?

Sit tight, wait it out. Forget whatever you saw tonight."

*Welcome to the monster club*, Bryan said.

Trefethen takes the soggy boxes once we're finished eating, exits the car and deposits them in a trash can on the street, then settles into the front seat again.

"You know you're wrong," I tell him. He raises his eyebrows. "You're wrong about what's happening."

"You think what you want, girl," he says, his expression thickening from disbelief to a dull anger. "But this won't be the last of it. If there's more of those things out there, by god, it won't just be rubber bullets they give us. Just you wait."

# 22

Trefethen parks on the street outside the house and insists on walking me to the door. I try to tell him there's no one in there, that Aunt Irene is away, but he doesn't believe me.

"I've heard that enough times," he says, chewing on his bottom lip, "you don't want your mum and dad to know what you've been up to. But I can't leave you here by yourself." I wonder if he's a little bit afraid of me, what I might do. He knocks at the door with three hard, short raps while I linger behind him. We wait a while together. I shuffle my feet, wondering what happens when no one comes. Will he have to bring me back to the station after all?

But then I hear footsteps. The door opens a crack. "Sophie? Is that you?" Mom's face is pale in the bald light of the porch and her eyes widen with surprise. There are lines I don't recognize. I want to hug her but the situation is so weird. Her gaze flicks to the man next to me. "And … you. What are you doing with my daughter?"

"PC Daniel Trefethen," he supplies.

"Right," she says slowly. "Police constable. Sorry, I. I

didn't realize." The door opens. Mom leans awkwardly against the frame, pulling unconsciously at a thread in the sleeve of her jumper. "What's all this about then?"

"I wanted to bring your daughter home. She was…" His gaze fastens on me. "Out past curfew. I knew you'd be worried, waiting up for her."

"I was, yes." She blinks again, looking lost. "Thank you, sir. I'm sorry if she's caused any problems."

"Is that it?" I ask him. "Can I go?"

"Right," he says. "Mind the curfew next time. The other officers aren't as soft as me. You don't want to spend the night at the station, hear?" He doesn't touch me, doesn't shake hands or anything like that. He just turns and marches down the steps. Mom's eyes continue to follow him as he gets into the squad car.

"Mom?" I say, shivering now. "When did you get home?"

"Hours ago." She looks as if she wants to say more but instead she nudges the door open and I follow her in. I wish she would yell at me. I wish she would look at me. But something stops her: guilt, maybe. It's almost as if she's afraid of me.

The house is quiet. Just inside the hall I see her suitcase, her shoes. I want to crawl into bed, bury my face in a pillow. Let the night drift away from me. But Mom is finally home and I know I can't.

"Mom?" I follow her into the kitchen. I hate this: the way she's treating me. Like I'm a stranger. "I'm sorry about all this. I was just out with friends and I lost track of the time. I didn't know you would be back tonight."

It's then I notice the mess. She has upended an album of photographs. They're scattered across the tablecloth, some spread out across the chairs, a few have drifted to the tiled floor. There are photographs of Kira by herself, playing in the garden at the old house in Toronto. Another with a face smeared with chocolate cake—her fourth birthday party maybe?—still that silly grin. Even one of her and Dad though you can't see much more than his hand, which I recognize immediately from the long fingers, the same fingers I have. I pick up a piece of glossy paper. The bottom edge has been cut in the shape of a crescent moon. It's a picture of me, young, staring at something outside of the frame now, but I have a look of thorough concentration on my face. I realize this is me holding Kira as a baby for the first time.

As I try to make sense of it, Mom pours herself a glass of water. "How long have you been back?" I ask at last.

"My train got in just before dinner. I didn't know where you were, where anyone was. Your phone wasn't on. Sophie, if anything happened to you—"

I don't let her finish. The evening has been too awful and for a moment I don't care about anything beyond that she's here with me now. I gather her in my arms. "I really missed you, Mom," I say and it's true. I want her to know that. After everything that's happened tonight I just want things to be the way they were before. When if I screwed up she could scold me and even if it made me angry I'd know eventually things would be good between us again.

"You aren't angry with me for leaving you?"

There's a wariness in her movements as if she's waiting for me to hurt her. And all at once I know I could. She's my mother but she left when I needed her. I could turn away now, cut her out—and she'd let me because some part of her thinks she deserves it.

The sudden swing in our relationship leaves me dizzy. "You did what you had to," I tell her at last. "It's okay, Mom. Really. I've been okay."

When I pull back I can see the damage the last months have inflicted in her lined face but there's something else. She looks stronger. Her muscles are toned, skin coppery from the sun. And when she looks at me I can see her relaxing visibly, despite the shine of tears in her eyes.

"Sit," she says.

"I'm sorry." I try again but she waves her hand.

"Hold on. I know we need to talk about this—you missing curfew when your aunt is away—but first, how are feeling? Is there any pain? Nausea?"

"On a scale of one to ten?" She's her old self again. A ghost of a smile crosses my face.

"You haven't been drinking, have you?"

"A little, yeah," I say at last.

"Sophie, you shouldn't…"

"I know," I tell her. "It was a dumb thing to do. But I'm okay." I don't let her see my hands. "Aunt Irene's been taking me to my appointments. There isn't much news though, nothing that anyone seems to be able to do for me. So mostly I've just been trying to get by. Keep it together, you know?"

"I do." She sighs, then glances at me. "It isn't easy, is it?"

"Maybe it shouldn't be."

We've both got things we're sorry for. We've both made mistakes with each other. But as the silence lengthens I'm glad she's here. Even if it means more questions. I thought I could do this by myself but what if I was wrong?

"What was it like up in Warwickshire?" I ask her.

She's hesitant at first but when I lean forward she begins to talk. "It was a warm winter. Jackie wanted to try out peaches, she thought they might grow now. They bloomed early and we had to pollinate them by hand because the bees hadn't come out yet. We used old paintbrushes for it. I had to press the bristles into each flower, one by one." She shakes her head at the absurdity of it.

"It looks as if it was good for you."

"It was." It's weird. She's talking to me as if I'm Aunt Irene, as if we're both adults. "Things moved more slowly up there. They've had floods too, particularly around the Avon, but it wasn't so bad. Everyone turned up to help with clearing the damage. There was glass in the fields, bits of debris. If we hadn't all pitched in they wouldn't have been able to start planting new crops. The government isn't moving fast enough. They can't cope with the scale of this."

"Aunt Irene's said the same thing," I tell her.

"Sophie, I want to be better now. For you. And for Kira too. I know she isn't … with us anymore. There are times I miss her so much it feels like I'm drowning and … and I just didn't want to pull you under as well."

"I know, Mom. It's just … you're staying now, right?"

She nods slowly.

"I want to be here with you. I couldn't protect Kira but I want us both to find a way to remember her that doesn't hurt so much. We can't give up on life, Sophie. We can't retreat from it. I don't want you to do that."

That's when I realize what the mess on the kitchen table is about, what she's beginning to make. A collage for Kira. Together the two of us look at the foundations of what she's been laying down.

"What is it?"

"I don't rightly know yet. We never scattered her ashes. It all feels unfinished." She touches one of the photos of Kira she has been reshaping. "I used to think that joy was an accretion, something you could build up and make physical. It was almost like a shell, a way of trying to ward off danger. But when your sister got sick the fear made that harder. It put a crack in things. I couldn't do it anymore."

"And now?"

"If there's anything of Kira left in the world, she'd want us to find a way to be happy, don't you think?"

I glance at her sharply but she's staring at the pictures. Does she feel something? Some trace of connection? Or is it just what all parents feel? I don't care. I hug her again and it's like touching a live wire, the voltage running back and forth, a shared moment of grief passing between the two of us. But dissipating afterward.

It's good. It feels really good. Maybe the only good thing that's happened today. It all comes back to me in a rush and I have to fight back tears.

"Will you tell me what happened tonight?" she asks me, catching the change in my expression. How she's behaving is different. She never would have given me a choice before. I wish I could share the truth with her but I can't. It would be too much, too soon. She's stronger now but would she understand? I remember how Trefethen reacted, disbelieving, angry.

"I met these students from the College. They were throwing a party. It's been ages since I've really talked to anyone so I decided to go. I just wanted things to feel normal for once."

She nods slowly, taking this in. I expect scolding but none comes.

"Are you going to ground me?"

"I don't know. I'll need to think about it."

"You can if you like."

Mom smiles at this, me offering to take on punishment. I wouldn't have done that back in Toronto.

"Things were different with Kira," she says. "She was so young when she got sick. But you'll be eighteen in a few months. I know you've had to make decisions for yourself but you can't be reckless. Last time, when I got the call from the police—"

"I'm okay. I promise you, I'll do better."

She picks up one of the photographs. "Your sister was beautiful, wasn't she?"

"She was," I tell her.

"You were a good sister, Sophie."

# 23

I'm finally alone in my room and I desperately want to sleep but my head is a cauldron of worries. Mom has begun to heal but for me nothing has been solved. There are gouges and dark bruises around my wrists from where the handcuffs bit into my skin. She didn't see them and I couldn't tell her what had happened.

*Sit tight, wait it out. Forget whatever you saw tonight.*

That was Trefethen's advice. Maybe it would be Mom's too—but I can't follow it. Kira is still at the cement works and Bryan could be dead. In the darkness all I can think about is the way that boot came down. The damage it might've done. And if he were to die, what then? There's a terrible blankness in my mind when I try to imagine it.

Only: *I can't lose someone else.*

The window is large, unsteady in its rotted frame, but I can pry it open with my fingernails.

"Sorry, Mom," I whisper. I hate that I can't tell her the whole truth when all I want is to find a way for us to rebuild our family. For a little while, in the churchyard, I felt joy. I understood it. Now all I can think about is survival: mine, Kira's, Bryan's.

The wind rushes in off the river, the amphibious smell of decay. The height makes my stomach turn as I crawl out into the night.

I ride toward the JR first. Trefethen said that's where the injured would be taken and I need to know if Bryan's alive. Kira can wait until after—at least that's what I tell myself.

On the way two ambulances pass me, their sirens blaring. There are police cars trailing them, but no one else on the road. More lights are on than I'd expect in the houses I pass and once I think I hear a sound above me but when I stop and look up there's nothing there. I squint into the night but the streetlights blind me. Eventually I get back on my bike and pedal faster.

At the hospital I find Liv by the nurse's station. Her dress is matted with mud, the hem slashed to ribbons. Limp strands of hair, gummed with dirt, frame a face made sharp by strain. "Sophie? What're you doing here?"

I shake my head, not bothering with the whole story. "I'm here for Bryan. Where is he? Do you have any news?"

"I've never seen him like that. He was covered in blood."

"I know, I saw him."

"That officer broke his ribs."

"Is he—?" My heart jumps.

"He's in intensive care. Martin too. I don't understand it. What happened out there?"

Her eyes wander, unable to fix on anything. I grab her shoulder. "You're okay?"

"My father woke someone up at the French embassy and had me released, but I don't know what's going to happen. The police took away my passport."

I guide her toward a chair, bring her a cup of coffee. The waiting room is unusually silent, tense. Clusters of staff gather around the television monitors. The newsreel shows footage of the nymph from what looks like cameras worn by the officers. What they capture is like something snagged from a fairy tale. Androgynous. Its golden eyes are flicking left, right, left in pure panic, and its body begins to—I don't know, *undulate* or bristle. The strange pearly white of its skin sucks in until I can make out the shape of its bones, the thin twig of its humerus, and a ridge that runs vertically down its chest. It leaps into flight.

"Oh my god," someone murmurs, sparking a frightened rumble of agreement.

Liv follows my gaze. "The story just broke. There have been sightings of them all around the country."

"Have they figured out what they are?"

Her eyes go soft. "It was beautiful, wasn't it? When we saw it? It wasn't terrifying. It felt…"

"Almost human."

"They're the ones who died, aren't they?" Her voice is full of wonder. "The ones who weren't cremated. They've changed. They're waking up."

She lapses into silence as a nurse heads toward us, an older woman with her grey hair tied into a loose bun. She has a familiar look about the face. "Mrs. Taite," Liv says, "how is he?" Of course, Bryan's mother.

"He's out of danger," she says to Liv. "You can see him if you want to."

"This is Sophie," Liv says, and the nurse's eyebrows rise. "You go on. He's why you're here."

"How's he doing?" I ask as Bryan's mother leads me through the hallway.

"Surviving," she says in a low voice. "I don't understand it. How my boy could attack a police officer."

Inside the room it's a shock to see him surrounded by machines, that ugly pattern of bruises on his face. She looks down at Bryan, and it's as if she is seeing the damage for the first time. She squeezes her eyes shut. "So you're Sophie then? I wondered when we'd meet."

"He told you about me?"

She nods. "I'll let you stay with him, love. But don't trouble him. My boy needs his rest."

Alone in the room, I watch the rise and fall of his chest. I want to touch his forehead, press my fingers against his skin and feel the heat rising underneath, but this seems intrusive, a breach of trust while he's so vulnerable. So I sit motionless, let the tension between these two impulses nag at one another: *wanting to touch him, afraid to touch him.*

He stirs, then his eyelids flutter open. His pupils contract against the light, then expand. They are ringed in a golden copper, darkening to a coffee-coloured band at the edges.

"Hey, freakazoid."

"Sophie." The word is a sigh. He struggles to sit up, but then his face goes white.

"Take it easy."

He collapses, panting.

"How did this happen?" I ask in a low voice.

He wears the same dazed expression that Liv did. "I don't know. I didn't feel scared. Just felt … good—even when I was on the ground and he was kicking me, I couldn't feel any pain." When he realizes I'm staring at him, his face flushes red with shame.

"Should I call your mom?"

"Not yet."

I catch his hand in mine. "Did you see it? The nymph?"

"Yeah."

"Did you feel it too?"

"What?"

"The connection. When it flew overhead, I could see, or feel, its memories. It was like I was hallucinating."

He shakes his head slowly. "It wasn't like that for me," he says. "It was … muted. Just a feeling. A sense of warmth, maybe."

"There are others," I tell him excitedly. "I saw it on the news. Liv said they're waking up. I think she's right." His fingers squeeze mine.

"Kira?" he asks.

"I don't know," I tell him. "I need to get to the cement works. But I had to see you first. I had to know you were okay."

Bryan looks as if he wants to say something but then there's a noise outside. Liv, I can recognize her voice. She's shouting for me.

"Go," he says. "Find out what's happening."


Liv is pacing in the waiting room, tears running down her cheeks. Her lipstick has smeared across her face.

"What's wrong? Liv?"

"It's Martin. He—the doctors say … he was hit in the head. Bleeding in the brain. He's dead."

I collapse next to her in a chair. "Oh god."

"He has … *had* a sister here in Oxford. She's a few years older than him. I know her a little." Liv's staring straight ahead. "Neither of their parents are still alive."

"I saw him out there. He was right next to me." His fingernails digging into mine. He was lost in the same wave of emotion that Bryan was. A terrible thought hits me. "Liv, what are they doing with his body?"

"Someone from the Centre is talking to his sister right now."

"You need to speak to her. You need to explain it to his sister, so they don't…" *Burn him up. Cut him up. Experiment on him.*

Liv turns to me with an expression somewhere between worry and wariness. "What are you talking about?"

"You were out there. You *saw* it, you felt it. We all did."

I realize I'm almost shouting at her. A security guard by the nurses' station is watching me and so is another one by the entrance way. Liv seems to realize it at the same time I do. Softly she says: "What am I supposed to do? Haven't you seen the news?"

The television is still playing. The host is interviewing one of the officers, early twenties. He's saying: "I brought it down. Three shots, didn't hesitate. It isn't for me to say what it is … but the training, you know, it kicks in right away."

*Downing Street authorizes army to take immediate action.*

"People are at risk, ma'am. I just did what I had to in the moment, and it made them wild, it did."

And then the image shifts to an aerial shot taken by

helicopter. Tower blocks lit up in Canary Wharf in London. Dark silhouettes passing. When the camera pulls back I realize the air is full of sleek bodies and alien faces. There are hundreds of them riding the currents over the Thames, spiralling like leaves caught up in a cyclone. So many of them!

"Liv, we have to do something."

"She won't listen to me. She's scared, Sophie. Everyone is panicking."

There's no time to help Martin. Kira is in danger. The image in my head is so clear. Her limp form, huddled in the darkness beneath the shelter, the open circle of sky above. For months her body has been shifting, preparing itself for escape. For this—*flight*!

"If there are more of them we'll be ready," says the officer on the screen and I know he's right. I can't let Kira be discovered, not now. If they find her they'll kill her.

I search for the exit. A security guard makes a move toward me, startled. His eyes fix on my medical ID bracelet and I can see his thoughts forming, slowly. The threat he sees when he looks at me—as if I might go wild at any moment.

But it isn't me I'm worried about anymore.

# 24

I toggle through the gears on my bike, trying to coax more speed from them, more power. Sweat streams down my face, stings my eyes. By the time I reach Kidlington, my palms are sliding on the handlebars.

There must be other nymphs, bodies that weren't cremated. If not here then in other places, across the Channel, across the ocean for all I know, in India where they dumped the victims of JI2 into the water. And now what? If they catch her, it will be worse than if they had cremated her in the first place.

Shit, shit, shit.

I turn onto the gravel road into the cement works, leaning forward to force extra weight into my exhausted thighs. Then—*snap!* Something whips lightning-fast against my shin. The bike stutters and I'm somersaulting over the handlebars. I hit gravel, flaying my jeans and shredding the skin of my knees, then my shoulder. I touch the back of my neck and my hand comes away varnished in red. Numbness, no pain yet. Nothing but a hot ache in my muscles as I stagger to my feet. The bike is completely mangled.

You have about ten seconds before the pain catches up with you.

*Right.* I begin to run.


The chimney is ahead of me, no one else in sight. *Good, good.* The first flare of pain sets my nerve endings on fire. My leg buckles but I force myself up. A red handprint on a concrete block, my contribution. Now I'm rounding what's left of the raw mixture plant and I can feel blood running down my back as well.

I crash into the metal door of the chimney but it doesn't budge.

The padlock.

I kneel to dig around for the hiding place we made for the key. A whimper escapes my lips, as my muscles spasm painfully. It should be just there ... god, I can't find it. The key. Where is it?

*Ka-thunk, ka-thunk, ka-thunk!* At first I think it's my heart pounding. But the sound is dully metallic. Coming from inside the chimney.

Blood pulses in my temples. My vision swims, replaced by an image of tiny hands pounding on a door. "Open the door, Soff! I wanna come in!" And my voice, high with irritation: "Go away, Kiki!" I blink and it vanishes. The key is tucked into my palm.

The padlock comes off in a single, abrupt motion. Then I'm pushing the door, hearing the squeal of the rusted hinges. I pull it shut behind me and slump inside, blinded by darkness.

She hits me in the chest so hard my filleted legs give out.

Instinctively, I wrap my arms around her. *Hold on, hold on!*

In that brief moment of contact: the slanted shape of bones, the hard keel of her welded ribs, her skin bristling with thousands of tiny pins, a soft layer of flocculent down, new growth. She is trembling, and it's as if she is growing larger, expanding toward me. It's her wings, bursting through the thin membrane of her skin. Those masses on her shoulders, those hulking deformities moving beneath the surface—now stretching out, unfolding.

Her eyes are lustrous, golden. They dart from left to right rapidly, observing everything in an instant, processing it all with avian intelligence. "Kira," I whisper. She stares at me, head cocked, her jaw a solid, expressionless shelf of bone. The gesture is recognizable, yet so alien it makes my chest hurt. She's gathering energy, bursting with it.

Then she explodes into action, somersaulting crazily away from me, battering herself against the side of the tower like a moth trapped against a screen.

*Ka-thunk!*

The problem is her wings. No space to extend them properly. She can't get enough lift, but she's trying.

Kira crashes into the tarpaulin structure Bryan built to protect her, scattering fairy lights and old two-by-fours. Then she slams against the side of the tower again. Her wings beat at the air, pinions spread like fingers. She doesn't know how to use them yet, not properly. She makes it halfway up the height of the chimney before they tangle. Newly grown feathers slice the air. It isn't enough to keep her up and she falls into the dirt.

I take a step toward her, but she's off again. This time she's learned something because when she collides with the wall, her legs are ready for it. They've become flexible, pneumatized shafts of bone. How did I ever think of them as brittle? She ricochets away and pirouettes in mid-air, her spine unexpectedly tensile, so that as she passes the centre-point she is already facing the other side, legs braced like mainsprings. She's adapting. A staccato, double beat of her wings keeps her hurtling higher. It's not flying, not exactly. More like a crazy game of leapfrog.

My head is jangling with thoughts, not all of them my own. Her confusion radiates out of her, but so does something else. Jubilation. How much she wants to be free.

"No! You can't!" My voice echoes in the tower. I don't know if she can understand me, but she continues to rise. She's going to make it all the way to the top—and when she does, she'll be gone.

She isn't going to stop for anything. Not unless I can stop her.

On the outside of the chimney is a decrepit utility ladder zippering up the full height.

The first few metres or so look like a mangled train track. The rungs hang askew in their locks, and the side rails twist this way and that. My shoulder glows with pain as I haul myself up.

Grunting, I pull and pull, feet planted on the chimney wall. Every couple of hand spans I reach another rung lock: a big knuckle of metal that carves up the inside of my hands. Pretty soon my palms are a lacerated mess of skin flaps and deep, gory runnels. Close to the top, the ladder has torn away from the wall so I can't quite get my feet against the side rail. I have to shimmy up like I'm on a rope, relying on the meagre strength in my arms alone while the ladder creaks ominously. The extra weight tears at my grip. I won't make it, I won't— and then I do.

One of my running shoes, the laces flapping wildly, slides off, and plummets to the ground. My gaze follows.

*You could jump.*

I recognize that wormy voice at the centre of me. *Jump*, it says again.

Nausea roils my stomach, but the fear is gone now. It

has been replaced by an ecstatic whisper. *Let go, Sophie.* There's a throbbing sensation in my palms, my groin, the arches of my feet. My body is bathed in a warm glow and my nipples have squeezed into hard pinpricks of sensation.

*Come with me.* A keening voice in my head.

I hear a thud from within the tower. Kira ramming her fledgling body from side to side, picking up momentum and speed. She's coming toward me. I close my eyes. When I force them open again, I start climbing again. One foot, and then the other. One foot, and then the other. All other thoughts slip away from me. There is only one: *Climb.*

And somehow I do. The height is dizzying, and from here I can make out a whistling noise. I become aware of shapes moving around me, the heavy beating of wings, flashes of white in the darkness. That noise thrumming through me, deep and wordless, a straining symphony that seems to come from every direction at once. I'm not alone—and neither is she. They have been waiting for her, just above the cloud cover, waiting and calling.

I haul myself over the edge of the chimney, and stare downward. I can see her gaining height, rocketing toward me.

"Kira!" I call to her. "You can't leave!"

Trace fragments of her memories muddle up with mine. Her fifth Christmas, tearing into presents before anyone was awake. Knowing she shouldn't but doing it anyway, both terrified and delighted to be discovered.

Standing on top of the toilet in the girl's room on her first day of third grade, missing Mrs. Laplant's roll call and then racing into the recess yard while no one was there. The space would be *hers*, all hers! She wouldn't have to share it. She wiggles her butt at Mrs. Laplant through the window, daring her to look, but she doesn't. No one in the classroom does. She is invisible. Totally free.

Then another. I'm staring down at her on the day she died. We are just within sight of the bridge to home. And I want her to go to it, away from the flooded Thames, but she knows, is utterly certain this is the wrong direction. But I won't listen to her. She's just a kid, she needs protecting.

Except she doesn't. Her body is alive with meaning, with wanting. I can't seem to understand it, but then sometimes it's like that. Sometimes she feels something so strongly she expects everyone around her to feel it too: joy, sadness, disappointment. But they don't—they're wrapped in their own bubble of protection, and nothing of hers bleeds into them. She knows I'm wrong, but there's no way to tell me, nothing I would believe. She loves me—I feel that—but she's impatient with me too. She knows what she wants and what needs to happen. I will only slow her down. She pulls away from me.

Suddenly Kira is coming at me fast. A final upward vault, and her wings stretch to full length with the speed of a switchblade. They lock into a rigid length of feathers and muscles.

"Please, Kira!" I call out, reaching for her. "No!"

She isn't mine to hold onto. They're waiting for her and she wants this. I know she does.

I let her go.

# THREE

Look at my image and see how I was once fresh and gay... When you least expect it death comes to conquer you. While your grave is still undug it is good to think on death.

*A disputation betwixt the body and worms,*
written in an anonymous hand
"in the season of huge mortality, of sundry
diseases, with the pestilence heavily reigning"

## 25

Martin's sister doesn't listen, of course she doesn't.

Liv calls to tell me the next morning, the chime of my phone dragging me out of a fitful sleep. Dreams of Kira, of dark shapes moving overhead. "I tried to explain but Cath just stared at me," she says, her voice seeming to come from miles away. I can imagine it perfectly—her bewildered look turning to distrust as she takes in Liv's hair, her mangled dress, her smeared lipstick. "She told me her brother was gone. Nothing could change that."

Martin wasn't the only casualty.

Seven people died in the Bartlemas churchyard riot. Six students, one officer. Someone tore off his helmet and heaved a rock into his head. The news alerts pop up continuously on my tablet while we talk, tiny flares of disaster in the corner of my screen. Blurry shots of our teeth, our rictus grins that night. Headlines screaming about *The Age of RAGE!*

I can still feel that raw jangling of emotion. A kind of *push*.

• • •

Mom comes down just before noon and from the look on her face I can tell she's been following the news in her bedroom.

"Were you there last night?" she demands. Whatever understanding we shared is gone now. I'm her child and I lied to her. I can't meet her gaze and she knows instantly what that means. "Jesus, Sophie. Why didn't you tell me?"

I expect her to yell but she doesn't. She turns on the television. Soon the two of us are huddled together in front of it. I watch her take in the appearance of the nymph, the dull gleam of its feathers—its *wings*, like sails. But what she sees is the wreckage of the human form, the monstrous transformation. "Oh god, oh Jesus," she whispers, over and over. "Did you see one of them last night?"

When I still don't answer, she makes a grab for my hand, not registering the lacerated palms, which I mended roughly with fibrin glue last night. The drugged haze of my stare, dirt crusted into the grooves of my skin. I've slept for maybe two hours.

"What are they?" she demands but it's the television presenter who answers her question. Officials have confirmed the results. The recovered body was human—or it had been human, once.

"They don't understand," I try to tell her.

"Understand what?"

"What happened out there. It wasn't our fault. They shouldn't have shot it down."

Her gaze has wandered to the urn with its ashes and the blood drains slowly from her face. I let her hold me.

Mom and I spent the day camped out in the living room watching the news. Aunt Irene appears like a ghost in the doorway late in the evening. Lane Ballard, the Centre's director, is trying to explain to a skeptical presenter what the nymphs are.

"What we're seeing is an advanced stage of the condition, which only one in ten, one in a hundred, will experience." He blinks at the light owlishly, looking unhappy, like this isn't a part of his job. "With the right post-mortem procedures we can control this. That's what we've been trying to do."

"So you were aware of what might happen? Who else knew?" the host asks. She's young, the kind of polished blond woman I'm used to seeing on American news channels. Reassuring, blandly pretty.

"We knew *something* was happening," he responds.

"But why now? Why haven't we seen this before?"

"We've been looking at comparable processes. Take locusts, as an example," he says, "they go through changes at the same time. Their eggs hatch when the conditions are right. Their life cycle is timed to the seasons, so when they swarm—"

"You think they're *swarming*?" Now the look on her face is incredulous, frightened.

"I didn't mean it like that!" Dr. Ballard pushes at his

glasses, reminding me of Martin, how nervous he looked in Aunt Irene's office.

The television flickers on and off, the power unsteady.

"That was Dr. Lane Ballard, an *expert* in the field." The last said with sarcasm. Nobody trusts them, not anymore.

We've seen footage from the Philippines and Malaysia, hundreds of nymphs moving over the South China Sea. Taiwan has already declared a state of emergency. No news from India yet but I remember the posts from the forum a few months ago—bodies tangled in bright sheets, unclaimed. Animals won't touch them, we've learned. Not carrion birds, not insects. It has something to do with the smell, that acetone—the starvation reflex. As if they knew the nymphs were still alive.

"You don't need to watch that," says Aunt Irene.

Mom asks, disbelieving, "Did you know about this? Did you know those children were still alive?"

Aunt Irene stares at the television and I can tell she didn't. Her face is white and her voice is tired, leached of the excitement she used to have. "I didn't have much contact with the medical researchers. If I'd known I would have told you." A grim look on her face.

"But there were people at the Centre who knew, weren't there?" I start to insist. "Friends of mine—some of your students, even—were talking about it. How the bodies were changing…"

"They're monsters," Mom says.

It takes me a moment to realize it's the doctors at the Centre she's talking about.

# 26

The next morning we hear from Mr. Coomes that Cherwell College is closing temporarily. He tries to reassure us it'll re-open, that they'll be able to make up the lost time before the A-level exams, but already the promises of that future seem so distant. It's impossible to imagine life going on as normal, me going to university next year.

For days Mom keeps me in the house and takes away my tablet and phone. My only escape route is cut off. Her rationale slides between a grounding for the police visit and a kind of makeshift quarantine, the best thing she can think of to do while she tries to get in touch with Dr. Varghese. But the phone lines to the hospital are always busy and when she and Aunt Irene drive down they're turned away by security guards. Medical personnel and emergencies only until further notice. My aunt looks furious at being cut out of the loop.

Bryan was released from the hospital but I haven't heard from him in days. The lack of information makes me nervous. What if there have been complications? Reports have been coming in across the country of teenagers like me taking sleeping pills, bleeding out in warm baths. Their parents have sick, bovine expressions on their faces afterward, an air of betrayal when they say *I never thought she'd do something like this. She was such a happy kid.*

When Mom hears about that, there's a nasty couple of hours when she considers removing my bedroom door. She stares for ages at the rusted hinges before Aunt Irene calls her off.

"You can't keep her locked up."

"She could've been hurt out there!"

My aunt answers her: "What are you going to do? Ground her for the rest of her life?"

"If I bloody well have to, I will!"

Unwilling to face them I stay in my bedroom anyway, staring outside at the sky. Searching for Kira.

In the following days, a creeping calm settles over the city. There are reports of a nation-wide register of people who have tested positive for JI2 but so far most of the doctors around the country have refused to share patient information. The prime minister addresses the nation, telling us he's temporarily closing the borders. Police officers have been authorized to carry weapons—lethal weapons, not just guns with rubber bullets. Trefethen was right. They've been ordered to shoot down the nymphs.

And they do.

The reports begin to filter in. They're filled with grotesque pictures of the nymphs, their strange attenuated bodies laid out on the pavement. Side by side they display images of dead teenagers, school photos cropped carefully to show their faces, the kind you see in missing child posters. I'm shocked when I see Lilee MacGilrea from Cherwell College among them, that wild mess of flame-coloured hair. It says she died two days ago of an aneurysm in her house. When her parents found her, the transformation had already begun. The image shows her immobile body lacquered in keratin.

Whatever is happening is happening faster. It took months for Kira to change, trapped in some kind of holding pattern. But nothing is holding them back now.

A week after the riot, we're all going stir crazy in the house. The power has been flickering on and off as the late March heat engulfs England, air conditioning little more than a dream. Aunt Irene tries to keep working but I can tell she's frustrated by her lack of access. With the university temporarily closed she holes up in her office, going over printed reports and trawling through her notes. I think she blames herself for not having more answers.

One afternoon Mom comes back from the shops with bags of fertilizer and potting soil. But for once she doesn't send me to my room to try to study. She lets me help her unload trays of starter plants and sort through seed packs: beans, beetroot, broccoli, carrots, celery, lettuce, peas, potatoes, spinach and spring onions. Together we start to prepare the soil beds but the garden is mostly overgrown with ivy. First we have to pull down the long strands that have crept up the side of the fence and dump them in a bin for composting, she says.

"What's all this for?" I ask her.

"I'm tired of sitting on my hands. This garden's been going to waste and we might as well fill it."

Mom never had much of a green thumb in Toronto but her time with Aunt Jackie seems to have taught her a thing or two. After we've disposed of the worst of the ivy we dig up the remaining weeds and mark the plots with stakes and wire. Then we work in the fertilizer by turning over the top foot of soil with a hoe.

It's as if she's channelling her fear, her frustration, into the simple task of fixing something. She doesn't look up, not once.

Soon Mom and I are both red-faced and out of breath from the heat. There's an ache in my muscles but it feels good to be doing something normal. Still I'm thinking about the empty houses out by the cement works, their lawns covered in massive clots of dandelion and borage. "We'll lose it all if the river breaks its banks here."

"Then we'll start over again," she says. "We'll salvage what we can and replant. There's no use in sitting around and waiting for things to get better. So good thoughts, Feef, okay?"

"Good thoughts."

When she smiles at me, it feels like the first time she's seen me properly since the news broke. Seen me and not my condition. For a moment our old closeness is rekindled.

For my good work I'm rewarded with the return of my phone and tablet and permission to leave the house. I tell her it will only be for an hour, just so I can stretch my legs. I'm information starved, desperate to see how Bryan is—Liv and Redmond too, anyone I can find.

I text Bryan to meet me in front of the Bodleian but there's no reply. I head out anyway before Mom can change her mind.

The first thing I notice when I get to the centre of town is the how different it feels. Like a war zone, the same shell-shocked expressions on the faces of all the people I pass. A dense, welcome drizzle has begun to soak everything grey. Grey skies, grey streets, grey faces. No one looks up. Like Mom, they keep their eyes fixed on the ground.

The College fences have been piled with makeshift memorials, old photographs and bright flowers, the expected things, along with exam books and school ties looped around the knuckly fleur-de-lis gate heads. But most of these have been wrecked. Someone has drawn $X$'s on the faces of the dead, draped banners with ugly messages across the debris of petals and torn paper.

There's a group of half-pissed men outside a pub across from the Bodleian gates, a stone's throw from New College. They have wrinkled, sunburnt faces and glazed expressions of despair. One of them lobs a half-full can of cider toward me. "It's you lot to blame!" he hollers as the liquid spirals out, splashing against my knees.

The drunk staggers to his feet and lumbers toward me. A scattering of grey hairs fuzzes his otherwise shiny pate. The other men avert their eyes, pretend not to see what's happening, and it's then I start to get scared. There's no one my age on the streets.

"You got it, then?" he says. His breath is rank, teeth yellowish. He lurches forward and grabs my wrist, twisting viciously. He stares at the medical ID bracelet. "Thought so, thought you might."

"Don't touch me." My words are strangled with fear. But he pulls me close. I try to get my elbow between us but his grip tightens. The rain thickens, hammering down on us.

"Please," I'm shouting, and then to anyone. "Please, he's hurting me."

"Same age, same age as her. I could show you a picture." He's drunk, I think, drunk and mourning. But then a police officer is between us, pushing him away from me.

"Leave off, let her alone."

"She shouldn't be out," the drunk mumbles as the cop shoves him away from me. "Not all on her own. Not now."

The officer is clean-shaven, courteous. "You shouldn't be wandering the streets by yourself. Is there anyone I can call to collect you?"

I don't want to head back, not yet, so I tell him I'm a student at New College. He walks me over to the front gates. "You be careful now, hear?" The solicitude he shows makes me want to cry more than the scare in the street did, both so unexpected.

Inside the College are security guards, which I didn't see last time I was here. They eye me suspiciously. "You're a student?" one of them asks but I shake my head. "I'm here to see my friend." Then I'm seated in a corner, the subject of intense whispers between the guards and the porter, a few sideways glances. I'm made to wait while the porter calls up to Liv's room.

"You know her?" the officer says as Liv makes her way across the quad in clothes that look as if they haven't been washed.

"Yes," she tells him. She takes me in, the dirty smears on my wrists where the man grabbed me. "Come on."

I follow Liv up a set of narrow stairs to the junior common room. She seems tense, concerned for me in a distracted way. She'd said she had rheumatic fever as a child, and I wonder if it's made her JI2 symptoms worse. Her skin is blanched and she doesn't look well.

She sits me beside the fireplace and pours me tea. "Drink this. It'll warm you up. Let's see if we can get hold of Bryan. I think I've got his landline number. He'll want to walk you home."

"Have you heard from him then?" I'm shivering bitterly—shock, I think, only there's a hot buzzing sensation beneath, a thrumming in my blood sparked by the near violence.

"Only that he's out of the hospital."

"What, no port? Shoddy service." Redmond gets up from one of the couches. I can feel it on him too, that same veil of anger Liv wears. But he smiles when he sees me, real warmth—so it isn't me he's angry with.

"Shut up, you," Liv snaps but Redmond shrugs it off. Both of them glance at me expectantly. Apart from the two of them the common room is deserted. There are shapes in the quad below, students shuffling across the long pathways through the green, but not many of them. Without Bryan I feel like someone's little sister crashing the party. Tolerated but not really one of the gang.

"Relax," Redmond says after a too long pause, "better in here than out there, eh? Bloody cretins."

"You can dry yourself off, if you want." Liv points out the washroom to me and then heads back to the common room to see if she can track down Bryan.

Inside, the mirror fogs with heat from the running water as I squeeze rain from dark twists of my hair. There are bruises I don't remember on my face, a scattering of them on my arms too, amid patches of dried skin. I have the same sickbed colouring that Kira had, that same otherworldly paleness, as if my blood has been leeched. I shove my hands beneath the taps, letting the scalding heat wash away the memory of that man, the rancid sheen of his grief.

When I return to the common room, Liv and Redmond are hunched over a tablet and I join them. I recognize the landscape in the video: the striped lawns lit by a low sun to the west, the grey-blue dome of the Radcliffe, and to the side, the gated walls of All Souls and Hertford College.

"What is it?"

"You'll see."

The screen goes white for a moment, but then the image clears again. Curving cloud cover, the slippery grey of zinc and mercury.

"Oh," says Liv.

Dark shapes have appeared. At first it seems like they could be blips in the footage, but then the clouds break open and we get a clear shot of the nymphs below. Massive, sporting plumage of different colours: ash and taupe, black, spots of reddish brown like terracotta.

"When was this taken?" I ask.

"Yesterday."

The nymphs themselves seem to glide effortlessly, as if they are fixed points in the sky, moving but unmovable. Then the screen crackles with static.

"Hold on. The battery's gone wonky. That surge a couple of days ago scrambled the circuits... but... let me..." Redmond raps the plastic casing smartly against the table and it jumps to life—but only for a second. "Shite."

"Reddy, it's wonderful," says Liv—and she's right. I haven't seen images like this, untainted by the commentary of the news. "Their wingspan, you see? Their wings must lock into place like an albatross's does. It's the only way they could support the weight of their bodies—but if that's true they must be able to fly for miles without landing. For *thousands* of miles."

Redmond grins, and circles her with his arm but Liv stiffens and looks away from him. "Poor Martin," she says, trying to stifle tears with her hand. Someone has set up a framed photo of him on a table. It's bedecked with notes of affection, a few cut flowers that look like they're from the garden below.

Redmond turns off the tablet, stands and heads toward the massive pool table that dominates the south side of the room. He starts racking up the balls. "Have you seen the tabloids? You'd have thought Cath had suffered enough, losing her brother and all, but there have been reporters banging on her door night and day, hoping for an interview."

I ask them what's happened, what they know that I may not.

"The tabloids have been publishing the names and addresses of anyone who's sick, saying the people have a right to know," says Liv. "They've been harassing Cath, wanting to know all sorts of things about him."

"The shitehawk bastards." This from Redmond.

"But why?" I want to know.

He sends the cue ball down the centre of the table with a smooth, effortless movement. The balls explode into motion. "Those ones thrive on disaster, getting people all riled up just so they can sell a few copies. They don't care a damn bit about who it hurts."

"It's all me first, and how do we protect our own? As if it won't happen to them, that somehow their children will be safe from it all."

"That's crazy. No one is safe from this," I say.

Redmond nods aggressively. "Everything's mad right now, isn't it? It's bedlam out there."

"I can't believe they're still shooting them down. Still cremating the dead," says Liv. "I thought—surely once they understood they'd stop. Once they realized that they're human."

"They *were* human. That's what they're saying, isn't it? Not now though. So they can do any damn thing they like." He sends another ball down the length of the table. *Snick plop*—the three-ball lands in the pocket. "But I'm not having it, not anymore. There's a group of students I've been talking to. Percy Herring and Tim Blackburn."

"What do *they* want?" Liv looks up at him, startled.

"They've been talking about the crematorium. The one out by Barton. Percy and Tim think there might be a way we can shut it down." Violence, action. That itchy feeling is back in my palms, adrenaline surging into my bloodstream at the thought of it—I don't trust it though, not after what I saw in the churchyard.

"What good would that do?" Liv says. "Beyond convincing the people the tabloids are right. That we can't be trusted, that we should be watched."

"We need to *do* something. Jesus—what we need is leverage, eh? A way to make them listen to us. We need to understand what those things are."

"Nymphs," I break in and they turn toward me. "Bryan told me. His mother works for the hospital. The word doesn't mean what you think though. It has something to do with the transformation. The Centre calls them that." I lower my voice. "They must have suspected something like this would happen."

"This is why we need to act," insists Redmond. "They still aren't telling us the truth, not about what they are. What this transformation is all about."

"You think you're the first to have thought of this,

Reddy?" Liv asks. "There have been protesters outside for
days—"

"I'm not talking about protesting."

"And it wouldn't stop anything. Do you know how
many crematoria there are in Oxford alone? Think about
how dangerous that would be. You're not a revolutionary,
Reddy, you're an English major. What are you going to do,
recite poetry at them?"

"Oh, love, how can you be so fecking cool about all this?
The new reality is *this*." He stabs his pool cue toward the picture
of Martin. "It's Martin with his bloody skull fractured. Them
against us. Why do you think they want a list of who is sick?
Haven't you heard about what's happening in China?
Mandatory registrations, heavy fines for any family that
disobeys or harbours a child without making weekly reports. If
you don't think they're going to round up those kids then you're
delusional. Liv, I know you don't want to talk about it but things
are getting worse. If something happened to you…"

I make a sound of distress. Redmond turns. "See," he
says, "Sophie understands."

"The nymphs matter." I stare at the two of them,
anxious to feel included in their plans. "You were out there
in the churchyard. You must have felt something? There's a
reason all of this started. There's a reason it's happening now.
There has to be." Even as I say this, the words feel inadequate,
naive, but Redmond nods eagerly until Liv rounds on him.

"Leave her out of this! If you want to risk your life acting stupid that's one thing. But—" She stares at me, close to tears. "She's too young."

"I'm not," I tell them, "I'm part of this too."

But then the common room phone rings. Bryan is with the porter, waiting for me.

Liv urges me toward the door. Redmond looks as if he wants to protest, to say more but she won't hear it. "You think you're invincible, that they can't touch you—"

"I don't."

"But the Centre wants to help us."

"Redmond's right," I tell her as we cross the quad toward the porter's lodge. "We can't just do nothing and wait for the situation to get better."

"Never mind about Reddy. Just pretend you didn't hear it," she says softly. "He's always going off half-cocked like this. You need to take care of yourself." I know that tone of voice, that protectiveness. And I wonder if back home she has a little sister, someone for whom she would give her life to keep safe.

# 27

"Hey," Bryan says when he sees us. "What's wrong?"

Liv shrugs, runs a hand through the tangle of her hair. Her gaze lingers pointedly on the glowing yellow bruise on Bryan's face. Finally, she shakes her head, kisses Bryan lightly on the cheek. "See you both around," she says quietly, as if we might meet each other on the streets like before.

"Sure." His tone is quizzical. "You take care of yourself, Liv. And Reddy too." She walks away.

When we're back out on the street Bryan turns, takes me in. "It's good to see you," he says, and there is a rise of sweet giddiness I can't control.

He still hasn't recovered, not entirely. I can tell that much at a glance. He has the short, hobbled steps of an old man and his movements are jerky. There's a glint in his eyes, a sort of inattention, as if his mind is wandering, he's listening to music in his head. Kira would get the same look sometimes. I wonder if I do too. If that's what Mom sees when she looks at me.

We walk along Broad Street. With him there, no one

bothers me. The rain has mostly dissipated now and the clouds are breaking up, chased by a strong-blowing wind that sends bits of refuse skirling over the pavement.

"What happened that night?" he asks at last. "After you left the hospital."

"I went back to the cement works. To find Kira. But it was too late to stop her. She'd already begun to change. I tried, though. I even climbed the side of the tower." His eyebrows lift in amazement. "After everything I realized I couldn't hold onto her."

We pass the gates of Trinity College, which are locked, forbidding. "You know you've never stopped surprising me," he says. "Not from the first day. You were just so—wild. So angry and in the moment but brave too, willing to take risks when everyone else seemed to just let things happen."

"I wasn't wild. She's my sister, my responsibility."

"Even so." To the west, toward Osney, the sun is hanging low in the sky, limning the clouds in soft orange and heliotrope. Amber light gleams off the busts of the emperors mounted on the gates outside the Bodleian Library. A shiver of homesickness skates down my body, a kind of reflexive sadness but even that doesn't last as long as it used to. He sees it and hesitatingly puts his arm around me.

"You all right?"

I shrug, shake my head but I say nothing. He understands. "Sometimes I think I'm still grieving. But grief doesn't feel like the right word for it anymore. Kira never really died. And grieving for her now feels—I don't know, somehow selfish. As if what I really missed was the place that she filled in my life, how it felt to be her protector."

There are two inches between us but Bryan doesn't close the gap. Still, being this close to him makes me feel as if my mind is a dark room filled with broken furniture, but he is slowly setting things right, clearing out the wreckage, opening the windows.

"We couldn't have kept her there forever. There's a point where protection just becomes another kind of imprisonment," he tells me.

"I don't know what to do now. How to reach her. I just feel so lost. As if all of this has been for nothing."

We head up St. Giles toward the Martyrs' Memorial, an old Victorian spire that looks like the blackened steeple of a cathedral sunk deep into the ground. Aunt Irene told me about it the first time we came into town, how three English prelates were burned alive here for opposing the Pope. We take a seat on the steps though the stone is damp. What must it have been like to have known so clearly what they wanted to do, even if it cost them everything?

"Did you ever used to watch zombie movies?" I pluck a daisy that's wedged itself between two stone slabs and stare at it for a moment, wondering how it got here, how it managed to root itself in such inhospitable soil.

Bryan makes a face but doesn't answer.

"It's hard not to think about them with everything that's happened."

"Never liked them much, to be honest. The gore, you know, and all that make-up. It seemed so artificial. I never understood how we were supposed to find them scary."

"I used to watch them back home. There was, I don't know, something liberating about them. How when shit got real, you had to figure out what you were capable of. Like, could you open up your boyfriend's skull with a shotgun when he was about to turn? In the end it was the survivors who knew who they were, where they stood with the world."

Bryan is quiet for a long time. "So, what? Could you put a bullet up here?" He raps his knuckle on his forehead, an uneasy look on his face. And it occurs to me this is one of the first times it's just been the two of us, no one else, no pressure or obligations. Kira is gone.

I tear off the petals from the daisy one by one.

The question is still hanging there and Bryan glances at me, waiting for an answer. His eyes are intense but shy too. I reach over and touch his forehead, thinking about making a quip, telling him what I'd be willing to do to survive. But it doesn't feel funny, not after what happened to Martin. To Kira. What could happen to any of us.

What I feel is so intense that my breath catches in my throat. He moves toward me, I can feel him doing it and I want him to kiss me. He's warm, so warm, as if someone lit a fire inside of him. But then his eyes widen and he jerks away. A huge shadow skates along the stone between us, across our legs and over the cobblestones.

From somewhere above comes a soft pfeffing sound, the noise a tablecloth makes when you snap it in the air to get rid of crumbs. Then I see it—like a wraith above the street. Its feathers are bluish-white with inky black at the tips, and there's something ancient about the machinery of its body. Alternating bands of light and darkness ripple across the surface.

"Sophie," he whispers but I shush him. We are both perfectly still, alone in the street. Are we the only ones who have seen it then?

The nymph rises above the peaks of the roofs, and turns a slow arc in the sky over the Ashmolean Museum. Then it passes by again, almost noiseless.

It isn't Kira—but for a moment I don't care, caught up in the vision of it. So otherworldly and strange. I search for a trace of humanity, a second self pinned to it like Peter Pan's shadow but I can't find it. It has given itself over entirely to its new form: a body shaped like a bullet, a long neck supporting a tapering skull. Its throat undulates. It makes a low, happy sound, a song in a minor key.

I see white, a flurry of feathers, then a different sort of whiteness.

Clouds, vast banks of them, stiff-peaked like meringue.

And I can feel the wind catching me, holding me aloft the way Dad used to swing me up in the air when I was younger. Restful, secure. My body is doing exactly what it is supposed to be doing.

There are other nymphs around me. Drifting through the smoke-grey sky, a slate ocean beneath them marred by choppy waves. I count twenty, thirty of them. There are more, I know there are, distant maybe but out there.

The sensation of their bodies moving alongside me, air ruffling our stiff feathers, making the soft down of our breasts and bellies tremble. My throat vibrates gently and the noise fills me up, not just noise, but something else—them, their thoughts. Ghost presences surrounding me, some close and some far, impossibly far.

But one among them is familiar. It's like catching sight of myself unexpectedly in a mirror. "Kira!" I call.

The connection is breaking—I want to hold onto it, but it's not enough. She's too far away and the world is turning below us. The contours of the air are as clear to me as an elevation map. Light too, an unexpected rainbow glowing above the water, a magnetic pull in my blood. We turn together, nerves whispering with the same reedy music.

And then I'm back in my own body.

The nymph vanishes into the clouds, a vision of silver and shadow. I want so much to go with it. The pulling sensation stays with me, the certainty of it, the calmness.

Then Bryan and I are both smiling, laughing almost. He squeezes my hand and it's as if the barrier between us is so thin I could jump from my body straight into his. But I'm crying too. The nymph has moved on: a crumpled linen ghost floating over the city. The only remnant of it is a thick acidic odor, chalky and sharp at the same time.

"She's out there, isn't she? I think I could feel her. Did you feel it too?"

"I don't know. I felt something but it was weak. Too weak. Just … like hearing music in another room. There was something but I couldn't make it out." He shakes his head.

"We need to find them."

"What?

My thoughts are beginning to coalesce, build into a purpose. "It's the only way we can understand what's happening. It feels like we've already passed a tipping point, doesn't it? We've crossed into some strange, new, dangerous territory and no one understands what it means. Reddy thinks violence is the answer but I don't know. When has it ever done much good? There has to be some other way."

He runs a hand through his hair. "How do we do that? It's just us, Sophie. Where would we even start?"

"I don't know. Not yet." There are still tears on my face, I can feel them. The nymph was trying to tell me something. It was as if it were trying to speak in a language of memory and dream. But the message was garbled, incomplete. Except for one thing: *Kira is out there.*

I know she is. This is my way forward.

The nymph has given me a gift, if only I can figure out exactly what it means.

# 28

The feeling stays with me, mingled certainty and fear, though I have no idea what to do about it.

Mom and Aunt Irene want me to keep working toward my A-level exams but nothing sticks in my brain. The news programs trumpet an endless flow of disasters. A hurricane has left most of Miami underwater and now it's heading across the Atlantic toward us, a second surely on the way behind it, and a third. Commercial air travel has been completely suspended. My dreams are filled with violence. Images of half-human bodies sucked into the engines, churned up and spat out again. The army shooting them down.

Then a letter arrives from Jaina and I stare at it. The postmark is from days ago. I rip it open and devour the contents:

> *Dear Sophie,*
> *This is strange huh? I haven't written a letter since*
> *i was seven, even holding a pen seems all kinds of*
> *weird now, like—how retro, right? But my*

*messages aren't getting through and I wanted to
tell you.*

*well, you get it don't you?*

*Mom says they look like angels.*

*There's this way she says it—like she's Carrie
White's mother. You remember us watching that,
ewwwing at the pig's blood and the way her eyes
opened and i screamed? Carrie never really scared
me—it was her mother, that crazy ole time Religion
she caught so she locked her daughter in that freaky
Jesus closet and the only happy part of the movie was
when Carrie stopped her friggin hateful heart... .*

*Mom got so happy when I finally tested
positive, she threw me this trippy sort of birthday
celebration with all her friends. They were chanting
this Rumi poem about the body being a guest house
and how I should welcome in the crowd of joys and
sorrows and meet them at the door laughing*

*which is great and all but it's my frigging
body right?*

*I dunno, feefs.*

*I used to love it how mom was different from
all the other moms but now she's talking about
mother Gaia and how we should all be moving out
east where there's a commune forming or
something. Somehow she's even got dad on board*

*with it. Maybe it's because Melanie Britnell died.*
*she drowned in her bath tub, i heard—but no one*
*knows how she did it.*

*T-dot is clearing out, all the big cities are.*
*Markeys is sick and Caroline and Aus and probably*
*a whole bunch more but no one is saying. Here you*
*can keep quiet if you want to and they have to treat*
*you the same. Mom says it's better this way because*
*everyone can choose but they don't tell us when*
*someone dies and there's this list we all started*
*keeping—just for ourselves and it's getting longer*
*every day.*

*I guess mostly why i'm writing this is to say*
*sorry because I get it now. What it must have been*
*like with kira. i didn't then. Sometimes i want to be*
*like mom and just believe it's all okay but I feel like*
*there's something rotten in me but maybe it's sweet*
*too. I don't know how to trust it.*

*I just wish you were still here—that it could've*
*been the two of us. I think you'd know what to do. You*
*always watched to the end of the movie, didn't you,*
*when I had to pull the covers up you just kept*
*watching. I'll see you on the other side fee fi fo fum*

For a while after I read it I can't concentrate on anything.
I sit on the bed, staring out the window at the Thames while

I try to compose my own letter in response, but nothing seems adequate. I don't even know where to send it. When Mom calls me down for dinner I tell her I'm not hungry. I try to reach Jaina on my tablet but all I get is an error message.

Suddenly the distance between here and Toronto feels monumental, uncrossable. I miss her so much. Her sharp laugh, talking in her bedroom, the smell of sagebrush all around us. I can't remember the last time I heard from Dad. What if I've lost them both already?

I slide the letter into my notebook. It's become its own archive, a way of remembering when the power goes out. It feels like we're travelling back in time, circling back to those dark ages of terror.

*And wonder*, a small voice in the back of my mind insists. *There were miracles too.*

As I page through my notebook, the word appears again and again. *Miraculum.* An object of marvels, a sign from the heavens, a message.

> *And since the conjunction was in Aquarius it signified great cold, heavy frosts, and thick clouds corrupting the air; and since this is a sign which represents the pouring out of water, the configuration signifies that rivers will burst their banks and the sea flood. For his part, Mars in that sign denotes the sudden death which comes among many races, especially among children.*

The first time I read the passage, I hadn't understood. I'd thought they were the ghostly declarations of those who couldn't grasp what was happening to them. They were terrified, searching for answers. But what if they weren't wrong?

Now those words seem oddly resonant. Microcosm and macrocosm. They were dreaming about a poetic cosmos, with every earthly body shifting according to the order of the heavens. Everything connected, everything in sync, everything moving toward some ultimate purpose.

Maybe Kira is part of it, just as I am, just as Jaina is—all of us connected to something sweet and rotten at the same time.

# 29

Finally there's a call from the Centre.

"There's nothing to be scared of." That's what Mom keeps telling me as we follow Headington Road. "You know that, right? I'm just glad they've got back to me. I've been ringing them every day."

Outside the hospital are furious swarms of protesters from all sides: students and their parents, environmental and antifascist groups, religious nuts. The noise is tremendous. Security guards have closed off the main gates, forcing them to the streets.

Most of the parking lot is taken up with massive inflatable structures—body storage. The deadpan murmur of portable generators spills out in a close radius. Mom waits impatiently while blue-clad staff wheel twenty-foot-long racks by us, then clutches my hand while we cross the pavement toward the entrance. A blast of cold air raises goose bumps all over my skin.

• • •

When we get to Dr. Varghese's office I see Nate Peverill from class coming out.

"Hey, Perella," he says, but his voice is quiet and he doesn't really look at me. He keeps scratching awkwardly at a rash that's begun to crawl up his arm. He's wearing a medical ID bracelet now.

"Did you hear about what happened to Lilee?"

He nods sharply but it doesn't look like he wants to talk. As he wanders down the hallway there's a moment when I almost feel good about the fact he's one of us now. He could be such a prick, always going along with whatever Evie Chudwell and that lot wanted! But mostly I just feel sorry for him.

A minute or two later Dr. Varghese greets us. I've never seen her so worn down, so removed. A partially rubbed-out jitterbug has been drawn on her door with permanent marker. I wonder who did that, how they got in.

Before she enters I tell Mom, "I want to do this by myself." There are things I need to know, things I won't be able to ask if she's around. She starts to protest but I hold up my hands. "This is how it's been since I was diagnosed." That seems to do the trick.

She lingers, a hurt look on her face, but there's no back-up from Dr. Varghese. "If this is what Sophie wants," she says, drawing it out into a question. I nod and slip inside.

"Tell me what you know about what's happening to us,"

I demand as soon as the door is closed behind us. Dr. Varghese shrinks away from my anger behind her desk. And I realize this must be her life right now, these same questions, over and over and over again.

"Please, Sophie, sit down. I'll try to answer whatever questions I can—but first, there are things you need to know." I hate the vaguely rehearsed feeling of this. Whatever pronouncement Dr. Varghese's about to make, she's made it before. She must have just made it to Nate. "This concerns you. And it's serious."

I swallow a thick bolus of fear.

"You know our assumption has always been that the hormone will dissipate past a certain point." Her fingers touch the edge of her desk, trembling. She sounds as if she's pleading with me now but I don't want to give her my sympathy. "That people like you, Sophie, will grow out of the condition if you pass a certain threshold. Our research suggested that your body eventually loses..." she pauses again here, searching for words, "a certain *plasticity*. The same plasticity that allows your body to change during puberty."

"I don't know what that means."

"Over the last week we've discovered a change in the progression of the symptoms of people like you," she says. "An escalation."

"What kind of escalation?"

"Your symptoms could get worse—much worse. All the

threats to your immune system we've been tracking. We were able to diagnose you because your body had begun to produce a hormone, which rewired the way your body works. Do you remember what I said about *Toxoplasma gondii*?"

"The parasite?"

She licks her lips, trying to judge my response, how much to tell me. "Suicidal thoughts, emotional swings, all designed to put you in harm's way, making you more vulnerable. It's happening faster, all of it. Your body is actively seeking the right conditions to—"

"Change," I finish and she nods. My fingers tap out a nervous tattoo against my leg. "But why? Why is it happening now?"

"We don't know, Sophie, only that the situation is different than it was before. We've never seen anything like this."

"How is it different?"

"It's like an inherited condition, something hardwired into your system. When a patient dies under certain conditions—when enough of the body is left intact—then the hormone activates new developmental processes. We think ... the potential for this was always present. In everyone, your mother, your aunt, me. But it doesn't affect adults, not in the same way." She sighs. "Your body isn't changing because you're sick, Sophie. You manifest as sick because your body has already begun to change, because certain genes have already been activated by the hormone."

"They're waking up," I whisper. "You said things are getting worse. How much worse will they get?"

"Some patients have fallen into trance states. They're completely immobile and unresponsive now. Others have shown signs of increased anxiety and aggression. Spontaneous hemorrhaging resulting in death. We don't know the full extent of it yet. But we're trying." She swallows. "We're trying to figure it out as quickly as possible. In the meantime we've been in talks with government officials and the World Health Organization. We're investigating the possibility of alternate means of care. A long-term care facility for people like you."

"You mean they'll lock me up." My voice is tinged with desperation. It's like Redmond said, exactly what he was afraid of.

"It isn't as bad as it sounds." A muscle twitches beneath her eye. "We're working on a treatment. But right now you're at risk and we have to take care of you. A long-term care facility will be able to monitor you much more closely. They'll be able to understand your sensitivities, to control your total environment. There will be medical staff on hand at all times. They will have better resources. They'll be able to *protect* you."

"Until the hormone dissipates, until we're older like you are."

"We think—yes."

"But you don't know?"

"You need to understand about the numbers. It's just—"

"Not many of us will live that long."

She says nothing but her eyes are wide, resigned. I know it's true.

I feel light-headed but oddly calm, as if something important has been cut away from me, some fragile grasping after hope. What's left is ... *propulsion*, maybe that's the best word for it. I should be frightened but instead I feel weightless. The sense that time is speeding up, running away from me.

"What will happen if I die? Will I be cremated?"

Her mouth trembles as a look close to sickness passes across her face. "Sophie, we need to focus on your health, on your options."

"This isn't about my options, don't you understand that? You told me that there was nothing that comes after. When Kira died, you said it would be easier on my family if we handed her over to you. You wanted me to trust you—but how can I now?"

"Please." Her voice is rising, taking on a higher pitch.

"I've seen them myself. It's clear they're alive. You had to know that—maybe not everything but some of it. You had to know they were changing, yet you still told us we should cremate Kira." My hands have bunched into fists and I can feel the adrenaline soaring, the sweet pulse of it in my veins—even as I try to stay in control. "What I don't understand is—why would you do that? Why would you ask us to do that?"

She won't look at me. Instead she stares out the window that overlooks the parking lot, those vast beehive structures barely visible from my angle. Over the sound of my breathing I can hear a faint susurrus. Chanting, I think, from the protestors. *No more lies! No more lies!* The whine of a siren cutting through the white noise of their voices. She has to listen to this every day.

"Sophie…"

"Just tell me the truth, Dr. Varghese. You owe me that, don't you?"

When she turns back to me there's a bright shimmer of tears in her eyes. She wipes them away with the back of her hand.

"When the crisis first started I thought I could help. But this? It's…" Her voice breaks. "I'm just trying to do the best I can for you."

"Then *tell* me. I was there when Martin Paisley died—he was this close to me. I—I couldn't help him. So please—enough about my symptoms, I know the danger. What I need to know is what happens next."

Her voice hitches: "Martin? You knew him?"

I nod slowly.

She closes her eyes for a moment. "I was his clinician too." She opens a drawer, pulls out a file and drops it on her desk. I wait for her to acknowledge it but she doesn't.

"What is that?" I ask her but she doesn't answer. The folder is unmarked. I pick it up gingerly and lift the cover.

The folder contains a chart, diagrams, pages of notes— an autopsy report.

> The clinical death of Martin Paisley was recorded at 1:27 am on March 11. **Cause of death:** blunt force trauma causing abrasions of the forehead. The skull casing was found to be fractured leading to hemorrhaging in the brain. Transition initiated upon cessation of vital functions.

"Take it," she says. Her gaze has wandered to the picture of the Lakhaniya Dari waterfall on her desk. She's smiling in that picture, young, elated with what she's accomplished. A completely different person. I remember telling her I wanted to go there. When I was older, when it was safe to travel.

"I'm sorry about your sister. And I'm sorry about Martin too. When Director Ballard said there were no alternatives, I believed him. That the severity of the crisis didn't leave us with any choice. But I became a doctor to relieve the pain and suffering of others. I promised to do nothing that might harm a patient."

A wave of anger rises up in me when she says that. I

don't want to acknowledge the pain in her eyes, the genuine regret. I don't want to have to forgive her anything.

She sees the atom of rage in my eyes and her gaze flicks down to the folder. "Leak it to the papers if you want. Maybe you're right. Maybe everyone should know."

When Mom sees the look on my face she lets me be. For a while anyway. We drive in silence, the sky lead-coloured and roiling above us. "What did she tell you?" she asks eventually.

"She said they're looking at long-term care options." My voice is flat.

"That's a good sign, isn't it?"

"They want to send us to a facility. All of the people like me."

Her knuckles whiten around the steering wheel. "You don't have to do that, Feef. They can't make you."

"Yet."

"I'm serious. I don't trust them. I don't care if they're the best doctors and scientists. They didn't tell us what was going on and they should have." Her voice rises. "They should have let us choose for ourselves."

I stare at her, surprised by her vociferousness.

Suddenly the urge to tell her the truth about Kira is so strong, but I don't know how to put the story together. And if I'm honest I'm scared too. Ever since the night of the riots I've been scanning the skyline, searching for her.

Am I doing the right thing by keeping this all from her? Or am I as bad as Dr. Varghese?

Soon, I think. I'll tell her when I know for sure.

Above us a growl of thunder sounds, rain pebbling the windshield. *Something is coming*, it seems to say to me and my body thrums in agreement, my blood thick in my veins, my pulse hammering in reply.

*Soon.*

# 30

**Name: PAISLEY, MARTIN**
**Clinician: DR. ANIL VARGHESE**
Martin Paisley, a 17-year-old male with JI2, presented unconscious on March 11, in critical condition due to acute cranial trauma caused by blunt injury to the head. Following cessation of vital signs and pronouncement of clinical death, activation of JI2 "post-mortem" changes began and Martin was recruited to the M-Plagge trial by Dr. Lane Ballard.

*General observations*
Martin was seventeen years old when first diagnosed with JI2 on January 3 and regular check-ups confirmed the continued presence of the juvenile hormone. He was a student at the Faculty of History at the University of Oxford where by all accounts he was flourishing. His sister Catherine Davis had been named his guardian, and encouraged him to defer for a year after his condition was reported to her, but he resisted.

*Initial progression of JI2*

13 MARCH. The first stage of the transition has proceeded along anticipated trajectory although much faster than previous observations have indicated. Muscle tremors have ceased. The epidermis has begun to develop a thick layer of keratin forcing rigidity but only briefly. Internally, there is a catastrophic destruction of the prior form's tissues, as lungs, kidney, spleen are being broken down into an autodigestible "mush" but only a limited period of stasis, much shorter than before. A needle biopsy has revealed that clusters of individual cells have returned to an embryonic state, embarking upon a secondary developmental path.

Research thus far has suggested that the fertilised human egg contains the hereditary programming for two very different and specialised patterns of body development. Humans have typically developed upon a singular path as witnessed by the standard phases (zygote, blastocyst, fetus, neonate, pre-adolescence, etc.) but this transition indicates a possible "branching" during puberty in which the secondary form might be triggered if certain conditions are fulfilled. But there are still questions I can't answer: What are they? Why is this happening *now*?

14 MARCH. Sac-like epithelial clusters detected, which will develop into the "wing-buds" over time. Already, bones have lightened considerably, faster than we've observed previously.

Multiple air sacs established, extending into the humerus, the femur, the vertebrae and the skull. The external layer of keratin has begun to resolve itself into the first layer of the nymph's plumage (dark brown). Rigidity of the body form is substantially reduced now that the initial interior re-organization has taken place. The new organs (heart, lungs, stomach, liver) have been established and are functioning smoothly. Martin blinks frequently during marked cycles of alertness and motor activity.

15 MARCH. At the request of Dr. Lane Ballard, Martin has been started on the M-Plagge trial.

*Course on M-Plagge*

The secondary instar—or growth stage—has been inhibited, as suspected. M-Plagge appears to be functioning successfully as a blocking agent, reducing substantially the effects of the juvenile hormone. If these tests bear out over time, then M-Plagge might offer some hope of stalling the development of early symptoms in JI2 patients and reducing the possibility of transformation.

16 MARCH. Martin shows striking changes. His expression is alert, and his rigidity is distinctly reduced. Small interactions include bouts of staring in which his eyes appear to track— or focus intensely—upon anyone who enters the room. But

I can't dismiss the feeling that he recognizes me. Dr. Ballard insists this is sentimentalizing but there is evidence that suggests otherwise. He has shown renewed signs of awareness, including frequent openings of the mouth as if to yawn or speak. It should be noted that the anatomy of the vocal cords has been significantly altered. All that remains of its previous function is a high chirruping sound.

17 MARCH. On a higher dosage, Martin shows improved posture. Despite the limitations of his body, he has begun to move. Gestures of the truncated metacarpus, something like little waves? His behaviour is remarkable. No prior patients have demonstrated anything like this responsivity. But what does it mean? The rapidity of metamorphosis in other patients means our tests are now of vital concern. Might there be a way to communicate with Martin? I think so.

First test shows a limited range of responses, but a basic method of communication (one blink for no, two blinks for yes) has been established. fMRI scans indicate that perhaps more of the language centres of the brain (Broca's area) have remained intact, or perhaps their function has been amalgamated into processes directed by an enlarged hippocampus? When questioned as to whether the subject could understand me, subject blinked twice.

If the subject's identity remains intact at any level, this raises serious concerns about current regulations re:

cremation. Previous subjects showed no signs of awareness but the speed of the instar development prior to M-Plagge is astonishing. Dr. Ballard has expressed unease with this line of questioning, fearing that evidence of subject identity may raise concerns with the Medical Research Council, which could jeopardize our primary trials. I have argued repeatedly that establishing the full nature of the condition is the only way to develop an appropriate treatment.

18 MARCH: M-Plagge dosage increased to 5 gm. daily. Initially Martin responded well, but over the course of several hours his movements became increasingly frenetic. Metacarpal gestures resumed but with some urgency. When restrained, he went through a series of muscular convulsions. Concerns over a possible seizure forced us to reduce the dosage.

*(transcription taken from 18 March video record)*

> **Dr. Varghese:** Martin, can you understand me?
> *(Two blinks.)*
> **Dr. Varghese:** Are you in pain?
> *(One blink. A long pause. A second blink.)*

Martin looked at me directly when I asked him that question. I could track his eye movements.

19 MARCH: A reduced dosage of M-Plagge has allowed us to reach a better balance with Martin. Responsiveness returned to previous levels. He seems to experience minor convulsions when I leave, followed by a series of flexing gestures, increasingly urgent. Martin becomes quiescent when I return.

I have commissioned an Eye-gaze Response Interface Computer Aid (ERICA), which will allow a camera and infrared light to track Martin's gaze on a computer screen as it focuses upon key icons, words and in some cases letters. Communication should be much more rapid and efficient.

The success of the ERICA unit has now allowed for a number of long conversations to be recorded. Martin has been able to identify images of members of his family: his living sister as well as his deceased parents. His memory, however, is not perfect, as at times he is unable to distinguish between past and present, imagining his parents still to be alive. When questioned about this, he indicated, "They are dead, I know they are dead, but sometimes I seem to remember clearly that they are not dead. My mind is lying to me." This sense of confusion has recurred throughout subsequent sessions. "I feel pulled by something," he indicated. "Like someone is in the room next to me, shouting for me. Sometimes it is very loud. They are impatient."

**20 MARCH:** Martin has indicated his sensations are "muddled." He feels "an absence, and sometimes a presence. A terrible shadow in his mind." Might this be the inhibiting agent itself? Dr. Ballard says there is no way to verify without reducing the dosage in which case he fears the transition—effectively inhibited thus far—might resume. He has expressed concerns that new treatment approvals are likely to be delayed by current regulatory uncertainties and has informed me the M-Plagge trial is set to expire in seven days.

**21 MARCH:** Martin is minimally response.

**23 MARCH:** Dr. Ballard and I met today to discuss Martin's progression. I've suggested we attempt to contact Martin's sister and obtain consent for the trial to be extended indefinitely. Dr. Ballard has refused, claiming DONATION agreement prevents any further contact with the family. He insists that the cremation order must be enforced as scheduled and that not enough evidence exists to demonstrate the presence of the host's identity. I suspect his concerns are for M-Plagge which has been expedited for further clinical trials in current JI2 patients. But surely Martin has demonstrated that our current frameworks for understanding the condition are inadequate? This is no disease.

*(transcription taken from 23 March video record)*

**Dr. Varghese:** Martin, do you know where you are?

**Martin:** Yes. At the Centre.

**Dr. Varghese:** Do you know what is happening to you?

**Martin:** Yes.

**Dr. Varghese:** Can you describe it?

**Martin:** Why?

**Dr. Varghese:** Because (a hesitation) there are others like you. You know that, don't you?

**Martin:** Yes.

**Dr. Varghese:** They've changed. We want to know what they might be experiencing.

**Martin:** Yes.

*(Twenty seconds elapse.)*

**Martin:** I know what is happening to me. At least, I think I know. I've stalled, haven't I? I've got stuck along the way. I can't tell if I'm going backwards or forwards, anymore. Or which way I'm supposed to go. I keep having dreams.

**Dr. Varghese:** What do you mean, Martin?

**Martin:** There was something I was supposed to do.

**Dr. Varghese:** What?

**Martin:** I feel as if I'm failing a test I didn't study for. I used to have dreams about that, you know. I had such awful dreams. Anxiety dreams.

**Dr. Varghese:** I've been having dreams as well.

**Martin:** I know.

**Dr. Varghese:** How do you know that, Martin?

**Martin:** Except they aren't dreams. They're more like memories. I am remembering something I was supposed to have done. A place I was supposed to go.

**Dr. Varghese:** Where?

**Martin:** I can't tell you. You wouldn't understand.

**Dr. Varghese:** Tell me about your memories, Martin.

**Martin:** Everyone got there ahead of me. Everyone is waiting for me.

**Dr. Varghese:** Does this frighten you?

**Martin:** I'm afraid of staying. I'm afraid they'll leave me behind now. They're out there and they are waiting for me. They want me to come with them. While there's still time. I want to go now. May I go now? I want to go now. Please.

25 MARCH: Today Dr. Ballard told me the termination will be processed despite all my arguments. He has not reviewed my transcript. I don't know what to do. Last night I had a dream. I felt as if someone was calling me. It was Martin's voice but I knew it wasn't Martin anymore. I don't understand how Ballard can go through with this, knowing what we know.

I have registered a complaint with the Medical Research Council but I have been told that regulatory procedures have been temporarily suspended and Ballard has been given authority to proceed. Security has been posted outside Martin's chamber and I have not been permitted any final contact.

27 MARCH: As per protocols, Martin P. was injected with a succession of saline, sodium thiopental, and a lethal mixture of potassium chloride and pancuronium bromide, a paralytic designed to prevent spasms. Time of secondary death recorded as 2:32 pm. His body was delivered for autopsy prior to cremation.

# 31

I read the report through twice then a third time, curled up in my bed while rain slashes the large bay window. I underline passages, make notes in the margins, my cramped scrawl underneath Dr. Varghese's surprisingly legible comments—the habits of reading Aunt Irene has taught me.

Tears blur the edges of the words until I have to wipe my face with the back of my hand. Afterward I stare outside as the setting sun casts bloody fingerprints on the surface of the river. The water is fast-moving, swollen with the runoff from the rain. Debris floats by, plastic bags and discarded soda bottles. I'm sickened by our carelessness, how humans are so willing to let something become someone else's problem.

All I can think about is Martin. How I left him there on the field when I should have done something, helped him to safety. How the Centre should have done something to help him. But Ballard wouldn't. He knew that Martin was alive but he didn't care.

I take pictures of the report but I'm at a complete loss of what to do with them. I doubt, despite what she said, that Dr.

Varghese would be willing to go on record if I leaked them. Would they believe me? I don't think so. No one trusts people like me. I understand that better now. They're cut off from what's happening to us. Nate Peverill seemed to hate Lilee and me before he got sick. He didn't want to believe he was just as vulnerable. Now he has JI2 he's one of us. He understands.

I decide to send the photos to Bryan and a few minutes later my phone buzzes.

BTaite: bloody hell
BTaite: sophie where did you get this?

FeeFeesFeed: my clinician gave it to me

BTaite: I don't understand it not all of it anyway but
BTaite: god poor Martin and they just

FeeFeesFeed: I know

A long pause.

BTaite: how could they do that to him?

FeeFeesFeed: they've been hiding this from us. they know something survives
FeeFeesFeed: they know that much about the nymphs and still

I stare at the phone, thinking about how different Dr. Varghese had looked from when I first saw her. Then she'd been professional, authoritative—but not always. Sometimes when I'd talked to her I'd see a chink in her armour, the sense of another person underneath: a sister, a friend. She'd cared about me—and maybe she'd cared about Martin too. She'd tried to fight on his behalf but it hadn't been enough to save him.

BTaite: what about m-plagge?

FeeFeesFeed: i wouldn't want that not in a million years

BTaite: not even if it would make you better ?

FeeFeesFeed: he was trapped they did that to him they didn't care about who he had been or what he was they just didn't care
FeeFeesFeed: the nymphs were talking to him
FeeFeesFeed: he wanted to go with them
FeeFeesFeed: then they killed him.
FeeFeesFeed: theyll do that to us won't they? if we die. if we let them

And now the tears are coming harder, so hard I can't see the screen anymore.

FeeFeesFeed: bryan u still there?

The carrier is up but he still doesn't answer. I wait half an hour, an hour, my frustration mounting. I feel so useless. All the things I used to count on are slowly disappearing and there's not a goddamn thing I can do about it.

The HemaPen is lying in its cradle. I pick it up, thinking about how I helped Kira to use this the first time. *It hurt*, she told me, and I'd insisted she use it anyway. I'd tracked her symptoms just like they told me to, tracked my own—because I thought they had my welfare at heart. From the bookshelf I search for the heaviest thing I can find: a Folio Society hardback of *The Deeds of the English Kings* wrapped in pebbled brown leather. It's expensive, beautiful—but I don't care. I slam it down against the device again and again until the frame cracks and the delicate filigree of its innards is revealed.

I stare at the ruined thing. And I know there won't be another. Whatever treatment the Centre has developed, I want no part of it.

"Sophie? Are you okay?" Aunt Irene knocks on the door. "I heard a crash."

"Hold on a second!" I sweep the fragments of the HemaPen under Kira's old bed along with the papers before I open the door. "It was nothing. You don't need to worry. I just slipped on the last rung coming down." I glance at the ladder leading up to my bed.

"I suppose you could always move to the bottom... ." She trails off when she notices my red eyes.

"Have you been crying?"

"I'm fine."

Fidgeting under my gaze, she tries the light switch but nothing happens. "No power, huh?" she murmurs.

"Nada."

"I just sent Charlotte to pick up more candles." Another long look. "Do you want to give me a hand with this? It's okay if you've ... got other things you're doing right now."

In the hall is what looks like a large fishing box.

"What's that?" I try to keep my voice level but there's that push again, the twitch in my blood when my emotions are intense.

"An emergency kit. There's a storm front building and I want to be prepared. Just in case."

"Just in case?" She doesn't respond. Instead she carries the box downstairs into the kitchen, me following behind. She places it on the counter and cracks the lid open. Inside are heavy duty flashlights, what looks like a hand-crank radio, a penknife and a whistle. She begins rooting around in the pantry cupboard, pulling out tins and stacking them on the table.

"So what do you reckon then, niece of mine?" she says in an overly chipper voice. "We've got peanut butter, some canned tuna, chili ... green beans or peas?" I don't answer her but she carries on as if I did. "I'm going to put in enough food for a week, so whatever we pack in here you better be willing to eat." Aunt Irene stacks the cans carefully.

I dig around further in her kit and come up with Ziploc bags filled with tablets. One of them is labelled WATER PURIFICATION. The other contains an assortment of prescription medications, plus ibuprofen, paracetamol, and a packaged tin of something called Queasy Drops.

"Where would we go?" There isn't enough here to last for long.

"The JR Hospital is the evacuation point. It's on high ground so it should be safe if there's a major flood. Safer than here anyway."

"And after that?"

"We'd wait until the water levels go down. Then we'd come back, I suppose, and get on with things. The same as always." She stops what she's doing and looks at me. "I'm sure we won't have to evacuate. This is just a precaution."

"That's not what they're saying."

"If it went on for very long we'd go inland. Wait it out in a shelter." She runs a hand through her hair, staring at me. "Come on, you. Help me finish this off?"

She's already got several two-gallon jugs of water as well as a knapsack with a couple of warm shirts and trousers wrapped in plastic bags. I try to distract myself by helping out. I add my own clothes, two old T-shirts I used to wear camping, a pair of jeans, and a Common Misfits sweatshirt from last year. Strange to hold it now—it used to be my favourite but I haven't worn it in months.

"You okay, sweetie?" She's looking at me, concerned, her hair loose, as long as mine. "Your mum said you had a difficult meeting at the Centre."

Tonelessly I answer, "Things have been pretty bad all around."

"I suppose they have." Wiping the sweat off her forehead, she gives me a sympathetic look. We shove the last of the things into the closet. "Let's go into my office."


Her office at home mirrors her office as the university. Her books are crammed haphazardly into makeshift shelves. To the right side of her desk hangs a corkboard bristling with a hodgepodge of clipped news articles, updates from the World Health Organization. She sits down in a large leather chair wedged in the angled space beneath the stairs. "So apart from the obvious, what's on your mind?"

I choose my words carefully, torn between my desire to trust her and some sort of deeper fear that maybe she won't understand, that she'd side with them. "I'm worried about the Centre, what they're doing. They want to set up long-term care facilities for people like me."

She looks up sharply.

"You didn't know?" I ask.

"No one has told me anything," she says, a trace of bitterness in her voice. "They've left me flying as blind as you. These are strange days—sometimes it feels difficult to be an adult. To know the right thing to do. Maybe your doctors are right. Maybe we just need to find a way to keep you safe until we can stop what's happening." She touches the objects on her desk as if they are charms. A way of warding off danger. But all this tells me is she doesn't understand at all. How can I get through to her?

"What if we shouldn't stop it?"

"What do you mean?"

"What if we need to let this happen? Let nature take its course?"

She stares out the window. "I thought I understood but this is unlike anything we've seen before. People are dying and I don't know." Her voice cracks with emotion and she squeezes her eyes shut.

"But it isn't death," I tell her. "That's what I'm trying to say."

She doesn't want to admit it. "It's worse."

"Nature finds a way when it's threatened, doesn't it? It changes itself so the next generation will survive and have a better chance. What if that's what's happening? You told me you thought it might be happening for a reason, didn't you? That maybe this has happened before?"

"Maybe." Her gaze returns to me but she still sounds

skeptical. "I've been searching through the records for anything that resembles what we're seeing. There are references to strange—unnatural—phenomena. In the Middle Ages, there was frequent flooding and freezing. Roses on the willow trees at Lent."

"Maybe they were clues."

"It's just speculation, Sophie. It still doesn't tell us what this is. Or what we should do about it."

"So speculate," I insist and the urgency of my tone makes her glance up. "What's the commonality? Why did it happen then? Why now?"

"The climate shifts, perhaps. Fluctuations in the temperature triggering an onset of the condition. I don't know, the ash in the air? Sophie, there's no way to be sure. We're still digging into the records, processing soil samples. We don't have enough information yet to say anything conclusively."

I brush this aside. "So you still think it was the environmental triggers?" I remember Lane Ballard on the television, talking about locusts, the announcer's frightened response. "But then why wasn't it as bad as this back then?"

"Diseases spread so much faster now, Sophie. Our population is bigger than it was then, crammed into smaller spaces. Pathogens can spread further and faster than ever before."

"You're still thinking about this as a disease. But it *isn't* a pathogen. That's what Dr. Varghese told me. It's something else, some sort of inherited condition. What if you've been looking at this wrong?"

"Fine. Perhaps things weren't so extreme then, so the condition wasn't so widespread. The ... triggers weren't as powerful."

What she's saying makes sense. Everyone has been talking for ages about how bad things are, how the storms are much worse than they used to be. What if this is it, the end? A shiver starts to build in the base of my spine but I flex my fingers, trying to follow the thought. "But why don't we have records of the nymphs then?"

She looks at me thoughtfully. "Maybe we do. In 1337, the chronicler Heinrich of Herford began the *Liber de rebus memorabilioribus*, the Book of Things That Must Be Remembered." Her gaze relaxes. She's on safer ground here, citing her sources. "He recounted the birth of piglets with human faces. Babies born with teeth. Visions of *fantasmata*, ghosts, who caroused in churchyards and meadows."

"So they existed."

"Sophie, you're jumping to conclusions. People thought they were superstitious."

Bird bones in the graves of the Greeks. The carvings of doves, a gift from one child to another. I start to bounce my leg in excitement, my pulse racing. Maybe there were other signs too, we just didn't know what they were. "But you don't."

"I don't want to be reductive. They were intelligent people

who were trying to make sense of the breakdown of their world. But their conceptual schema was different than ours."

"So if they were seeing nymphs, what happened to them?"

"I don't know," she insists.

One possibility hits me hard and my leg stills. "They were wiped out."

She jerks her head up.

"It's what we're doing now, isn't it?" I whisper.

"The Centre has good reasons for the approach they're taking, even if I don't always like it. Sophie, above all, our souls—if we can call them that—live in our minds, our memories and experiences. But the structure of the human brain is delicate. It can't survive the kind of trauma those bodies are going through. So whatever lives on, even if biologically it's alive, it isn't the same. Don't you think I want to believe as well that something continues on? But that's false hope, Sophie. It's a trick. And it's dangerous for you to think that way."

"Why?"

"Because it means you might to do something stupid," she says bluntly. "You can't trust your instincts right now. What your body is telling you, it's chemical. It isn't real." When she sees the stubborn look on my face she sighs. "Even if what you're saying is true—even if this has happened before—then we still need to look at the evidence. Millions of people died from the Black Death. It's hard to comprehend how terrible a loss of life that was. We need to prevent a global catastrophe. You understand that, don't you?"

"But what about what you said? That things change and we grow stronger from them."

"This isn't another disaster we could survive. It's as if the rules of nature have been rewritten." She shakes her head. "Death is understandable. It's part of a natural cycle of destruction of growth. We're *meant* to die, Sophie—but this? I don't understand it."

"That's not how history works though, is it?" I argue. "We don't get to put things back to how they should be just because it makes life easier to understand. You told me not to trust despair and I don't. But the flip side of immersing yourself in history is false nostalgia, thinking things were better before when they weren't. The planet was in a tailspin before my diagnosis. There isn't safety in the way things were. So what if there's an answer here, something radical and new?"

"What do you mean?" Her eyes are wide.

"Maybe this was supposed to happen."

"Magical thinking, sweetheart. Nothing is ordained. If this were supposed to happen…" She hesitates and a shadow of grief crosses her face. "Then why you? Why *now*?" And buried within that question are others: *Why not me? Why not my daughter too?*

"I don't know. I don't know what any of it means, only it isn't what they're saying."

"Sophie."

Her eyes slide away from mine. For a moment I felt she almost grasped my line of thought but now she's shifting away, her mind rejecting what I told her, antibodies pushing out a foreign bacterium. I guess that's one way of living, of protecting yourself. But there's another way too: you could take what it brought you, let it break through your defences, and you could find a way to use it. But she can't bring herself to do it. Not yet.

I could show her Martin's file. Would that be enough to convince her? I don't know. I need to talk to someone who understands first. Bryan. Still I want to mollify her. "Look. I'll think about what you've said, what the Centre said."

"Good girl." My aunt looks faintly relieved. She tries to smile but I can't bring myself to do the same. I want her to understand but after everything we're at odds with each other. She doesn't want to listen.

Outside the sky has begun to dim, casting long shadows. The heady scent of paraffin wafts into the room. The wind starts to moan like a live thing.

# 32

I hear nothing from Bryan all night, though I check my phone until late, just in case. But the next day, just as Mom is opening a can of beans for lunch, he shows up at our front door.

"Hello?" Mom asks, a tad suspiciously, when she opens it. I can see her taking him in, the collared shirt I haven't seen before. An air of respectability. After he introduces himself, a thoughtful expression replaces her irritated broodiness and she lets him inside. That dressed-up College look is working. She's warming to him.

"The place is a bit of a pig-sty," she apologizes. There are drifts of laundry draped over the radiators, ready to be hung outside. No one's had the energy to do it.

"I was hoping I could borrow Sophie for a few hours." Mom glances outside, a small frown creasing her lips when she sees his truck.

"You have a licence?"

He smiles. "Passed it on my first go."

"Well…" she says. I watch her eyes travel to his wrist,

searching for a medical ID bracelet. But he's either shucked it off or hidden it beneath his cuff. I slip into my shoes before she has a chance to interrogate him further.

"Bye, Mom," I tell her, planting a kiss on her cheek as I walk past.

Even with the windows down it's hot in the truck. Bryan doesn't say anything about what prompted him to show up at the house. But for me it feels strange. For so long I kept him separate from the rest of my life, a secret. But now my worlds are colliding.

We turn onto Banbury Road toward the cement works. There's a kind of easy trust between us that's been strengthened since the riot. But I can sense a familiar anxious energy in him as well. He blinks too often, licks his lips—it's almost a nervous tick. He takes the roads slowly, carefully checking and double-checking before he turns or changes lanes.

It seems like it has been months since I was last at the cement works though it's only been a few weeks. Still, it feels good to be going back, just the two of us. This is *our* place, a sanctuary.

The air is scorching away from the river, the grass brittle beneath our feet. I head straight for the tower, which still has the faint sour smell of acetone. My bloody handprint on the door, flaking at the edges. Inside, Kira's blanket, the dusty-looking fairy lights lying on the dirt near the wreckage of the tarpaulin shelter. Her absence feels strange, like the ache after a tooth's been pulled.

Bryan walks toward the raw mixture plant, about thirty paces from the tower. When I join him, through the gaps between the oversized, chalk-white support pillars, I see a large shape drawn on the concrete floor. It reminds me of an ancient petroglyph, stark, like the ones I saw back home in Ontario—turtles, snakes, birds and humans, all carved by hand into the gneiss-flecked rock. This has the same mysterious quality, a giant disk with either a rocket or a throne sketched inside.

He says, "This is what I wanted you to see."

"What is it?"

He stares at the drawing for a moment as if lost in thought and then picks up two slender silver tubes about two inches thick stamped with the letters EMT on them. When it's clear I still have no idea what he's talking about, he shows me how they might fit together. "I found Da's old brazing torch in the shed this morning. I managed to work these bits together without much trouble. It's not much, but it gives us a frame, yeah? And there's loads more EMT conduits from back when he rewired the house. See? That rectangle in the centre will be where we mount the harness." I have the odd sense that it isn't Bryan I'm talking too, or not the Bryan that I know. This one is expansive in his gestures, loosened, unknotted. There's a … *too-muchness* about him, too much pressure, too much force.

"Bryan." I want to summon him back to me. "What about Martin? What should we do about the report? There's things I need to tell you."

His face goes cloudy with something close to rage. I feel it too, reacting to him. That crawling sensation under my skin, a feedback loop, reflecting his excitement and his anger both.

"Martin," he says, "that's why…" But he's shaking his head as if he's trying to block out a terrible sound. "That's where I got the idea for this. Listen. That feeling Martin talked about … You've had it too, haven't you?"

I nod slowly. "Like they're out there. In the sky, somewhere, maybe over the ocean, calling us."

"We need to do something about this ourselves," he says. "We can't trust the media. The Centre isn't trying to understand this. They're trying to stop it."

"I know. But how exactly does *this* help? What is it?"

"A paramotor." He says at last, as if he can't understand why I haven't been able to keep up with him. "A powered paraglider. I saw a bunch of students using them over Port Meadow once, in the old days. They're surprisingly simple when you break them down, simple enough that you could build one yourself if you had the tools." A long pause, as if he's waiting for me to respond. Which I don't, until he says, "We could go up there."

I take in the new angularity of his face, the compact muscles of his shoulders and arms. He looks as if he has been pressurized like coal beneath the heavy crust of the earth. He positively glitters, hard, sharp. I pry my gaze away to look at the thing he has begun to create.

"We can reach Kira up there," I say. My heart staccatos at the possibility. A gleam of hope. "We could communicate with them. We could find out what they are." I could get proof, something Mom and Aunt Irene would have to believe. *Magical thinking*, she told me. But I know it isn't.

Bryan presses on as if he's tuned into my thoughts. "Martin knew they were waiting for him. That means there's intelligence behind what they're doing. They must have a way of communicating with each other. And with us as well—outside of a lab, I mean."

"I've felt it." When I'm close to them—at the riot, with Kira, with the nymph that Bryan and I saw. "But there's a fuzziness to it, hints and images, memories, dreams, out of focus." He nods and I can't help grinning. "Getting closer to them—this could be a way to strengthen the signal."

"All we need is a motor, a propeller, and some sort of fabric sail. Like an aerofoil or a parachute."

Bryan fills the space between us with his plans. I'm shaking with anticipation. This is insane, I know it's insane, but it also feels right. What if we could *find* her? What if I could see her again?

I'm coming untethered. I could drift away, except for this: my hand in Bryan's, heat in my wrist, my neck, my cheeks. The two of us here, as it has been from the start. I pull him closer. My lips graze his.

His eyes widen and then his mouth presses against mine, he sucks the oxygen out of my lungs. He traces the outline of my hip, buries his hand in my hair. Our teeth knock together. Our second kiss is exploratory, the pressure of his tongue, sweet. Still surprising, but not just surprise.

And then he pulls me into him, harder. His skin is feverish. "Oh, you," he murmurs and his voice melts my inside. I want to run my fingers over every inch of him. But beneath the elation, some part of me is frightened by the suddenness of this, the strength of his arousal. He jams my back against the cement wall and sparks crowd my vision. "Wait!" But his mouth is against mine. "Bryan, wait—" He doesn't. Neither do I. My eyes are closed, and a furious white light burns behind them. I rise up onto my tiptoes to meet him, thinking: *I could breathe underwater if it only felt like this, I could grow gills and deep-sea dive.*

But then he's gone, slipped out of my arms. "Sophie," he says, "I'm so sorry. This isn't me. This isn't how I wanted it to be. I want to, but I just—"

"I know—it's the bug." My stomach collapses in on

itself, hollowed out by disappointment.

Fist clenching and unclenching, Bryan walks a slow circuit away from me. "I don't want to hurt you." When he turns to face me again, his smile is small, bitter. "It gets into everything, doesn't it? Fuck."

As I shift away from the wall, an ache deep in my bones, the beginnings of a bruise, I still want him. His smell is so thick around me, the feel of him imprinted on my skin.

"That's why we need to do this," he says, half to himself. "It's why we need to *know* what's happening. What's us and what's—"

"Something else." He's as far away as I have ever known him to be.

"It's coming. Can't you feel it? In the air, in the earth, as if the world is shifting. But my symptoms are getting worse." His eyes are dark and coppery, the colour of molasses. "My mum said she's noticed changes. She said I passed out yesterday. While I was talking to you. She wanted to take me to the hospital but when I woke up I wouldn't let her. You know they're talking about long-term facilities?"

I nod slowly. "Dr. Varghese told me that."

"Someone from the Centre called. After reviewing the blood tests from my HemaPen they said they were making arrangements. Said they were opening a facility up north, somewhere near York."

"Jesus, Bryan!" I reach for him but he wards me off.

"I know, I know. My mum's scared too, but she doesn't know what else to suggest. In the meantime she's started stockpiling supplies from the JR, just in case. But someone's bound to notice."

"What can I do? What do you need right now?"

"I need this," he says, staring at the paramotor. "I need this to work. I need some reason to think there might be a way forward. Until then, I don't—I can't—" His voice is strangled. "I can't risk you getting hurt if something bad happens to me."

The desire has drained out of me entirely. I know he's right. There's a growing heat between us but what chance does it have right now? I want it to be real, to be pure—not just the product of our condition. We need to choose it for ourselves. Because that's all we really have, isn't it? It's what we've been fighting for: the power to choose.

# 33

Something's coming, Bryan said, and he was right.

A storm breaks over London three days later, in the evening, whipping the sky into bruised eddies of purple and yellow, the rainfall like a flowing river and chunks of hail the size of golf balls. Where we are further inland, in Oxford, the rain is lighter but the air picks up an electric gloss that charges the hairs on the back of my neck. It's frightening, but also thrilling. The air smells burnt.

Somehow the power is still on so Mom and I gather around the television to watch while Aunt Irene fries fresh ground beef, adding in a can of chili. She managed to get to the store early in the day to load up on fresh food before they ran out, and we have to cook the meat before losing power again. It's a treat, rich and textured the way that nothing that comes out of a can ever is.

On the TV, helicopter coverage shows a great swell of water advancing upon the Thames Barrier, a series of steel gates and massive hydraulic piers stretching the breadth of the river. It almost looks as if it's happening in slow motion.

The wave crashes into the barrier—weird that there's no sound, or so little of it, just the breathing of the newscaster—and then it creeps up and over.

"The problem," announces the newscaster, "is that the storm arrived at high tide when the Thames was already at higher-than-expected levels. The flood damage is expected to be severe. Twenty-six underground stations are in high risk—we have live footage from a reporter, please excuse the poor quality."

The image on the screen dissolves into a shot of a black metro sign with the following words lit up in dull, orange dots:

Welcome to NORTH GREENWICH Station

JUBILEE LINE: Good service operating.

The camera, lens spotted with condensation, shows a wave of seawater pouring across the walkway, splashing against the glass that encircles the escalators. The water flows down the escalators and smashes against the plastic partitions at the platform. The camera tilts as blue-tiled columns chart the flood's depths on the concourse. Water begins to surge through the open doors into a stalled train.

Mom is shaking so hard the vibrations travel across the couch. None of us can stand to eat anymore.

Aunt Irene makes a move to turn the TV off, but then

the image snaps back into focus, the colours tinted blue, briefly bleeding into one another. Amongst the crowd of trapped passengers in the train is a girl close to my age: a pale face framed by a close-cropped blond bob. The deluge drags her off her feet, her arms flail, she grabs the edge of the door. There's a moment when it seems like she'll manage to swim forward, against the current, but she's slowed by the weight of her clothing, a floral skirt and ivory cardigan. She manages to haul herself halfway out of the train before the foamy crest of a second wave collapses into her.

The news anchor, his voice tinny and distant: "There are reports of people trapped in buildings as well as in Tube stations like this one. They've made desperate calls, asking for help, asking for rescue, but the rescuers can't get in. It's simply too dangerous."

The camera catches an image of the girl kissing a bubble of air trapped against the ceiling of the Tube train. Her face is dreamy with terror—and something else, longing maybe. Has she been waiting for this? A tiny stud in her ear winks at me.

"Please, will you just turn it off, Irene? I can't—I can't…" Mom moans.

The image shrinks to a single point of light, then vanishes. Mom fidgets, pulls up the edge of a thin coral throw into her lap. Her legs are tucked underneath her, and she looks like a little kid watching a horror movie. "Thank god," she says. "Thank god we're safe."

"Do you think she survived?" I know she didn't. "They can't show us something like that without letting us know whether she made it or not."

The chili lurches in my stomach. We sit in silence and I hold in my thoughts: *How old was that girl?* and *no one could have got her out in time* and even after everything, *thank god, thank god, it wasn't me.*

But at the same time there's a part of me that understands, a part that recognized that look in her eyes. She wanted it to happen. And finally I understand. This is what the nymphs have been waiting for: the beginning of the end.

# 34

At the cement works traces of the storm are everywhere. The wind has ripped handfuls of wildflowers out of the ground, leaving bald patches of soil. Saplings are shattered like kindling. In London, thousands of people are missing. Downing Street is mostly underwater.

Our work on the paramotor is a welcome distraction. Bryan hauled out a portable welder before his mum told him not to risk driving. Our bikes are leaned up against the concrete wall, the smell of burnt ozone all around us.

Bryan's got the frame mostly finished: a giant steel circle of welded pipes. I leave him to it, for the most part. I have to prepare for my job, which is just as difficult. We've agreed that I'll be the one to fly the thing when it's ready.

We've hung a practice harness from a secure pipe about ten feet off the ground, its copper underside dappled with lichen. Being inside the harness is like being on a swing, but with more support from the foam seat. Pairs of recycled seatbelts encircle my thighs—they're more comfortable than I would've expected. The hang point of the harness has been set so the supporting straps attach to carabiners just above my shoulders. Mostly I've been focused on getting the sense of the straps, how easily the harness adjusts to my movement, how I hold the throttle and brake lines. Sweat greases my palms, but the movements are becoming more natural, automatic.

It's not even close to how it'll feel to be airborne, but I don't want to think about that too much right now. Today is a day for mindless routine. I lean back into the harness, and my bare feet lift in the air. I've painted my toenails bright orange, the brightest I could find, the orange of safety vests and warning signs.

When I look at the paramotor—nylon straps, a square of plywood, a fuel hose leading to a tank—a feeling of calmness washes over me, of hope. It is the only chance I have to see Kira again, even if it is a long shot. A leap of faith. I don't know what comes next but I have to try.

"We'll attach the parachute to the back," Bryan says, "but the propeller should keep you in the air. Give you direction, all your control." He touches it, and the blades begin to rotate.

"How long before it's finished?" I ask.

"Not long." Bryan says.

"How long is that?"

"Soon."

• • •

The sun rides lower in the sky as we cut along Five Mile Drive. The spokes of Bryan's bicycle wheels flash like a spinning silver plate. I'm close behind. Past the Perch Inn, the Thames is swollen, but slow-moving as it twists its way east toward London. We follow the edge of Port Meadow where cows low in the field, their tails flicking half-heartedly at the flies that swarm whenever the wind dies down.

We hear the noise of people before we can see them.

There are maybe forty of them, massed on the field, blankets checkering it. The music is loud, blasted from a portable speaker system, and the smell of kerosene is everywhere. As we get closer to the footbridge over the river, Bryan holds up his hand warningly. When we see it's mostly students and younger people, no police, he relaxes.

"How do you think this all came together?" I'm thinking of how few young people I've seen on the street, the violence at the last gathering.

Some littler kids are chasing ducks by the river's edge, their elbows scabby and shoulders peeling with sunburn. A dark-haired boy in an unbuttoned linen shirt, maybe fifteen or so, grins at me over the remains of a watermelon as we pass him. As I watch he spits something into his palm: a seed, I think at first, but it's white and gleaming. A tooth. He seems surprised to see it.

There's a drugged, blissed-out quality to the party. All the faces are thin and hollow, hematomas blooming beneath the skin. They are sick, all of them. *We* are sick—but strangely euphoric too, an electric spark jumping from person to person.

*Us, us, us.*

Someone offers us tinned frankfurters cooked on a camp stove and I take one, eating it quickly, then licking the grease from my fingers. I want to laugh, feeling light-headed and dreamy among them.

We spot Redmond near the shallows of the Thames. "Bryan!" He waves us over. "My good fellow, you've decided to join us!"

Bryan shrugs. Redmond comes toward me, Liv next to him. "And you, Sophie, what a pretty young thing you are." He kisses me lightly on the cheek.

"Hey, Redmond. Keeping well?"

"Better than some. I'm glad to see you, love." I wonder what happened to his plans, if he's made a decision. I want to tell him we've been making our own plans but the way his eyes glitter makes me nervous.

"What is this?" I ask them.

"We wanted to celebrate!" Redmond says, offering us each a cup filled with something that smells sweet and medicinal.

"Celebrate what?" I call.

He takes a swig from his own cup. "It's not quite May Day but we're pretending, aren't we? The first day of summer—or it might as well be. Who knows if we'll get another. So linger a while, will you?"

With that he strips off his shirt. A flash of pale skin, his sun-darkened wrists, fingers working at the buttons of his jeans, then he's down to his trunks. A spring-heeled leap sends him into the river. He comes up sputtering. "It's lovely. Join me!"

*Eat, drink and be merry…*

I strip down to my underwear, and throw myself in after him. The water is cool, a blessed relief after the heat. My toes dig for the bottom, barely managing to graze the slick mud of the riverbed. The current whips me around— I'm breathless, weightless, invisible, free.

Bryan lowers himself slowly into the water from a makeshift wooden platform. I wedge my nails between the planks and haul myself up, letting the river run over my thighs.

Only Liv keeps herself on the bank. "You shouldn't be in there. It isn't safe."

"Aye, but where is it safe now?" Redmond says. He gets hold of my ankle and drags me back into the water. My head goes under, and I come up sputtering as he laughs.

The current carries me downstream and I crawl up onto the bank next to Liv, my skin glistening with water. The crowd of people seems to give her a wide berth. When I look more closely I notice dark bruises underneath her eyes, a feeling of wrongness. She looks fragile, bone-thin in her tattered skirt and blouse.

"Liv, what's happened?"

"You know what's happened."

"No, I mean—you look like you're going to be sick."

Suddenly her breath hitches. "I'm pregnant."

"God, Liv, with—"

"Yes, with Reddy. We were very careful. But…"

This is the last thing I expected her to tell me. "What can I do? Are you okay?"

"At first I thought it was my childhood illness coming back. I was sick when I was younger, I told you that. They warned me that JI2 could cause complications even now, that my heart might have been weakened by the fever. So when my temperature started running high and I felt nauseous all the time, I thought—well, it wasn't that after all." She laughs, but it's a strange, unhappy sound.

"Does Redmond know?"

She looks me in the eye. "I don't want to tell him. Not yet, anyway. Things between us never seemed … permanent. He's charming and clever, sweet when he wants to be. But I don't know how he'll react. His head is full of mad ideas right now and he doesn't trust the Centre."

"What're you going to do then?"

"My clinician says I'm at a high risk for all sorts of complications." She picks up a handful of stones and stares at them, letting them drop one by one from between her fingers. "He offered me choices. They're trialing a new drug called M-Plagge. It's not approved yet but he thinks I'm a good candidate for it."

M-Plagge—the drug they tested on Martin.

"Liv, you need to listen to me." Urgency makes me stumble. "You can't take M-Plagge. You don't know what this drug will do to you, or to the baby."

"I was told it will inhibit the juvenile hormone. My symptoms are supposed to improve almost immediately." She's staring at the rocks, out at the swimmers, the sky, looking anywhere other than at me. I grab her wrist but I feel no shimmer of connection. Her skin is cold, leaden.

"I know all about M-Plagge. It isn't some wonder drug that will make everything better. It doesn't eradicate JI2. It just stalls it, stops the body from taking its natural course. They have no idea what the side effects will be, no idea how it will work on people like us."

"How do you know that?"

"It's what happened to Martin."

"Martin?" she says with surprise. "But he's dead. What are you talking about?"

"He signed a donation agreement. My clinician gave me a copy of the report. They tested M-Plagge on him. It trapped him in his own body, left him halfway between one form and the next. He wasn't him but he wasn't … one of them. A nymph. He was somewhere in between."

"I don't believe you," she says, on the verge of tears again.

"Why would I lie about this? The donation term

expired. Liv, they cremated him, what was left of him. Even though they could tell he was still alive. That some part of him had survived."

"But that's wrong," she whispers.

"It's inhuman. That's why you need to find another option, we can figure something out."

"Sophie." She shakes her head. "What you're saying is horrible but … but it also proves that M-Plagge works, doesn't it? It stalls the transition. And if I continue taking it…"

"What're you talking about?"

"They gave me the first injection this morning. I'm going back to the Centre tomorrow. After that they'll move me to a facility where they can monitor my health. Don't you understand? Whatever risks there are, they're worth it. This isn't just about me."

"You're talking about a containment facility."

"Maybe that's what we need. Maybe we need somewhere we can be safe." She wraps her arms around her legs, tugging them close.

"What if they won't let you keep the baby?"

"It doesn't matter. At least the baby will have a chance." Her voice is frightened and the tears come hard. I fold her up in my arms, trying to comfort her. The sharp press of her nose against my shoulder as she sobs in short, shallow gasps.

"I'm sorry, Liv, I'm so sorry," I tell her and then when she doesn't stop I try again with the same thing Mom keeps telling me: "Everything'll turn out all right, I know it will." Around us I can see evidence of the lie: the sheen of spoilage, of bodies beginning to break down. But it doesn't scare me the way it used to. There's something mesmerizing about it, an alien beauty that Liv can't seem to see.

When she's cried herself out Liv pulls away from me and pushes herself from the ground.

"Please, Sophie, don't tell anyone."

"Redmond deserves to know. I'm sure he'll surprise you. I can tell how much he cares for you."

I want to believe my own words but I can tell she's drifting away from me, spiralling off in a different direction. I wish I could help her see what I see but she's made her choice.

I wander back into the crowd, uneasy, searching for Bryan. There are dark clouds gathering overhead. When the first few drops of rain fall, Redmond cries, "It's raining, everybody in!"

And I don't understand it entirely but they listen, all of them crashing into the water now, whooping and hollering, knowing their clothes will be soaked anyway. Their mood is contagious. Before I know it I'm in the water too, feeling the current rush around me, the blur of legs kicking furiously beneath the surface.

Liv is on the bank a stone's throw away, watching

us—but distant somehow, separated from it all. She isn't part of it, I realize, she doesn't feel the intense bleed of emotions. The drug is already changing her.

But it's different for me. I can feel something growing inside of me, an awareness. Something as thick and urgent and overpowering as desire. What Liv's choosing is wrong, I know it is. Trying to clear my head I swim out into the middle of the Thames where everything moves faster. My arms carve out strange geometric shapes as I push against the current, away from shore—if I stop moving for an instant then I'll be whisked downstream.

Redmond swims after me and when he breaks the surface, his grin has changed, is less convincing. "Come back to the shore, love." I shake my head, frog-kick once, twice in the direction of the dock but my legs have taken on the weight of lead.

But the feeling is with me, that whispering in my blood. As if someone is calling to me from the other side of some thin and insubstantial barrier. I push myself under, just for a moment, just to see what it looks like, those pale limbs flashing, shimmering. It hurts to keep my eyes open, but I do anyway, wanting to see the river all black and sunlit at the same time. Its power is phenomenal, swallowing me up in a dizzy welter. Pressure sucks at my ears and my hands are otherworldly, mottled in silver and shadow.

A trickle of lacy bubbles rushes out of my nose. My feet

touch bottom for a moment, skittering over pebbles, old coins, lost fish hooks anchoring colourless threads. What if I stayed under? What would it be like to feel the water overtake me?

My ears ache with pressure and my vision is stippled with dark spots and bright chromatic bursts. There is no sense of alarm—what I feel instead is an unexpected ebullience. The death wish, the jitterbug. My whole body begins to pound like the taut skin of a drum, pushing oxygen-poor blood to my extremities. A slight tremor in my fingertips, numbness in my toes.

Distant noises. There are other faces around me, like bright moons. The pug-nosed girl, her hair floating like a wreath around her. Darkness pushes down on me from all sides, but I'm glowing, golden, full of light. This is what I want. This is—

Then Bryan's face is hovering over mine, angry and frightened. He pushes down with both hands on my chest, and it *hurts*. Water bubbles over my lips, gritty with silt. I suck in air, choke, spit again.

"What the bloody hell were you doing?" He's close to shouting at me.

I'm exhausted, exhilarated, but sad too, the feeling after you wake up from a good dream, knowing something irretrievable has been lost. It felt as if I was coming into some special form of knowledge.

Redmond is still treading water, a streak of black hair plastered to his forehead. But Liv looks furious. "Come in, Reddy," she snaps. "Right now!" In three strokes he covers the distance, and she practically yanks him onto the platform.

I'm shivering even though the air is still hazy with heat: "I'm fine," I whisper, "really. Nothing happened, I wouldn't have let it." I push myself up, chest still heavy, fatigued, black spots dotting my vision.

Liv is glaring at Redmond now. "You can't take chances. You *know* that."

"I'm fine," I repeat, shaking my head, trying to clear it. And then: "It's fine." But I don't know what's fine, not exactly. Too many feelings crowd my head: embarrassment, dismay, regret but the last traces of joy too, the sense I was close to understanding.

"I'll take her home," Bryan says. I don't want him to look at me. I force myself to stand.

"I wasn't going to do anything."

"Liv's right. Someone could've got hurt, don't you understand?" he replies.

"Didn't you hear them?" I ask. He stares at me helplessly, and I can tell he didn't. Not the way I did. Redmond and Liv are giving us space, but neither of them looks happy. Finally Bryan shakes his head. "Let me take you home." I don't want to fight him, not now.

I search out my dusty cut-offs and espadrilles, swing

my leg over my bike and pause to look around. The others have dragged themselves from the water and are now knotted in clusters on the bank. They look small and fragile, pigeon-chested boys, girls with slender legs, hair glistening with dampness. It hurts me to see them, to think about what's coming. I shiver with a premonition: *I'll never see them again.*

Liv sighs, then leans forward and takes my shoulder. An unexpected, protective gesture. "Don't be so quick to give up on the world." Her face is pale. She glances at Redmond.

I tell her, "It isn't that. I promise."

# 35

Just the two of us now. Bryan rides his bike along the towpath from Port Meadow, me a short distance behind. We pass over Fiddler's Island, water lapping close on either side of the narrow causeway. Our tires make slow clacking sounds as we cross the footbridge.

"This is where I lost Kira," I say, and he stops, turns back to me.

"You never told me that."

I shrug, still feeling hurt by his anger, unsure of myself. "I was holding onto her. At least I was trying to. But she didn't want me to."

Bryan's voice is tense. "We need to keep going. The weather is turning."

"I kept playing it over and over in my mind. She had this look in her eyes. She wanted me to let her go." I can make out a thin stretch of sky through the branches of creeper-cluttered hawthorn and willow. "I don't want to go home." What I mean is I don't want to leave him with this hanging between us. "I wouldn't ... I mean, nothing was going to happen to me."

He runs a hand through his wet hair. "Not yet."

"I can't turn back from what's happening to us."

"And I don't want to lose you."

"I thought you said—"

"It doesn't bloody well matter what I said before!" Water trickles down his chin. We're both thoroughly soaked. Finally, he shakes his head. "My house then, okay? The rain is getting worse."

His place is a part of an old council property on the opposite side of the Thames. Decaying terraced houses and empty parking lots, debris that hasn't been cleared from the communal gardens. Most of the ground floor flats have been abandoned, and the windows are boarded up but damp darkens the frames. The signs of neglect are everywhere.

Bryan leads me up a concrete external staircase. "The funding goes to flood defences in posher areas," he mutters. "Places like Osney. The river broke the bank close to here, but they still haven't been able to afford proper repairs. Da bought this place when he was young and thought it'd see Mum taken care of. But now? If the banks break again, the foundations may not last. We could lose everything." He pushes the door open. "Mum won't be back tonight. She's just started her shift at the hospital."

Inside, there's plenty of space, but somehow we're still

bumping into each other in the hallway. The ceiling is low, webbed with tendrils of black mould above the windows. Bryan tries the light switch and sighs when nothing happens. "I'd offer you tea, but."

Nervousness makes me want to hold my body tight, compact.

"It won't be long before the power's back, I reckon. But you need to get dry at least."

"Bryan…"

He doesn't answer. Instead he turns and disappears into the room on the left, returning a minute later with an oversized Glastonbury T-shirt. It smells thickly of him. "Sorry, I don't have much that's clean," he says.

"It's fine, really."

He steers me toward the bathroom, which is lit only by a small window, looking out toward the river. I change out of my clothes quickly. A slug of toothpaste is crusted against the drain of the porcelain sink and plastic pill bottles are lined up along the wall, exposed, all with Bryan's name on the label. Paroxetine, an antidepressant that Mom has used, Haloperidol, and others I don't recognize. Fibrin sealant glue like I have to carry, in case of cuts that won't stop bleeding. I wonder what else his mother might be hoarding, what contingency plans she has made.

After I'm finished I find Bryan in the living room, where he has opened all the windows and got a small heater going to dry my clothes. He takes my shirt and cut-offs, and hangs them on a rack. A small puddle begins to form beneath the edge of the pane, and he sets out an old cake pan to catch it.

The T-shirt is long, but it doesn't leave much to the imagination. My thighs prickle with a shivery warmth. I take a seat on the ground, enjoying the coolness of the floorboards. The heady smell of naphtha fills the room, reminding me of the camping trips my family used to take to Algonquin, good memories.

"I've always loved this smell. It reminds me of autumn, going back to school. I was always excited about September."

"Never was much for school," he says. "Except for sports."

I try to imagine him hurtling down the field, tussling with the other boys on the team. It makes me smile. "Our street always smells like this, you know."

"It's the houseboats. They use lamps like these."

He shifts next to me. There's an undercurrent between us, as if the air itself is vibrating. "Freakazoid," I whisper.

Bryan's mouth relaxes. The ghost of a smile, but it's enough.

"I was wondering…" I'm looking for words now. I know nothing has changed between us but something has changed inside me. I don't want him to hold back. All I can do is trust these moods, the impulses, trust where they are taking me.

"Yeah?"

"Can I kiss you? Would that be all right?"

"That's not why I brought you here!" he said in a half-strangled voice. "Not for—that."

"Even so. I want to."

He sits perfectly still as I pull myself an inch toward him. The floor is sandpapery, grit in the crevices between the floorboards. The rain drips into the cake pan, *ping ping ping*. I rest a hand on Bryan's knee, then I touch his cheek. His eyes are very wide, but he doesn't stop me.

"You have to give me permission. Okay?"

"Yes," he breathes.

Gently, I touch his lips. He tastes rich and earthy. I lose myself in the sensation of it. Flecks of emotion, like fireflies sparking in my brain. Mine or his, I can't tell.

"Is this—?"

"Yes," he says in a different pitch than I'm used to. "Yeah, it is."

The warmth from the heater is sweltering, crisping my face. *This should be easy*, I think, *easier than it is*. How do I summon him out of himself? The two of us are satellites, half glaring, half in shadow, as we circle one another. But then his mouth fits against mine, his tongue brushes the inside of my lower lip. My senses expand to take hold of everything: the chipped-lacquer lamp, a tablecloth slipped too far at one end, the size and shape of every room above us, around us, beneath us, the water whispering through the pipes.

He leans toward me, covers my body with his. My shoulders touch the floorboards and I'm finding it difficult to breathe. I've never been kissed like this before, never felt another body pressed against me this way, the crook of his hips, the velvety hairs on the back of his neck.

He slides off the T-shirt and kisses my shoulders, my neck. His blunt nails graze my nipple. *Oh.*

"I thought you didn't want this," I whisper, which is stupid, because I don't want him to stop. But there is an image in my mind of someone a year older than me, pretty. Very pretty. Skin like silk when he touched her.

"I never said that."

A faint popping noise, then all the lights in the room flare on at once. The radio crackles to life, spitting out static and then the hint of a melody, words floating: *I always knew you'd take me back.*

"Bloody hell," he murmurs.

"I thought it was your mum!" I start to giggle.

"Let me check the fuses."

"No. Stay." Jangly pop music fades in and out and for a moment he doesn't move.

"Sophie…" He rolls off me, kills the radio. Blood rushes in to fill all the squeezed out places. The heat is intense but I feel colder without him.

"Do you want to kiss me again?" I ask. His hesitation is

back, that wariness you see in certain trapped animals torn between fight or flight.

"No. Yes." And then, thuddingly: "No. I want to—"

"You never manage to find your way to the end of that sentence." I balance on my knees beside him, reaching for my own shirt. The heater has made it brittle without drying it all the way through.

"Let me try, will you? Please?" He tugs me down next to him onto the blanket. "It isn't just … this." He holds out his hand for me and it's shaking. "I was in love once."

"I know." I can't help the hurt from creeping into my voice.

He sits up. "Have you ever been in love before?"

"No."

Bryan brushes a lock of hair behind my ears and gives me a happy-sad look.

"You don't know what it's like then."

"So tell me."

His eyes cloud over, lost in his own thoughts. "I didn't always live out here. When I was growing up we lived out in the woods. In a house surrounded by bluebells, woods— an old gamekeeper's cottage. In the springtime it was lovely. You could hear muntjac deer calling. Ha-*ha*! Like someone breathing. I hated it when they were out in the night. I'd lie awake listening, thinking there were people outside. In the winter the lake would skim over with ice.

If you tossed a coin on it would ring like a bell."

He's never talked much about his childhood. It makes me realize there's so much I don't know about him, about who he was before he was sick. "Go on, Bryan. Please."

"I loved it out there but it was lonely. There weren't many buses. We moved here a few years ago. Mum thought it would be easier for me to go to school. But I was never good at making friends."

"You didn't want to go to university?"

"Astrid was accepted here but there was no way my grades were good enough. I didn't have much saved up so I thought I would work for a year. I loved her. She was this bright, fantastic force in my life. She brought me out of myself. When she—died, I fell apart. I didn't go to the funeral, couldn't bring myself to. Her father came round, but I couldn't talk to him. I couldn't speak to any of them, not one. It was as if I'd fallen into a dark hole. I could see people around me, could hear them, but I shut them out. Didn't know why talking about it would even matter."

"How did she die?"

"It was August of last year. There hadn't been many JI2 cases here in Britain. Or maybe there had been others but they hadn't been diagnosed. It was sudden. An ischemic stroke. They said it was very rare for someone as young as her. Anyway, the doctors weren't checking for JI2 back then—so her parents had her buried, see? When the cremation order came through, it ... had to be applied retroactively. They had to dig up anyone who might've had JI2. Astrid was one of them."

"Oh."

"Her da came to me. He said he wanted me to come when they reinterred her ashes. I never got to see her body."

Neither of us says anything for a while.

"That's why when I saw you with Kira—"

"You helped me save her."

"Sometimes I think about what it must have been like for Astrid, underground. I used to have these dreams, you know? That I was trapped in this black space, burning up. Every part of me hurt. I could hear voices. And now I wonder if that was her. If she was trying to tell me."

"You couldn't have known. What could you have done?"

"I could've done what you did. I don't have those dreams anymore. Not since they cremated and reinterred her. Her da was glad I was there. Her mum? She hugged me, but it was cold, you know? I don't think she wanted me to come. And I can't blame her."

I reach out and touch his hand. His knuckles are laced with small cuts from the work he's been doing on the paramotor. His body is close to mine, but his mind is far away, drifting. And when I withdraw my hand he looks at me as if he's seeing me for the first time.

"What was home like for you?"

"Different. Normal, I guess. Dad was always working long hours and Mom didn't like it. At school things were fine but…" Back then high school had been everything: me dreaming about whether Markeys would kiss me, Jaina egging me on. "It seemed like there was so much I was supposed to do. There were all these straight lines between one point and the next. Volunteer work. Sports. Projects for extra credit. Life was happening around me, happening to me. Until Kira got sick."

He nods.

"At first it was almost exciting. Suddenly we were special. But then things dragged on and on. Mom was always after the doctors for a diagnosis, Dad wanted to pretend it wasn't happening. No one knew what was wrong with her and when they figured it out no one knew what it meant. So they got scared—first of her, then of me.

"The only person who stuck by me was Jaina. She was—well, cool." Her close-cropped hot pink hair, the jut of her chin when she was angry. Dimples when she smiled. "I had a letter from her. It sounds like things are pretty bad back home. And there's no way for me to talk to her now." He folds his fingers around mine. "You know, I would give anything to stay here with you." I mean it.

"But?"

"Don't you feel it? This … can't be forever. Maybe the world worked one way for our parents, for their parents—but not for us. It isn't the same."

"You don't know that."

"I do, though. We're at the start of something new."

He touches my hair, smooths it back and the feel of it makes me shiver. "The way you look at me sometimes, it's like lightning. But I'm afraid of something happening to you." A long pause, then: "I don't want to die, Sophie."

"Me neither."

"It seems like you're rushing toward it. As if you're waiting for it."

"I'm not." Thinking about Liv and the choice she has made—Kira too, that look in her eyes as she slipped from the bank. "But I'm not turning away, either. I'm not pretending."

"I never used to be afraid of dying," he says. "When I was a kid people would say it was like going to sleep, and if that's what it was, I thought, why are people so afraid? And as I got older I figured maybe it wasn't so bad if you just—stopped. No heaven, no hell. The lights go out and you're done. It meant how you lived was the important thing, not because of what happened after, but because of what it meant to the people around you." He grits his teeth. "But when Astrid died it was as if she'd never existed. Her family was devastated and it nearly destroyed me. We couldn't just take the good things and move on with our lives. And I'm afraid of what'll happen if I die, how much it'll hurt the people I love.

"When I saw the nymph I felt something—I know it

wasn't as strong as you but it meant something to me. It means something comes after. It isn't over. Still I'm scared because I don't know what they *are*. What we might become."

I squeeze his hand. "I know. It's why I want to go up there. I just feel like a candle, you know. Melting away. Like my time is running out."

"It doesn't seem as if there are any good choices."

"Maybe not." A shudder runs through me, sweet, but also sad. "So maybe we should just grab hold of what we can while we're still here." I kiss him softly and when I pull away, I can still taste him on me, salt and copper—a good taste.

He brings his lips to mine again, with more urgency, and a warm shiver runs down my spine as if I've slipped into a hot bath. "Will you stay?"

"For a little while."

# 36

It isn't like I thought it would be, like I used to imagine it would be. Bryan is very, very gentle so much so that eventually it's me who pulls him close, helps him ease into me. It's strange and it's sweet and it hurts more than I thought it would. When I'm ready, he begins to rock into me. At first I don't feel anything but the pain of it—then something in my body shifts. It's as if my body is a bell that's been struck, singing out one long note.

We have to remove the sheets after because of the blood. It scares Bryan, seeing it there, and for a moment it scares me too. I wonder about anti-coagulants, how what we just did must be dangerous. It was for Liv. But I don't regret it.

I stay over. Some time after, the power goes off and Bryan rests fitfully as I listen to the rain slamming against the roof. My body aches with a pleasant dullness. I watch his chest rise and fall as he sleeps. There's a kind of magic in the intimacy he's granted me.

In the morning we're both awkward with each other. He makes something he calls builders' tea on a camp stove.

I cradle my mug against my belly, imagining what Liv might have been going through, why she was willing to take the risk. The longer I stay with Bryan the more I have to lose.

But I don't want to leave yet.

When Bryan takes my empty mug I pull him close and kiss him. I laugh as he strips my shirt away and neither of us flinches at each other's scars. We make love again, and it's better than the first time. We're both more certain of ourselves, less self-conscious.

Mom and Aunt Irene will be wondering where I am but my time with Bryan is running out. I want to seize hold of it while I can.

It's late morning when I finally head home. The rain has nearly stopped and the sunlight is just a smear of light on the wet pavement. The footbridge over the Thames is slippery, pounded by the rain and the thin spray thrown off by the churning river.

I walk my bike along the towpath past the derelict mill buildings. Raindrops *splonk* into the river beside me, stippling the surface. In the distance I spot two emergency service officers in bright, Day-Glo vests. One of them, a woman in her forties with a ruddy complexion and fawn-brown hair pulled back into a ponytail, waves me toward her. "What're you doing out here?" she demands. "Where do you live?"

"South Street." A tight feeling in my chest. "On Osney Island."

"We've just come from there. Have you checked in?" I shake my head and she scowls. "You need to get home as soon as you can. They'll be evacuating Osney soon. We're going door to door to let people know, in case they haven't heard the announcements."

"What announcements?"

"There's a major storm coming." Her partner's lips are compressed into a hard line. "We're worried the flood defences might fail. With what happened in London … if the rain keeps coming down like this, it's going to get a lot worse very quickly." I want to ask her more but already she and her partner are shouldering past me.

*God*, I think, *oh god. It's happening.*


When I make it back to the house, Mom is pulling open a suitcase on the kitchen floor.

"What's going on?" A tipped-over dresser worth of clothes lies in piles. My eyes land on a cream blouse with bright pink trim—Mom used to wear it at home in Toronto all the time. I didn't know she'd brought it with her.

Aunt Irene rushes into the kitchen carrying a giant

stack of papers. A binder skitters out from where it was wedged under her arm and smacks onto the tiles. "For chrissakes, where have you been? Turn on your damn phone, will you? I've been trying to call you for hours." I look and she's right: there are over thirty missed calls.

"But what're you doing?"

"We've been ordered to evacuate, Sophie. So get moving, please," Aunt Irene says.

I pick up the binder and flip it open: lists of names and dates, a copy of the map of England that hangs in her office with the old county lines and towns, some of them crossed out, others circled.

"The rail link north has already been flooded out," she's saying. "Didn't you see it? Tewkesbury is practically underwater, and the power is out as far as Cheltenham and Gloucester. They think the Thames will burst its banks here." Aunt Irene clamps down on my wrist, surprising me with the strength of her grip. It hurts.

I gawk at the wreckage of the house. "But—you said we'd be coming back."

Aunt Irene takes the binder and slips it into a duffel bag where she's stacked dozens of them. She and Mom exchange taut glances.

"Please, Sophie," says Mom. "We don't have time to discuss this. The roads will be dangerous soon. Take what you need, okay? Only what's important." She pushes me up the stairs, calling after me as an afterthought, "Everything's going to be okay."

A lie—we both know everything's falling apart.


The wind whistles, squeezed through the hollow spaces of the house and into my bedroom. Outside the rain is slowing, now a grey curtain over the river, but I know it's a brief lull. The quality of darkness shifts, expands. Sandbags and slats of wood have been laid across doorways to catch the mud and detritus. Soon these homes will be as empty as the villages on Aunt Irene's map. I pull my dusty suitcase from the closet. How did those people choose what to take with them? What was necessary?

I pick up my favourite sweater, a pilled, sheepy grey thing with extra-long sleeves. Do I need this? The shelves are crowded with keepsakes. A charm bracelet with a jewelled heart that Jaina gave me for my fourteenth birthday, a straw hat I wore camping in Algonquin, a frayed toque with a ratty looking pompom. I swore I would throw it out, but I never did. Not those, what then? I yank out a cream-coloured sweatshirt with an appliquéd owl on it that says "Owlsome." It's so dorky, when would I have ever worn this? Then I remember—Dad gave it to me. Why didn't I keep anything else from him? The sweatshirt goes into the suitcase as well. I could leave all of this behind. None of it really matters. But at the same time I want to take all of it, to hoard these memories.

I dig through my chest of drawers, searching for my notebook with its inscriptions, scrawled poetry and fragments of translated Latin, Jaina's unanswered letter folded between the pages. Also newspaper cuttings about JI2, the names of the dead. Sketches of maps, abandoned villages. A strand of Kira's hair I found curled in her pillow and pressed between the pages for safekeeping. Martin's report is there as well, folded in half and held in place with a paperclip.

Fear glides down my spine like meltwater. But not just fear—a presentiment. Dreams of something chasing me, darkness descending and Kira calling out my name.

"We can't stay much longer." Mom's voice drifts up from downstairs, ghostly and panicked.

In a plaintive tone, Aunt Irene answering hers: "This is my home. I have to salvage what I can."

That's when I know I will never see this place again. We're leaving for good.

And I don't want to let go of it, of any of it. The river, this room, the sketch above my bed, a well-thumbed collection of old fairy tales, gilt-edged. And also slanting sunlight on cold mornings, our laughter, the two of us perched on our suitcases on our first day, both eager to go home. Except home is here now.

Cool air from the crack in the window chills my bare

arms, riffles through the pages of my notebook. The words dance in front of my eyes, vivid in the greying light.

*Things return to us.*

There's a feeling inside of me, a tension, as if I'm being wound up like a spring. If I leave with them now, I'll never know the truth.

I trudge downstairs with my suitcase, place it carefully beside the stack of luggage in the hall beside the evacuation kit.

"Sophie, can you start loading the bags into the car?" calls Mom. She and Aunt Irene are unplugging all the electrical appliances in the kitchen, one by one. The chairs are being stood on the table, everything upside-down, to avoid water damage.

"Mom." I say it quietly, watching them from the doorway.

It's Aunt Irene who comes to me first, hands on her hips, impatient as all teachers are with those who don't seem to be listening. "Sophie, get moving! We have to go."

"Mom," I repeat slowly. "I can't come."

I expect hysterics. There aren't any, only the slow turning of Mom's face toward me. "Of course you can."

"We won't be back, will we?"

"In a couple of weeks, maybe. We hope."

"But you don't think so."

She doesn't answer.

"I can't go yet."

Aunt Irene stares at the two of us as if we're mad. "What are you talking about?"

"There's something I need to do."

"It'll have to wait, Feef." But a look of fear has come into her eyes, the same look I saw when we talked after PC Trefethen brought me home. But I can't hold back now. There's no more putting it off, no more room for lies.

"I can't. Kira is out there. She isn't dead."

For a moment she doesn't say anything, just stares at me, eyes wide. Then she bends forward, caught between hope and fear. "What do you mean?"

"It wasn't her body. They cremated another girl. I fixed it." Aunt Irene gives me an incredulous look. "I'm telling the truth. Kira is up there. In the storm. And this is my only chance if I want to…" *Find her. Save her. Say goodbye.* "Keep her safe."

"Kira's alive?" Mom demands.

"I think so."

"I've been dreaming about her," she says, her voice almost lost in the howl of the wind outside.

"She didn't die. She just … changed. The same way I will."

"Sophie, don't," says Aunt Irene but I shake my head.

"Listen to me. I need you to understand what's happening to me, what I am."

I pull the cuff of my cotton blouse away from my wrist, revealing first the JI2 bracelet, then higher up, the seam of the scar from the night of the crash. Mom lets me take her hand, lets me touch the pad of two of her fingers against it.

"I'm still alive, despite the infection I'm still *me*." She tries to pull her hand away but I keep hold, not forcing her, just letting her know I'm not finished yet. "When Kira got sick I didn't understand, not really. Deep down. I thought her body was weakening. That's what the doctors told us. In Canada. Here, too—like Dr. Varghese said. But that's not right, is it? Dr. Varghese told me our bodies *want* this to happen. There's a reason all this is happening."

I flex my fingers and the muscles ripple, the scar dances.

"I can't leave without finding out what she is."

"If you're going then I'm going with you," Mom insists stubbornly.

"You can't."

"Like hell I'm going to let you go on your own."

"I need to do this alone. You have to trust me. I know I don't deserve it but Kira's out there and I can find her. I know I can."

"Will you come back?"

My hands are trembling. "I'll meet you at the evacuation point."

She makes a small noise and moves away from me to the window where she can see the storm clouds thick and heavy, swirling as if someone has stirred them with a spoon.

I turn to Aunt Irene. "You said that something will come after. You took me to see the survivors in Ashwell. You told me you didn't know where the nymphs had gone."

"We still don't, Sophie."

"Listen, this isn't magical thinking, no matter what you believe. It's just a new way of thinking. We're caught in a cycle. This has happened before—during the Black Death, during those earlier cycles of sickness and calamity—because whatever's causing it is a part of us. We can't keep doing the same thing we've done before. You said you wanted to help me. This is how."

"You're only seventeen, how do you…" She still thinks this is her choice to make.

"I'll be eighteen soon."

"I wanted to solve this for you. I wanted to help."

Gently, I say to her: "It doesn't work like that, not this time. It's just—the only alternative is nothing. Waiting for the collapse. Shoving coins soaked in vinegar into the boundary stones and hoping someone will see them. Surviving isn't enough, not anymore."

"This is crazy, Sophie. Let us come with you."

"Keep this safe. For me." I push my notebook into Aunt Irene's hand. It's not enough, I know, but it's something—and she's used to sorting through the debris. She opens it, hands trembling ever so slightly. Then she sees the report with Martin's name.

"What is this?"

"It's everything I have. Just in case. I need you to read it. Maybe then you'll understand."

Mom is staring out the window, losing herself, then returning like a tidal flow. She turns to me and tucks a few strands of hair behind my ears, the gesture so casual, so familiar. "I love you," she says. "You know that, right? And Kira too—so much. You have to promise me you won't get hurt out there."

"You mustn't let her go, Char. It's too dangerous."

"You were right before," Mom answers. "I can't keep her locked up, can I? Not now. Not when…" Her eyes search for mine. She says: "But promise me anyway."

"I can't," I answer her as honestly as I can.

"Please."

"I love you too."

"Come back, Sophie." A fierce smile, a blue smile—and then she lets me go.

# 37

"Sod that," is all Bryan can say when I show up at his door, drenched through, telling him we need to go to the cement works now. "No bloody way. I need to meet my mum at the hospital. She's already there."

But I'm nothing if not persistent. Stubborn as the will of kings, Dad used to say. He could never talk me round to what I didn't want to do. There's no screaming this time though, no arguments, no rationales or mulish indifference, just me saying: "Please. It's now or never."

And Bryan saying: "Get inside at least. I'll bring round my truck. This is madness, yeah? You know that?"

"I know."

Ten minutes later I'm crawling into the front of the truck. He has tucked a pair of workman's boots under the seat as well as a heavy wool jacket. My feet are dwarfed by the boots, so I lace them up tight. Bryan shifts us into gear, and the Ford growls onto the street.

"All right?"

"Maybe." The pungent sting of ozone sends a charge

shooting through my body. Some part of me craves the storm, revels in it, but it isn't just that. It's sitting here next to Bryan, the new feeling between us. It warms my skin, grips me in effervescence.

"I wasn't going to let you walk with that land-lash blowing in, was I?" A spatter of rain flecks the windshield. One wipe is enough to clear it but we both know the worst is yet to come. "Leastwise I can help you use the damn thing. But you think it's worth it? Your family will be wondering where you took off to."

"They know all they need to for now."

"Everything?"

"I told them about Kira. I gave them Martin's report. The rest I'll tell them when we're done here."

"*If* nothing goes wrong."

"It'll be fine."

The lie hangs between us, neither of us wanting to acknowledge the litany of things that could go wrong. My phone beeps with a notification: Mom is trying to call me but I can't talk to her. I'm afraid she'll convince me to turn back. I thumb it to "silent" as Bryan shifts into second. We take off down Banbury Road.


"It's a bodge job," Bryan says, "but it'll fly pretty well. I mean, it *should*."

The cement works is glistening, slicked in the last downpour. The graffiti looks fresh, shiny. The rain is dying down to a sullen spatter, but we both know it's the eye of the storm, and worse is on its way. Brownish rivulets of water thread the gravel beneath our feet, as we load the paramotor onto the bed of the truck.

Bryan drives us down the potholed road until we find a clear spot. We exit the car, gently lift out the paramotor and unfold the wings. The wind catches them, fills them with pockets of air. There could be hail, I think. It fell in London, chunks as big as duck eggs. I imagine them catching in the wings, tearing them apart, me plunging to the ground.

"Too windy," Bryan says but all I can do is shrug. Nothing about the circumstances is ideal, but we have to act now, I know that.

He spends a good long time untangling the harness. His tongue pokes out between his teeth as he concentrates, muttering instructions at me. "This is the leading edge here. It has these openings, see, that'll let the air inflate the wing, yeah? And this is the trailing edge where the brakes are attached."

"I *know* all this."

He shuts me up with a glance. "You know it when you're hanging two feet off the ground. It'll be different up there."

After fastening me into the harness, he touches my

face, cups my chin. There's tenderness in him, but also fear smouldering beneath the surface. His eyes are lambent, nervy. "Like when you were practicing, hold onto the brakes." He curls both of my hands around the handles. I'm wearing his heavy work gloves, but the leather is supple enough I can hold the handles without any problems. Everything fits snugly against me, the straps pulled taut but with enough slack for me to move a bit and adjust my weight. "How're you feeling?" he asks.

"Scared."

"Good, stay scared," he grunts. "What you're doing is *dangerous*."

He grips my shoulders for a moment. We can both feel it: the terror of hurtling toward some unknown extreme, the necessity of it.

"At least I met you. I'm glad about that. If I'm going to die young, kissing you was worth five years." He's kneeling in front of me, his mouth is close enough that the warmth of his breath reaches me. I lean forward, kiss him again.

He pulls away, standing, steeling himself. He'll survive, I think. Even if I fall, he'll survive. He has to.

"Just remember. You'll need a lot of air speed for the landing. Don't touch the brakes until the last minute. If you pull too hard you'll end up back in the air. You've got a radio headset. I'll stay in contact the whole time, yeah?" He's calm now, intent, focused.

"Yeah," I tell him. Wanting to kiss him again, never going to kiss him again.

I breathe out slowly, trying to keep all the instructions straight in my head. The field is clear of obstructions, the tall grass snapping in the wind. Grey-green light glitters on bent saplings as tall as my shoulder, a tangle of briars and brambles, far enough away I should be in the air before I reach them. I position myself so that I'm facing straight into the wind.

"Just like practice," I say into the radio, even though it isn't.

"When the storm starts to break you get down here as quick as you can—but not the hard way. Obviously." A tinge of humour in his voice. Good, good.

*Th-rumble* goes the engine, the vibrations running up my spine. The paramotor weighs less than I thought it would, but I still grunt as I swing it off the ground using my hips. My arms are wide overhead, the throttle gripped in my right hand.

I start jogging against the wind and the boots are awkward, too large, sinking into the damp soil. I try to gain speed. Then—*thwump!* The sail snaps into place in a smooth motion behind me and the lines pull with tension, throwing me off balance. I shift, ducking downward, hoping I can keep the damn thing straight. Momentum drags me forward, legs still pumping. I creep the throttle up until the grass skates away beneath my boots. The barest squeeze on the brake lifts the leading edge. Up, up, up, it sends me.

The first couple of seconds in the air are pure panic and pure joy, more like falling upward than flying. I have to grab height as fast as I can. The trees are coming toward me but then I'm arcing upward, over them. The canopy of leaves shivers beneath me. It's only noon but it's dark up here, storm clouds blotting out light, releasing it in snatches. I catch sight of the truck's headlights carving out bright yellow divots in the shadows, and pass beyond them.

"You all right up there?" Bryan's voice crackles in my ears. It's a comfort to hear him.

"It's dark, I didn't think…" What I see is deep wood beneath me, the crook of the road somewhere to my left, the travellers few and far between. Empty houses, the power lines useless, strung like streamers from maypoles. The landscape, its rounded hills and flat valleys, formed from the giant beds of hard limestone, the churned-up deposits from an ancient coral reef. I can see the Colleges below, the city walls, centuries old. Built to last forever. Or until the water's come flooding back.

In the distance, the storm gathers strength, dark and greasy-looking. I feel permeable, as if the world is flowing through me.

"Sophie?" The radio snaps and snarls but I don't answer.

The sky has turned into white clouds around me. Salty droplets of water sting my face, wrapping me in sea fog. The wind is whistling in my ear, a low keening note. Stronger, picking up speed. My sail has gone crooked, it ripples behind me—this is exactly what Bryan warned me about. The harness shakes and bucks, as I tug on the brake line to straighten myself, wondering about dropping lower, getting below the storm. But I don't.

*This, this*, my body whispers. *What you came for. What you knew was out here.*

They burst through the vaporous gloom, gliding around me. Like shadows, ghosts, a shoal of sleek, lustrous fish.

At first I can only sense those closest to me, but then I become aware of hundreds of them. It's as if a thousand eyes have opened over every inch of my body, sight and sensation merge. I'm attuned to them, snapping into place like a magnet. I realize they've been here all along, hidden in the skies, the wild places where they are unreachable. Kernels of beauty in the hurricane.

And Kira is with them. Part of me has been asleep since she disappeared, but now it revives, feeling creeps back in, pins and needles. I hadn't known I was waiting but now the waiting is over, I'm free of it.

"Kira," I'm saying into the radio, "she's here!"

A fluid shape coasts below me, its edges indistinct. White—or not white, not exactly. Whiteness can mean so many different things: clouds, salt, cream, fleece, paper, porcelain. This is the white of feathers, of bone, of eggshells.

Closer now, I know that it's her. I've dreamed about her every night since she left. But not like this. I saw her as she was, my sister. But she is something else too: her wings spread out in a delicate but rigid arc. She is buoyant, perfectly still, a creature of the air inside and out.

She has been made for the storm—not just to survive, but to flourish in it. She will never need to land.

"Sophie!" Crackle and hiss. I think I can hear the town siren blaring in the distance, warning of an emergency.

*Go back, go on, go back, go on ...* Bryan is too far away, earth-bound. And the earth is passing away from me, the earth is an egg, the earth has hatched me. It's hatched both of us. I can feel her closer now. The hair on my arms is standing on end, every part of me vibrating, like a plucked string, every part of me singing, calling out, echoed, answered in full. Beautiful, she's so beautiful! And I'm riding the storm with her.

At last I am with her.

## 38

Memory is a twisty thing, a snake that's half shed its skin. What I'm remembering is important, necessary—as clear and urgent as if I were reliving it anew.

Snow, a white blanket of it. Last December, the night we left Toronto.

The plane has been delayed, first for twenty minutes, then two hours. At the terminal gate, Kira and I press our faces against the windows overlooking the runway, watching the heavy snowflakes stick to the glass. We breathe on it and draw sad cartoon faces with our fingers.

"It won't be so bad," I tell her. She glances at me, doesn't answer. She breathes out another perfect circle of condensation and touches her thumb against it.

Later, she clutches my hand as we board. Normally confident, the bustle of people filtering through the narrow aisles has turned her shy. She tugs a small suitcase behind her. Mom settles in the row behind us.

"I'm scared," Kira whispers to me.

"I know. Me too." My fingers brush her green flannel

shirt, so soft it could be her pyjamas. "Here. Cuddle against me."

"I'm too old for that," she says, even though we both know she isn't. Instead she pulls the hood of the shirt up, and rests her head against my shoulder, shaky with exhaustion. We should have left hours ago. It's coming up on midnight by now.

But the plane doesn't take off.

"Sorry, folks." The captain's voice over the speaker is abrupt, filled with false friendliness. "They need to clear the runway again. We'll have you in the air as soon as possible."

"Does that mean we won't be able to go, Soff?"

"I don't know. We'll have to wait and see."

"Let's just stay," she says. "I want us to stay."

The same bright hope is flaring in my mind. Perhaps the flight will be cancelled. Perhaps the whole thing will be called off.

Slowly, the snow begins to pile up against the window. It gets thicker and thicker as the plane stays motionless. I feel afraid, looking through the fluff of Kira's hair, watching the world beyond the window disappear. What if we get buried in the snow? Equally terrifying: *What if we don't?* What if the runway is cleared, what if the plane takes off, what if it lands at Heathrow just like it was supposed to? I have no idea what our life will look like.

The light of the plows streaks the glass in blue, almost

obscured by the snow. Time seems to stand still, everything erased.

"I had a dream we were underwater," Kira murmurs. The same dream she has always had, since she was very small. "It was scary not to breathe anymore, but it was okay too. You were there."

"It's just a dream, Kira." I touch the fine, staticky hairs on her head, smooth them down again.

"It wasn't a bad dream." This last statement is devoured by a yawn, her fear giving way to sleepiness. She's going back to that place, the dream place. Going back underwater. But she resists, stays awake. "I'm sorry that I hurt you."

But this isn't right. This isn't part of the memory.

"You've been so worried about me," she says.

I'm afraid to look at her. I'm afraid I'll see black eyes, rimmed in yellow, a body that has already begun to change. Past and present are blurring, merging. Memory and dream.

"I could hear you, Soff. I could hear you whispering to me. Telling me stories. You called me back to myself."

I force myself to meet her gaze but it isn't what I thought. She is still herself. Her eyes are the light blue verging on grey they've always been. "I didn't mean to leave you alone like that. I just wasn't really thinking." And she smiles the same smile I've always known, rueful and apologetic. "I should've held onto you longer."

"You've been calling me," I manage. "Why?"

As if she hasn't heard me: "Do you remember the story about the birds?"

"Which story?"

"All the stories. You know them, Soff. You told them to me."

Singing. I can hear them singing. Birds like smoke, birds like weather.

"The lark's mother died…" I begin.

She finishes it for me: "But there was nowhere to bury her body. No earth, only water. And so she lived in grief. Then on the third day she buried her mother in the back of her head." Then she smiles. "All stories have a seed of truth inside them. Look."

She reaches over, her finger hovering just between my eyes.

And I can see the world as she sees it. Below is water, a vast ocean stretching toward the horizon in every direction. As the sun rises it smears colours across the surface, orange and yellow, amethyst, pale blue. The light is extraordinary, clear and unimpeded. There is nothing but this, all else vanished, all else sunk beneath the waves. A vision of heaven—but not weightless, not changeless. The sky is teeming with life: great feathered bodies, their wings made to tame the storms. They are buoyed up by rising columns of warm air that move like cyclones across the open space. And they sing to one another of the storm that has passed. An endless note, going on and on and on.

"That is what we are, Sophie. Our bodies have changed but we remember. We're a way of remembering. So we can survive."

How do we take what we love with us? Our bodies remember, imprinted by pain and joy. We bury it all inside of us: memories of disaster, memories of joy, shored up against loss. And from those memories, comes what? Change, I think, a way to survive when all hope seems lost. A fresh start. As I watch the waters recede and the earth is revealed again, rocky and black-green beneath us, gleaming in the sunlight.

"Is this what's coming?"

"None of us know what comes next," she says.

"I'm scared."

"You don't have to be." She's the big sister now, trying to comfort me. "You can bring everything with you. Nothing needs to be left behind. Whatever you can carry." She unbuckles herself from her seat, pulls herself up close to me so her face is almost touching mine. Her eyelashes brush lightly against my cheek.

I put my arms around her. I don't want to say goodbye even though I can feel that she's leaving me. Sinking away, back into slumber. I watch the shadow of heavy machinery moving outside. I listen to the rising babble of the passengers. They're trapped, they know it. The delay has made them skittish.

Then the speakers jump to life. "Sorry about the delay,

folks. We're cleared for take-off now. Cabin crew, please prepare for gate departure."

Kira's body feels thin and bony through the green flannel shirt. The cabin is shaking. "It'll be okay," she whispers. A premonition, a prophecy, a command.

And I hold her close to me as the plane leaps into the air.

## 39

"Sophie? You have to—"

Bryan's voice crackles in my ear.

"You have to come down now."

I don't want to go yet. I still feel them around me, their voices, their thoughts. I could lose myself in the low noises they make, lose myself in everything they are. *We are going*, they say, *we are going. Come with us, come with us, come with us.*

Promise. Hope. That's what Kira wanted to tell me. What's happening is a way for us to survive. Some of us. Enough for us to continue until something better will come: *one day, one day, one day.*

But until then I must keep hold of my memories. I must bury them in the back of my skull. My time with Bryan, the sweetest thing. Mom's trust in me, her artist's vision. Aunt Irene, always wanting to solve the problems of others. Liv. Redmond. Martin. Jaina. Dad. Everyone who has passed out of sight. Out of sight, but not out of mind. I will take them with me, share them. Nothing will be lost.

Lost like I am lost. Lost like I'm losing altitude, sinking beneath the cloud cover.

The air is clearer, like a cool drink in my mouth, light and misty. But above me the sky has turned into an ink-black gloom, veins of lightning spark and vanish. I hear a noise: something churning very far away—then very close up, almost right on top of me. I can't see the nymphs anymore.

The wind sends tremors through the sail, dropping me ten feet in one dizzying plunge. Bryan is right. I've done what I needed to do.

"Where do I—how am I going to land?" I yell into the radio.

"Here!" His voice is sharp with fear. "Follow the lights. I'll guide you through it as best I can. But you should cut your engine—*now*."

The wing of the paraglider twists and curls and the ground telescopes toward me. Yellow light washes over the flat stretch of farmland below. The wormy line of a hedge illuminated by the headlights from the truck. Bryan's been following me, trying to track my movements. *Poor Bryan. I must tell him, I must...*

But there's a second set of headlights. As I try to make sense of it, the paramotor's engine chokes off. Every movement I make is translated into sweeping curves. I lurch in the sky, a hundred feet above ground.

"Don't touch the brakes now, hear? Whatever you do.

Just wait for it. See if you can straighten out."

The ground is coming up at me very fast now, the landscape a blur of yellow, not just the headlights, but golden, a field of rapeseed like an oversized yellow brick road. *Follow, follow, follow*, sang Dorothy Gale. Memories of childhood, curled up in front of the TV with Kira, memories strong enough they could suck me in the way a current carries a swimmer out to sea. *Not yet*. The dust is gritty on my tongue, flecks pelting my cheeks. The straps keep me steady, which is good, because the speed makes me dizzy. I slip off the seat so that I'm hanging in the straps alone, able to manoeuvre and catch my weight properly when I hit the ground. But I'm going fast, way too fast. The acid taste of fear coats the inside of my mouth.

"Get ready to pull the brakes. Okay, okay, okay, and go!"

I give a vicious tug, and the wing flares up behind me. Yellow all around me, my feet colliding with the heads of the flowers. Then I snap backwards in the harness and my knees take the brunt of the force as I hit the ground and am thrown forward. I haven't detached the sail! And the storm has got it, the storm is dragging me up again like a dog with a rope in its teeth. Back on my feet I run to keep up, but the rapeseed is too high. Thousands of tiny blossoms explode damply against me, releasing their dense, mustardy scent.

Then I'm spinning, spinning. Ten feet up, twenty feet up. Mud spirals off my boots in a galaxy pattern. I'm screaming: "Oh god, oh god!" Pulling on the brake line, flailing my arms as the ground begins to rush toward me again. I can't get my legs up properly this time, so I land heavily and some part of me gives out, breaks open. Like the flowers, too fragile for this. Busted up. The back of the propeller cage hits the earth and ricochets upward, flipping me over. I tuck my head down. The field rolls and jags around me, brown earth, black sky, brown earth. Mud sucks at my cheek, spatters my elbow, squishes between my fingers. A heavy *thwooping*. The sail has collapsed at last.

My chest aches, like someone punched it. I gag, cough, all of the air behind a locked door I can't open. I struggle against the straps, finally unhooking myself, rolling out of the twisted cage. Blackness. Then Bryan is beside me. His face is close, the faint line of dark stubble on his chin. Brown eyes, copper streaks around the pupil. His hand cradles the back of my head.

"So much for the landing," I tell him. A bad joke. He isn't laughing.

He isn't alone either. For a moment I think I'm dreaming, that the past and the present have bled into one another. Because Mom is above me, her face a mask of bright light and shadow.

But then she takes my hand and I know she's real.

"You came," I tell her, slurring the words. "How did you find me?"

"Your phone, Sophie, I tracked it. But none of that matters now. I'm here," she tells me. "I've got you. I've got you. Please don't let go."


Rain pings against the roof of the truck and Bryan's in the driver's seat, throttling the steering wheel.

In the rear-view mirror I can make out the front of the Renault following close behind but I can't concentrate on it. There's a high-pitched squeal as the tires find a stretch of slickness, spin out, touch the ground again. Mom is holding me against her and I'm concentrating on the grit worked into the seams of the seats, how smooth the seats are, shiny as the skin of a grape. Not letting the pain in, not feeling it, or feeling too much of it, feeling everything.

"I saw her. Kira was up there. Did you see?"

"Oh god, there's so much blood," Mom says.

I follow her gaze. My cut-offs are soaked through with red, my thighs sticky with it. A bright ribbon of blood loops my wrist where the scarred flesh has gone soft as wax, and peeled away from the veins. I'm coming undone.

"I'm fine," I tell her, what I say whenever she's fussing too much.

Except.

# 40

Temporary shelters have been set up in the park next to the JR Hospital, dome tents made of inflated PVC tarpaulin. They look like igloos, and the rain crackles against them, a sound like deep-frying meat. This is the safest place the city council could think of, high ground.

They're ready for us. Medical staff and emergency volunteers direct bedraggled evacuees and hand out blue fleece blankets, makeshift bedding. "No space in the hospital," one of them says, so Bryan carries me into the closest igloo, cradling me. Pain in my abdomen, a wrenching of bone. *No good.* I leave a red imprint of myself against his body for the second time. A hazy numbness creeping into my limbs, like I'm disconnecting, detaching, drifting away.

*Goodbye, fingers. Goodbye, toes.*

Bryan is scared, I can tell by his thudding heartbeat. He feels responsible, he found me. Not just here, now, but on Bunkers Hill months ago. He found me. I don't know how, except the right people always find you, don't they? That's what makes them the right people. At the cement works, that first time: *wasn't sure if you were going to make it, you know how it is, pleased you did…*

I'm on a cot in a tent, waiting for doctors. Mom is beside me and Aunt Irene too. They fold and unfold their arms in unison, mirrors of grief and worry. The floor is soaked and there's chaos around us. The pale maniac faces of other children as orderlies restrain them. They want to get out. The storm is calling them. I can feel it too, a surging of adrenaline. Bryan's eyes are panicked.

Someone tries to pull him away but he won't leave my side. He settles down beside me, elbows springing into the mattress of the cot. Shielding me.

"It wasn't your fault," I tell him.

"Shut up," he says. "You bloody fool. Just stop it, will you? You can't die on me!"

"I know." He doesn't understand, can't.

*This is not me dying. Not dying. Not me.*


"Broken femur for sure," someone is saying. "The right—a compound fracture. Several ribs too." A nurse? He's ashy with fatigue, hair close-shaven. "Her BP … she's lost a lot of blood." I can't see who he's talking to, chanting, incanting. "Let's assume injuries, likely a liver lac, maybe—splenic rupture?"

Bryan is holding my hand but I can't feel it. The nurse speaks in a soft voice as if he is talking to a small child.

"We're taking her into surgery." He sounds like Dad in the living room, telling us goodbye. "There are bound to be complications. In her state, with her condition." Telling us he loves us, but not enough. Not enough to come with us. "There's so many of them," the nurse says, voice breaking with frustration. "I don't know how we're going to cope."

I feel like a telephone line cradling thousands and thousands of crows. Claws hooked into me, the bustle of their wings, voices. A thick residue running through me, a noiseless vibration. New signals filling me up, if I can tune myself to them. *Tune in, tune out.* Easier to hear them now. As if I was listening through muffling cloth before, through water.

Struggling to speak to Bryan, to tell him: "I understand it now. What Kira said. How she wanted to go even if— oh—" It's lovely. So bright. "It's okay, Bryan. You don't have to be afraid."

I'm hollow on the inside. You could put your ear to me and hear the ocean, hear roaring. This world is imprinted upon me. Everything nestled inside everything else, everything falling open.

I'm half flesh, half ether. I'm made up of insubstantial things: air, lightness, thought, memory. A different kind of memory, the memory of cells, the memory of bone. My hand in Bryan's, him gripping me. Sparks cross, little zigzags of lightning. We're sharing molecules, spreading energy between us. I have caught him inside of me.

I can see him clearly now, him but not just him. He is hollow too, hiding his own secret world. His cells are storerooms, miniature temples. All these pieces of him, his father, his mother, his grandmother.

I travel back, ages and ages, from one cell to another. It's like turning a page, reading what has been written into him, heartbreak and joy, trauma, recovery. A village called Dowde with roofs of yellow-grey thatch, mud, and furze. A thick peaty smell in the air. The fine ash of a bonfire. I see how the survivors moved in grief and a slow stupor, talking to each other about what they had seen. The dead climbing out of the earth, angels with the faces of their kin. This memory, a seed. *A remarkable thing was noticed ... everyone born had two fewer teeth than people had had before ...* He knows, some part of him knows. Some part of it has been imprinted inside his body.

*This has happened before...*

Further, I could go, eons into the past. Would I see the same thing? A way of surviving, hiding, travelling, starting over, passed on from generation to generation.

Bryan is wrenched away from me, the contact broken. They're taking me somewhere, through a long tunnel. Mom grips me, running alongside the gurney. Her skin is soft, transparent. It breaks open like an egg. I can sense the silky course of her blood, the yolk of each cell. Those cells and mine, singing to one another. Gifts passed between them.

Her, calling out to her sister, to her daughters, both of us.

I remember this. I remember Kira going to the same place, through this hallway. The strange look on her face, the absence of fear. My fingers twitch. "Stay with me!" Mom pleads.

Too late for that. My cells have opened, the doors have been flung wide. I am rushing forward, laughing, to greet whatever lies inside. And then I'm moving beyond them, not forward but upward, into the open air where the rain is moving, lovely, lovely, dissolving me like sugar on the tongue. And all around me, the sound of birds, their wings carving up the night, endless birds. Birds like wind, birds like weather. A swarm of them, glossy in the moonlight, radiant eyes, radiant throats, the music pouring out of them and into me, all of it, everything. I'm pouring out of my body and into the darkness, spread so thin, thin as electrons spinning and spinning, shifting, becoming this: the hidden world, it is me, it is all of us.

# AFTER

When you were younger you used to play dead.

Sometimes when I knocked on your door in the morning, I'd see you there, with the light streaming in through the window, and you'd be pretending not to breathe. Your eyes would be closed and you'd be so still. A terrible fear would come over me that *this* time, maybe it wasn't just playing, this time maybe it was real. I'd want to rush in and shake you until your eyes opened.

"It's just a phase," your dad used to tell me, "children do all sorts of things that don't make sense to adults." He never understood how scary it was. Even when he saw how the panic left me shaking and he'd rub the spot between my thumb and index finger, a thing he'd done to help with the pain when I was in labour.

You were unexpected from the very first moment and everything that's happened along the way has had an aura of unpredictability. The fall, you coming into the world ten weeks early, blue skin, struggling to breathe.

"Can't we just put her back inside?" I don't remember

saying it but your dad says I asked the doctors that. There wasn't enough of you. You were half-formed and I thought if I could just swaddle you up in another layer of skin—and another and another—you'd get better. You did eventually but after there was always a shine about you. I'd look at you and I'd see blue. I'd see the web of your veins and they were blue. I'd see how pale you were, how your skin was almost transparent.

As we rush you into surgery, a part of me believes this isn't real. You'll blink your eyes, you'll wake up when I touch you. But an austere doctor with silver spectacles is talking to me. His voice is crisp and emotionless. Lane Ballard. He was there when Kira died—but this time when he speaks I feel like a misbehaving child.

He tells me the procedure was a success. You have a heartbeat, there's brain activity. But no one knows how long you will last. You've lost a lot of blood and your immune system is badly compromised. He tells me you might not get better, he wants to send you to a research facility near York. When I ask about Dr. Varghese, he frowns and informs me she's been suspended.

Talking to him I feel so many things. Shame, anger, frustration. I shouldn't have let you go out. I should have come after you sooner. I never should have left. Beneath it is a dull rage. My body glows as if it's made from burning metal.

"Don't you touch her!" I snap.

There are procedures in place for this, he tries to tell

me. He says I've seen what can happen if they aren't followed. That this is for the best. He has two orderlies with him with the look of men prepared for violence.

Suddenly Irene is beside me. "Do you think she gives a damn about your procedures?" she says. "We know what you've been doing here and if you come near Sophie I'll kill you."

I stare in wonder at her. She was always the calm one, infinitely reasonable. Now her face is scarlet and her hands are shaking. We both know what we saw out there, those shapes in the sky. How many there were. You told me Kira is with them. You told me she is alive.

I'd have given anything to have her back. I'd do anything for you now.

Police in fluorescent vests load a crowd of evacuees into a bus headed inland. Bryan is still here, his mother too, treating the injured, the children and teenagers who lie motionless on cots. There are so many with JI2—more than I would have imagined. Bryan helps direct the flow of evacuees, breaking up fights when the crowding gets too bad. But he comes back to me when they can spare him, splattered in mud up to his thighs. He brings me tea from a thermos.

"It's cold now," he says, "sorry."

I can see the way he is staring at you. Breathing like he doesn't really want the oxygen. I know how he feels. Dr.

Ballard told me I shouldn't touch you but I do anyway. I hold you, I scrub my hands and then I reach out for you again. No one tries to stop me.

Eventually the place is almost empty.

There are only a few of us left, huddled under blankets, looking like the last people alive in the universe. I tell Bryan it's time to go. At first he resists and I understand that. You look so fragile. It seems impossible that we could go anywhere but I know we have to. We can't stay.

It's Bryan who finds the four-by-four ambulance, me pushing your stretcher behind. It makes me almost laugh, the sheer craziness of what we're doing, but there's no time to think about it. All I know is that you're my responsibility and I won't leave you.

There are five of us in the end: Irene and me, Bryan, his mother and you. Bryan takes the front seat while the rest of us load into the back. There isn't much room. In the chaos no one pays attention to us until he's driving. Then I can hear shouts, people yelling at us to slow down. But we keep going, silent and afraid.

We have to stop twice to figure out if the road is passable and once we have to backtrack because the main road has been completely washed out. But when we head north on the M40 toward Warwick things are easier. No one says much. There is no plan, just the hope that maybe we'll find safety there. For a little while. You're breathing still and I watch your chest rising and falling, willing you to live, remembering your birth.

You in the incubator at thirty weeks, a machine showing you how to breathe. "Live," I whispered as I looked at you behind the glass, "please, live." But it doesn't always work like that, does it? Only in fairy tales does it work like that.

All at once I feel like I'm going to be sick and I ask Bryan to pull over. The rain is finally beginning to lighten. He opens the back of the ambulance and I climb out.

After everything, it's turned into a clear night. None of the streetlights are working and I can see the stars—there are so many of them! Ditches and divots cradle rainwater, reflecting moonlight. It gives the landscape this otherworldly glow.

I remember a story you used to read Kira. From Egypt, maybe? It was about the world, how it was submerged. And when the land rose the first thing to appear was a heron. And the heron created the universe. It made the gods and the goddesses, it made the men and the women, everything. It made them all anew. Kira loved that story. So did you.

I know you're almost gone. In my blood and bones. The ambulance is stopped. I don't want it to happen here so I tell Bryan to carry you outside where the air is cool and fresh and there are stars overhead. We're all around you, waiting. For what I don't know. When does waiting become something else?

"I don't think she's breathing, Char," Irene whispers.

She's right. It's coming now and I want to be ready for it, but how can I be? I search your face for a sign, some last signal that you know what's happening even if I don't. But there's nothing. The terror, the hopes are mine to sort through. To take up or discard.

For a moment you're perfectly still but then your body begins to shake. Is this it then? Everything seems as if it's moving fast and slow at the same time. Too fast, too slow.

I hold you in my arms as it happens. It's as if you're shedding layers now, coming undone. And I have this feeling of being lifted up and out of myself. There isn't any clear way to explain it, only the sense that overhead is something important, something hypnotic. I imagine I can see dark shapes in the sky above me. The ones like Kira. But they aren't here for me, are they? They're here for you. All of this is for you.

The rain is falling, washing everything away. You're changing, becoming something new. I don't want to be afraid of it—but I am. I can't help it. Because you're young. What you did was so stupid and brave in the way I suppose all young people are stupid and brave, thinking they were the first people to ever really live. I could've helped you if you'd let me.

We stand there, all of us—hopeful, curious, desperate. And all at once I want to take them into my arms. I want to take the whole world in my arms, all the scared people, the mothers and daughters, the fathers and sons, and whisper to them what I used to say to both you and Kira when you were small enough you still believed me, hoping it will be true.

*Shhh, baby girl, the storm is passing. It's going to be all right.*

# ACKNOWLEDGEMENTS

Worldly things will sink and stagger. So wrote the medieval clerk, Nicholas Grantham. He was tasked with copying the records of London a hundred years after the city had been wracked with plague. The task of putting pen to paper calls to mind this fact.

He was right. This novel has sunk and staggered many times. Thanks are due to the numerous people who lent their support when it did: Sally Harding, Ron Eckel, and the whole team of Cooke McDermid Literary Management, who threw their weight behind it; Amanda Betts and Anne Collins of Random House Canada, who shepherded me through the editorial phase with wisdom and forbearance; Vince Haig, who has been tireless and kind and quick to bring chocolate; Nina Allan, Chris Priest, Rob Shearman, M. Huw Evans, Nathan Ballingrud, Bryan Camp, Laura Friis West, Greg West, Carlie St. George, Georgina Kamsika, Sarah Dodd, Henry Lien, Blythe Woolston and Tiffani Angus, all of whom offered valuable feedback, sometimes at length, sometimes more than once; my colleagues and students at Anglia Ruskin University; Sandra Kasturi, Brett Savory, Simon Strantzas, Gemma Files, David Nickle, Michael Kelly and the whole Canadian gang; Peter Buchanan, Alex Gillespie and Daniel Wakelin for helping with my own period of transition; and, of course, my family— especially my sister, Laura, to whom this book is dedicated, who never let me stop.

The Canada Council supported a draft of this novel through the Grants for Creative Writing Program as did the Ontario Arts Council with their Writers' Reserve. I could not have written this without them. I'd also like to thank the Social Sciences and Humanities Research Council for their support of my academic research through a Canada Graduate Scholarship, a Michael Smith Foreign Supplement for travel to Oxford and for a postdoctoral fellowship.

A number of historical quotations have been included in this book. The first appears in the epigraph to section one, taken from J. F. C. Hecker and B. G. Babington's *The Black Death in the Fourteenth Century* (1833). A number of others are drawn from Rosemary Horrox's brilliant edited collection of eyewitness accounts and source materials, *The Black Death* (Manchester University Press, 2007). These include passages from Bengt Knutsson's *A Little Book for the Pestilence* in chapter two, Robert of Avesbury's *De Gestis Mirabilibus* in chapter three, from John of Reading's *Chronica* in chapter sixteen, from the anonymous *A disputation betwixt the body and worms* quoted as the epigraph for section three, and from a manuscript by Geoffrey de Meaux in chapter twenty-eight. In chapter seventeen Sophie reads a passage from *The Journal of the Statistical Society of London*, vol. 9 (John William Parker, 1846).

The novel begins with an epigraph from Wolf Erlbruch's astonishing picture book *Duck, Death and the Tulip* (Gecko Press, 2007). In chapter two Sophie reads from Charlotte Perkins Gilman's short story "The Yellow Wallpaper" (first published in January 1892 in *The New England Magazine*). In chapter seven she remembers a line from "Buffalo Bill's" by E. E. Cummings, first published in *Tulips and Chimneys* (Thomas Seltzer, 1923). Lastly, in chapter sixteen she reads to Kira from J. M. Barrie's *Peter Pan* (Hodder and Stoughton, 1911).

This novel is more dream vision than fact. At times I've run roughshod over history. Excuse me, if I've spoken amiss. My intent was good.

*Hoc opus est scriptum magister da mihi potum; Dextera scriptoris careat grauitate doloris.*